Praise For
Whoa, Nelly!

"... A must-read for risk-takers and dream-weavers who create whole cloth with homespun desire." [1]
[1] Sorry, not sorry, Ma

—Kate Farrell, storyteller, author of *Story Power* and *The Fairy Tale Heroine*

"Tracey is a quick-witted, snappy writer who misses nothing and tells a hell of a story. More, please!"

—Billie Thomas, author of *Murder on the First Day of Christmas*

"... Nelly is the greatest of company for a witty immersion into the Little House world with a powerful love story of her own. A delight in all departments."

—Diana Birchall, author of *Mrs. Elton in America* and *The Bride of Northanger*

"*Whoa, Nelly!* is more than a love story. It's a story that shows how fiction can serve as a guidebook for life."

—Deborah Luskin, *Reviving Artemis*

"This authentic, angst-ridden, anxious, though funny voice is a hook that drags you in as much as the triumph of narration. We root for Nelly as she wrangles things most of us take for granted: people to exchange ideas with, friends to share pain with, even romance.
Whoa, Nelly? More like *go, Nelly!*"

—Eric Turowski, author of *Willing Servants, Inhuman Interest,* and the Irons series.

PRAISE FOR
The Bereaved

"In *The Bereaved*, Julia Park Tracey reopens America's wounds in prose that is propulsive and resonant. Theodore Dreiser comes to mind, but so, too, the fine contemporary novels of Jo Baker and Maggie O'Farrell."

—Christian Kiefer, *The Heart of It All* and *Phantoms*

OTHER BOOKS BY JULIA PARK TRACEY

The Bereaved: A Novel

Silence: A Novel

Tongues of Angels: A Novel

Veronika Layne Gets the Scoop —
#1 in the *Hot off the Press series*

Veronika Layne Has a Nose for News —
#2 in the *Hot off the Press series*

I've Got Some Lovin' to Do: 1925-1926 —
#1 in the *Doris Diaries series*

Reaching for the Moon: 1927-1929 —
#2 in the *Doris Diaries series*

Amaryllis: Collected Poems

Whoa, Nelly!

*A Love Story**

**with Footnotes*

JULIA PARK TRACEY

Sibylline Press

Copyright © 2025 by Julia Park Tracey
All Rights Reserved.

Published in the United States by Sibylline Press,
an imprint of All Things Book LLC, California.

Sibylline Press is dedicated to publishing the
brilliant work of women authors ages 50 and older.
www.sibyllinepress.com

Sibylline Digital First Edition
eBook ISBN: 9798897409853
Print ISBN: 9798897409860
Library of Congress Control Number: 2025938481

Cover Design: Alicia Feltman
Book Production: Aaron Laughlin

Sibylline
Press

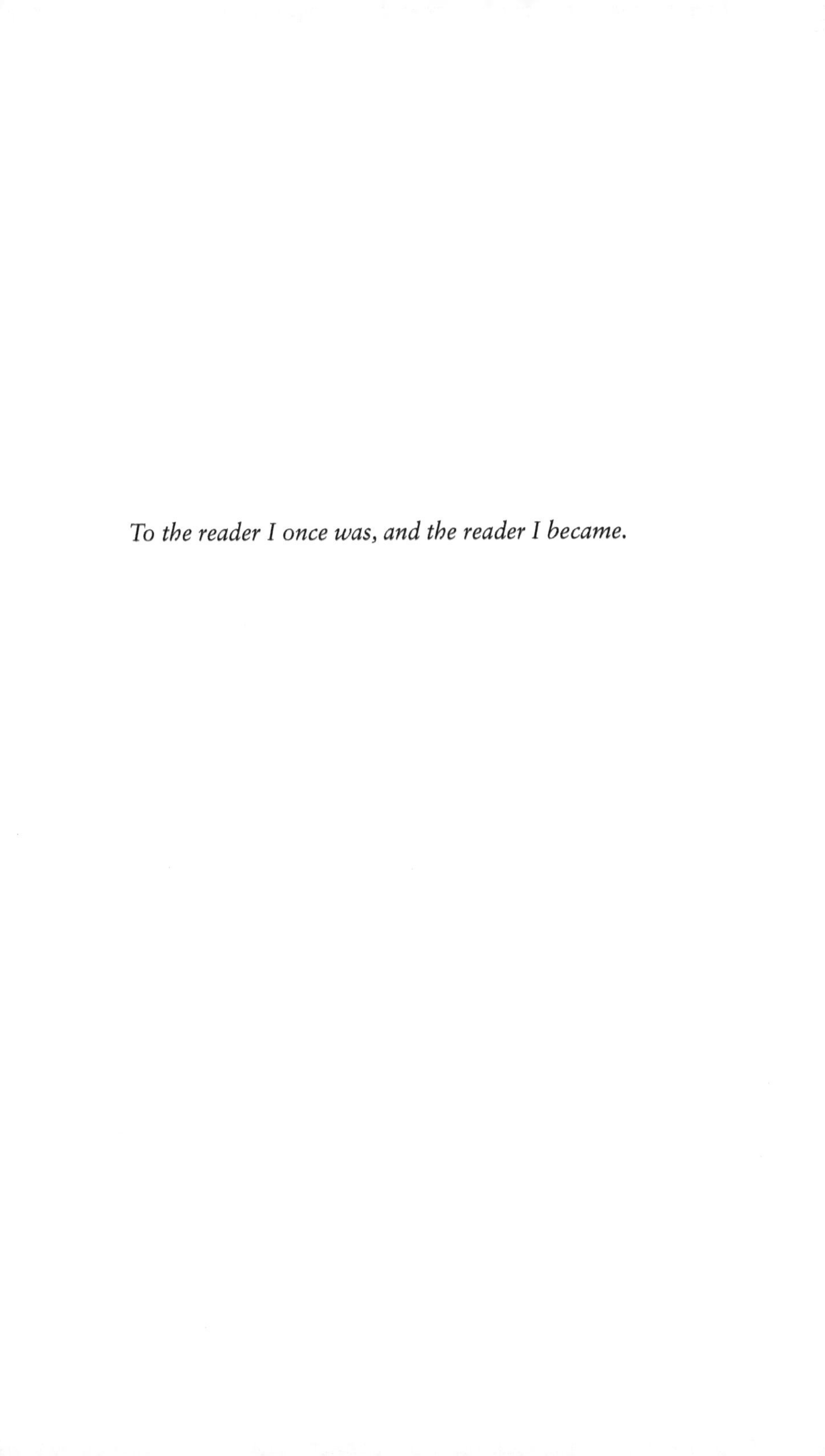

To the reader I once was, and the reader I became.

PART ONE

LITTLE HOUSE IN A BIG TOWN

CHAPTER 1

Sixty years ago, or forty, if you want to be a stickler, there lived a little girl in a house in the suburbs. She didn't call her parents Mother and Father, nor Mama and Papa, nor Ma and Pa, although she wished she could have. They were Ellen and Jerry, and the little girl's name was Penelope, but they called her Nelly. They lived on a quiet street in Northern California, with a neighbor who was a terrible creep so we won't talk about him now, until Ellen and Jerry split up, and then it was just Mom and Nelly.

Nelly loved Laura.

Laura Ingalls Wilder, that is.

I'm Nelly. I was about six when I discovered *The Little House in the Big Woods*. Our city library owned an edition that was larger than the usual, maybe two feet tall and twelve inches wide. The print was large, but it was a real chapter book, with those beautiful Garth Williams drawings of Laura in her nightgown with rag doll Charlotte in her arms, and Mary, bright blue-eyed Mary, with her arms slung around Pa's neck. I wished my Pa was around so I could do that.

On the cover, Ma curves a smile and Jack the brindle bulldog wriggles happily nearby. Maybe there's more happening off the page, I don't know. Maybe a pot boiling over in the fireplace.

A new reader in first grade, I took off like a runaway ox. When I got a rope around the sense of the words, I could drop my finger from the page and just dissolve into the story, become one, *om shanti shanti*, with the written word. I entered the world of the Little House books, and became Laura.

I loved Laura then.

I still do.

Laura was strong and smart, good-hearted and modest, and yet very brave. She was no Mary Ingalls, to be sure—not prim, not fearful, and not Biblically inclined toward rote memorization. Laura was jealous of her sisters, yet plagued with guilt when Mary went blind and Laura had to step up and teach school in Mary's place. Mary's blue eyes! Those golden ringlets! Laura's jealousy was a revelation to me—sometimes she hated her sister! Real feelings from imaginary characters! I think the first time I ever saw the words "shut up" in print was Laura yelling at Carrie when Baby Grace was lost on the prairie.

My dad didn't make bullets, nor tell long stories that lasted a whole chapter, nor whip me with a strap like Pa Ingalls. My dad worked in an office downtown doing things with numbers and files, so I heard, but I saw him rarely after my parents split up. So what did I know? Probably he didn't love us all that much. Maybe my mom drove him away, like how Laura and the Norwegian boy kept the cows out of Pa's haystacks. But by gosh, I'd better not ask about my dad if I wanted to stay up and watch *Little House on the Prairie* starring Melissa Gilbert[1] at 8 p.m. It made Mom angry when I asked about my dad, and she said things she didn't mean, or maybe she meant them. How would I know? I was just a kid.

Back to now.

The city library is open six days a week and although I had started working there part-time while earning my master's degree,

---

[1] Her buck-toothed gaze!

as a stepping-stone toward my brilliant career as a novelist[2] and women's literature professor, I somehow got sort of stuck and had been there ever since. Like, for eons. Novels written? Zero. Classes taught? Not many.

I do teach middle schoolers how to use the library a couple of times a year. That counts. It's not nothing. It's not much, but it's—well, anyway. I get to read. I keep working toward my project of creating a Laura Ingalls Wilder bible of sorts: everything they ate, made, grew, wore, owned, lost, or dreamed of. All of the things in their world, clamped into a three-ring binder or two. Or seven. I wanted to taste all their flavors, feel my breath constrict as Ma pulls my corset strings, sew a button on a boot, roll in hay, make maple candy in the snow. Ride behind those elegant horses. Fall in love with a farmer or a horseman. I wanted all of it.

I work on my Laura-binders in the same way that Laura and Mary knitted Carrie's Fourth of July mittens in *The Long Winter*—in snatches here and there, when my boss is out of the back office and no one is panting down my neck about gathering up board books after Toddler Storytime like Laura gathering ripe plums. And of course, I read everything new about Laura, her family, her world, not that there's much. It's not as if she were America's Jane Austen, about whom there is a new spin-off, TV series, or "modern take" each year.

Alas, with government shutdowns and budget crises and tax revolts and such, it's a wonder I get to read anything at all at the library. There's always a chance we'll be shuttered here, conglomerated with the other two branch libraries into one and our hours cut, our wages slashed, our benefits evaporating. You'd think I could lap at the public trough for years and bank my fat state pension later, but no—those days are over, and I'm surfing the edge of my paycheck like everyone else in the country. So

---

[2] "I, write a book?" she hooted.

reshelving I do. I push that damned cart of vampire novels around the first floor and try to look busy while I sneak-read from the books I'm shelving.

Today the new books came. Since Sage was out sick (hang-over) and Makenzie never had to leave Children's, and Shawn enjoyed sneering down his stubby nose at patrons stuck at the always-on-the-fritz self-check-out kiosk, I happened to be in the right spot when the boxes came.

There's a UPS delivery guy who looks like Joe Strummer from the Pogues, and he still sports that kind of scrub-brush hair that stands on end no matter how he smashes it down with a brown cap. He wears mirrored sunglasses like some dude from the 80s and at Halloween, he wore a blue metallic wig that looked basically like his usual hair, except blue and metallic. He wears shorts year-round. Dead sexy. A woman can dream, right?

Did I mention that I'm a 45-year-old virgin? Imaginary lovers are safe, and they don't break your heart or your spirit. Well, anyway.

I was in the right spot at the right time (hello, UPS dude!) and thus, took myself to the back office to open the box and catalog the new books into the system. Always such a delight. So much pleasure to handle and smell the new books with their genuine hard bindings and new glue and paper scent, that we always tussled for the perk. And it was all mine today.

I slit the tape on the first box with familiar ease. I could have been a surgeon with these moves. The packing slip on top enumerated the contents: Young Adult novels. I lifted those out, then the new children's books beneath. Replacement copies of *Pat the Bunny*, always, every month. *Goodnight Moon. Time for Bed, Sleepyhead!* Out of the box and into the pile. Later, the bar code. The library disclaimer and warning. Random page stamps with my embosser and my ink pad. If a librarian were a villain, you know she'd have some kind of poisonous stamp pad to kill her enemies. No flying powers necessary—not when you've got that sweet rolling cart to do your bidding. Why, I—

"Nelly."

I came back to the moment. Supervisor Dave Turner filled the doorframe. He used to be a very large man, but he'd lost weight, so much so that he looked Bassett houndish to me, with folds of skin at his neck, under his eyes. His once-plump ears sagged a little. He's still tall, though. The effort of losing weight has turned his hair gray, emphasizing his sad doggy look. I'm never quite sure if I trust him or not. He's a man, for one thing. You know how they are.

"New books? Good, good. Staff meeting at 4. Your report?"

"Got it," I said, trying to recall if I had it or not. Which report was it? "You want me to make copies, or save the trees?"

"Save the trees and the money." He hitched up his sagging suit pants a little on each side. "I hear we're getting our supply budget cut again. Just tell the staff about it."

I nodded and he left. I finished logging in to the main catalog to confirm the new entries, checked my email to remind myself of the report I had promised, and typed up a page of notes to read if necessary. I nicked my finger on a staple, though, and had to pause for a bandage. It stung, more than it should, stupid thing, and a flash from my childhood Girl Scout camping trip came to mind.

"I am the Bloody Finger," I said, *sotto vocce.*

There was still a quarter hour before the meeting, so I opened up the second box of new books. Glossy photography, dreamy landscapes, few words—coffee table books. Love them. They're heavy, but they don't pile well or sit on the shelves long. As shifty as a rolling log, tumbling upon poor Ma, crushing her foot under its weight—I save her by not stacking them, by shelving these oversized tomes correctly, on a lower shelf. Beautiful books. *New England's Autumn Colors. Tugboats of California. Vintage Postcards. The Doors of Jane Austen.*

I paused. *The Doors of Jane Austen.* What the hell? Who thinks of these things? I flipped the cover open, turned pages. On one page, a pretty purple door. A brass kickplate, with a shiny handle in the center of the door, Hobbit-like.

... where lived the former resident of 25 Gay Street, Miss Jane Austen. The shiny plum-colored door with its polished brass would have pleased her. She lived for a time in the stylish house in 1805, which was up the hill from the River Avon and less prone to damp, but it proved too expensive for a retired clergyman and his wife and two daughters, so after less than a year, the Austens moved to other quarters.

A few pages later, another photograph, more inane description.

From the Upper Rooms it is downhill, at last, toward Queen Square, where the Austens rented a house for six weeks in May 1799. Number 13, on the corner, has a terribly English shiny black door; the current resident, a tax office, has kindly printed a pamphlet describing the interior. Jane was pleased with the house: "I like our situation very much; it is far more cheerful than Paragon, and the prospect from the drawing-room window, at which I now write, is rather picturesque, as it commands a perspective view of the left side of Brock Street, broken by three Lombardy poplars in the garden of the last house in Queen's Parade." To think that Jane wrote her letters there, in her own hand, and now nothing but dull accountants and tax attorneys and duller-still clients come to call. It makes one want to weep.

The things people publish. Seriously? A book about the doors of Jane Austen? Nothing wrong with that *per se*, I'm sure, but Jane Austen is no Laura Ingalls Wilder. Now *that* would be a book worth reading. All the doors of all the places she lived? The log cabin in the Big Woods. The surveyors' house near Silver Lake. The dugout on Plum Creek. The Rock House that Rose built for her parents in 1928, and onward. All the houses. All the many little houses, in woods, on prairies, by lakes and on the way home—so many houses that a devotee like me could truly appreciate. I have half a mind to write that book myself. But then, I have only half a mind to do anything.

I closed the book and left the barcoding for later.

* * *

Work meetings are kind of like family dinners. Not the good kind. Dave is Pa, kindly, with brown eyes that don't twinkle. In fact, he's no Pa at all. Maria is Mary, I guess, just because of the name similarity, but Makenzie is Eliza Jane, and I feel like Laura when Miss Wilder picked on her in class. I want to make the meeting-room chair *whump* and *bang* when I am told off. But I don't. Instead, I'm Carrie, shy, pale and prone to attacks of faintness.

When I had to give my report, they didn't understand how hard it is for me to speak[3] before a group, even if just a few coworkers. I feel their judgment, I feel the gaslighting before it even begins. I'm sensitive that way (a lifetime of practice: Thanks, Mom).

"Statistically, the values of home users in comparison to branch users—"

"Could you speak a little louder?" Makenzie sighed from the far end of the conference table. My inner Laura snapped her blue eyes and pulled Mary over the woodpile, but I lost my place in my report and paused a minute.

"I can't hear you," Makenzie added unnecessarily. "She's so quiet."

---

[3] How do you speak with your dress buttons done up all inside out, like poor Carrie at the School Exhibition? Her hair in two tight plaits, her white scalp showing vulnerable and meek. *Chisel in hand stands the sculptor boy.*

I am the Bloody Finger and I'm on your street.

"Go on, Nell." Dave looked over the tops of his glasses.

"The number of home users has increased since March so that—" I finished my insipidly dull report about online catalog users and willed myself to pause at the end and ask for questions. None. No one cared. No one listened.

Dave thanked me and I sat, a hot flush slowly seeping from my face as the horror ended. I got the whip this time, but not from Pa. *Thanks a lot, Eliza Jane, you twentysomething pipsqueak.* I squared the edges of my papers.

Maria gave her report on finance and ended it with the kind of pause that makes it clear there is more to come. She made eye contact with Dave.

Dave cleared his throat and pushed his glasses up the bridge of his nose with his index finger. "I'm sorry to say that I've got some bad news. With the latest rounds of cuts, the City put a couple of options on the table. One is to close one of the branches, leaving us with just two in town. Another option is to cut back the days we're open, and our hours, as well. The third is to maintain all three branches with a smaller staff, which means letting go of some of the team at each branch. And because we can't maintain the service we have with fewer staff members, we would still have to cut hours and days. So I have the unfortunate task of cutting staff here."

He played with his loose neck skin, pausing. "Uh, at this time I'm going to dismiss the meeting until next Tuesday, when we will reconvene and go over new staff assignments. Everyone can go back to work now."

Well, that went over like leeches at a tea party, I thought, collecting my file folder and grabbing for the pen rolling across the slightly tilted table. The pen rolled right off the table and onto the floor, and I squatted to fetch it as the others left the room.

"Nelly, will you stay behind a minute?"

Oh, crap. I stood.

Dave looked past me to where Maria was leaving the room. "Close the door, will you, Maria?"

I met her eyes for a moment as she pulled the door closed. Her glance was sympathetic, and I knew what was coming.

* * *

I had an hour till the end of the workday, and I knew what I wanted to do—finish logging in the new books. I might be unemployed tomorrow, but today, I got to touch these books for the first time, before anyone else in the library. I affixed the barcode sticker and library sensor to each and made a few random stamps with my purple ink-stamper. Then I sat back and flipped through the Jane Austen book again.

Walk along Argyle Street and through Laura Place, where the Austens aspired to live but couldn't quite afford, and then down Great Pultney Street to the end, where it meets Sidney Gardens and Sidney Place. The Austens eventually took a house at 4 Sidney Place, which pleased Jane and her sister Cassandra mightily: "It will be very pleasant to be near Sidney Gardens! We might go into the Labyrinth every day." In Austen's day, there were concerts, strolls and other entertainment to be had in the public gardens, and it is a pleasure to read of her joy and contentment in the house.

Number 4 itself is the only house that commemorates Jane's dwelling with a plaque...

I thought about the doors of Jane's houses and the doors of Laura's houses, and the blue door of my own little house in the suburbs, the foreclosed-on cottage I had scrimped to buy with my retirement savings account, a cashed-in life insurance policy, and some savings bonds I'd had since birth. It wasn't much, but it was all mine, not the bank's, and I could at least be grateful that I wouldn't lose it with my sudden unemployed status.

Laid off. Well, that stank. I looked at the calendar and did a little math on the distance my last paycheck would take me. A month, maybe. Plus my unemployment. A little savings, too, but I had been here long enough that my resume was far out of date. I hadn't even seen this coming.

Snap out of it, Nelly. Look alive! The grasshoppers have eaten the crops and Pa has holes in his boots. What are we gonna do now?

I packed my rucksack with my personal belongings and, though as tempted to steal it as Laura with an abandoned Charlotte doll, I left the Jane Austen book behind. I would find my own doors upon which to fixate.

CHAPTER 2

Let's address the issue forthwith.

I must admit, it's problematic being named Nelly. Nelly—it just won't do. Here I am, perhaps the world's biggest Laura Ingalls Wilder fan, and I have the worst possible name. Of course, Laura's biggest enemy was Nellie. Awful, horrible Nellie Olesen—and she wasn't even real! The fictional Nellie was a composite figure of three of Laura's most annoying classmates and rivals. Seriously? I'm co-named with a nemesis who didn't even exist?

As it happens, I was named for my great-aunt Penelope, and Nelly is better than Penny, a little. It was just an unhappy coincidence that the books I chose to love had an antagonist named Nellie. I could change my name, I suppose. But I wouldn't feel like myself if I were Penny. So Nelly I stay.

Unemployed Nelly. Nelly the Nonworker. Numb-nuts Nelly.

My cats awaited my arrival after work. They anticipated the food I give them, not *me* in particular; being mercenary little beasts, they want the food, not my love, and oh, the cliché of unmarried librarian with cats is so excruciatingly accurate. Cat lady? Me? I'm a woman with cats, so it must be true. And the unmarried part? I saw a cartoon the other day, with Gollum from *Lord of the Rings* holding his ring, saying, *"My Preciousss!"* and the caption, "Every single woman over 40."

Ouch. Whatever. So I'm not married and I have cats. Some people have made a career out of this lifestyle. Marian the

Librarian in *The Music Man*, for one. Mary Richards of *The Mary Tyler Moore Show*, for another. And the spinster of spinsters (till later in life), Miss Eliza Jane Wilder. Whether they had cats or not, I cannot say, but unmarried and proud? Or only slightly demented?[4]

Fergus is the elder cat. He's a black and white tuxedo-boy and drools when petted. Hates his belly rubbed and will tear the bones out of your hand if you try. Tommy is the younger, my baby. He's an orange tiger-cat, super smiley, and as lovey-dovey and snuggle-icious as possible for a cat to be. And he has Fergus under his kitten paw. Fergus sleeps on top of the covers, behind my knees. Tommy, given the chance, will snake down under and curl up on my lap or against my belly. Both of them together keep me pinned in an impossible position, but I'm used to it. Luckily, I'm a side sleeper anyway.

I realize I just went all cat-goofy there, but that's what happens when you don't have a lover or kids. You go nuts over your pets.

They were happy (I guess) to see me when I got home, and did their damnedest to trip me and get fur on my black work clothes. Tommy thinks it a solemn duty to sharpen his claws on my leg. Which is okay in jeans but not cool when I'm wearing a skirt. Not cool at all.

A scoop of kibble and a bowl of fresh water distracted them, and I slumped into the sofa. Mail was the usual bills, sales, and pleas for money for starving children. I don't watch TV unless there's a disaster to watch unfold, or a decent PBS program on.

My laptop awaited. And so did my virtual friends online.

But the phone rang. My mother. I didn't want to pick up, but I was too well-trained not to respond to her calls. Like Pavlov's dog, I answered at the second ring, working on my explanation

---

[4] As no one has yet locked me in the attic, true. Not demented.

of the job loss through no fault of my own. But there wasn't time to tell her.

"Nelly."

"Hi, Mom."

"Did you get the book I wanted?" She had asked for a library book and I had forgotten. Because, of course, I did.

"Oh, Mom—I'm so sorry, I didn't get it. It was crazy at work today—in fact—"

"Well, for Cris*sakes*, Penelope, I don't ask for much. Couldn't you remember this one thing?"

I got the full-on Penelope. She was in a mood. "I'm totally sorry, Mom, but today—"

"Now what am I supposed to read? Book group is this week-end and I was counting on it. Well, you'll just have to pick it up tomorrow."

"I'm not working tomorrow."

"I thought you worked on Saturdays."

"Well, I do, normally, but they had layoffs. I was laid off. So I'm not going in—"

"That can't be right. They're supposed to give you two weeks' notice!"

"No, I would have to give them two weeks if I were leaving, but they laid me off because of the budget."

"Well, that's terrible. I suppose they had to get rid of the least competent[5]. Isn't that how it goes? What am I supposed to do about book group, anyway?"

All the things I couldn't say burbled up inside of me. For once, just once, couldn't she give a crap about me?

"Nelly? The book?"

---

[5] <insert string of curses here> <shrink slowly into the swamp>

"I'm not going back to the library, Mom. I'm laid off. I don't want to just sashay in the door the next day. That would be too weird."

"I suppose I'll have to go buy the damned book now. Is World of Books open on Saturdays?"

"I wouldn't know. I don't work there. I think so."

"Well, maybe you should go try them? Now that you're free—you could work in a bookstore now. That's just like the library."

"It's not, actually." I could taste my heartbeat in the back of my throat. Maybe that's not physically possible but that's how it felt.

"Library, bookstore—same difference! You always had your nose in a book. That's why you have glasses now—you ruined your eyes reading in the dark."

Wait for it. Here it comes. Say nothing.

"I don't know why you insist on wearing those creepy cat-eye glasses. They went out with saddle shoes and bobby socks. Get some contact lenses and maybe you'll get yourself a boyfriend. Or a man-friend, I suppose they call it at your age. It's not too late. You're not bad-looking without glasses!"

Say goodbye, Nelly. "Mom, I have to go now. My tea kettle is whistling."

"I don't hear it. Is it one of those quiet ones?"

"I'll talk to you later, Mom."

"Well, what about—oh, never mind. I'll go get it *myself*. I was going to get my nails done anyway. I might as well just go next door."

"Bye, Mom—gotta go!" But I couldn't hang up on her. I couldn't. No matter how much I wanted to.

"Well, goodbye. I'll talk to you tomorrow!"

"Bye!"

The line was dead before I hit the button.

Naughty Nellie blew her Ma's chance of reading the book before Book Group met. Disappointing Mom again, like every other day of the week. Nellie, the Bloody Finger, dripping on the white carpet. *Nellie the Numbskull.*

Back to my imaginary internet friends, at last.

I logged in to the *LauraLand* website. There were a number of conversations going on, some private messages, some scholarly, some ridiculous. The usual running arguments about bipolar Rose Wilder Lane, on *Let the Hurricane Roar* versus *Free Land*, and what feminist critic Ann Romines had the effrontery to say about Laura's incestuous infatuation with Pa. What Pa's twinkling blue eyes meant to their Electra-complex relationship. The sister-sister bond in *Little Town on the Prairie* when Mary goes away and Carrie has to step in and step up. And the authorship wars: How much had Laura written and how much had Rose written? How much had Rose pressured Laura, and how much did Laura rewrite after Rose got her mitts on the manuscript? How a smart, fast-thinking, kind woman like Laura could have given birth to such an out-of-control brat like Rose. Was it childhood trauma, or was it genetics?

The website carried on the ridiculous and the farcical: If the Ingalls family had gone to Oregon with the cousins, would they have gotten trapped with the Donner Party, and if so, would they have eaten each other? Who would have they eaten first? Is soil really an efficacious treatment for bee stings, *vis a vis* Cousin Charley's infamous dance on the hornet nest in *the Big Woods*? What if the ice had cracked while the wagon was crossing Lake Pepin, and under the ice there was a whole underwater pioneer world in the lake, and sea monsters were part of that world, would Laura have taught school just the same?

You think I kid? You know nothing about the *Mary and the Mummy* spinoff-fanfic that continues on the Internet. You've missed out on Carrie and Grace turning into vampire-slayers. To say nothing of *LustyLaura*, the erotica fansite where pioneering penises get their first experience with *Girlz Gone WILDER*. Slash fic[6] with Willie (heh) Oleson and Mr. Owen, the stern young schoolteacher who whipped him. Please. The world of Little House fans is odd, quirky, and—strangely enough, very much like a warm log cabin in winter.

It's cozy, a little isolated, but it's probably better that way.

Anyhoo, I logged in because I had nothing left in my pathetic life, *Nelly the Knucklehead* with no flipping job, a disappointing daughter, and I wanted to see what was going on. I saw a few messages, one from *TheRealLaura*, who started the site, again asking all members to refrain from flaming each other on the boards. Good luck, lady. Internet trolls are with us forever. Like grasshoppers and crows and striped gophers, they are here to make life a little miserable, and we have to figure out how to live with them. Plant four kernels of corn instead of just one, as Pa said. *Four don't go'fer.*

Another message, from *Almanzoor*, was an invitation to go on one of those literary book tours, visiting the sites of interest to Laura fans. I liked this *Almanzoor*, this unknown "invisible" friend who often posted about farming, horses, and pioneering. He knew a lot about fireplace cooking, for example, and often chimed in with recipes from the 1800s that he had researched from who-knows-where, but when I cross-checked, because, *hello, librarian here*, he was correct. I'd learned from him.

Almanzoor invited any and all to join him on a tour of the Mecca for all *LauraLanders*, the literal Little Town on the

---

[6] Slash fiction is when two unlikely same-sex characters are paired up, like David and Goliath in a romance. David/Goliath, with a slash between them. Ergo, slash fic. You're welcome.

Prairie—De Smet, South Dakota—for a private group tour he had set up.

I've never been to any of Laura's special places.

I've ridden in a stagecoach, though. Every California school kid learns about the Gold Rush in fourth grade, and if you live close enough to make a day trip to San Francisco, you go to the headquarters of Wells Fargo, where they have a stagecoach in their lobby, and everyone gets a chance to sit in it and a lucky few get to sit on top and ride shotgun[7]. There are long straps of woven cord outside the coach, that a few strong kids hold and jerk on, to simulate the rugged ride. It all involves a lot of yelling, whooping, and a few blasts from cap guns. Very exciting if you're nine years old. Probably gets really old for the tellers in the bank next door, though.

I've ridden in a stagecoach out of doors, too. My Girl Scout troop went to the historic town of Columbia, up in Gold Country, when I was about eleven, and we saw the Wild West show, including the man who gets "shot" and falls off the top of a building into a pile of mattresses. We panned for gold and bought hoarhound candy (oh, delight of delights, the candy that Laura ate!) at the general store. And we took the stagecoach ride that included a "real" holdup on the road outside of the town. Columbia was cool.

In junior high we all participated in the local town's Founder's Day activities, like marching in the parade and making candles by dipping string into wax. I rode for three days in a covered wagon as part of Wagon Days, on a 50-mile ride to celebrate the nation's 200th birthday. Not sure how that all was connected, but I was told to get a sunbonnet and a long dress, and my mother duly found me one. The 100 kids participating were divvied into

---

[7] Literally where the term came from.

"families" and then into wagons, and we ate together, sang songs along the way, snuggled in our sleeping bags together, and so on. We had skits at night around the campfire and took turns performing for the whole camp.

That was as close as I imagined I'd ever get to the true Laura-pioneer-prairie experience, out here in California. And I never go anywhere. I stay home. I'm a librarian cat-lady. I'm a 45-year-old virgin obsessed with a dead lady from 150 years ago. Where the hell would I go except the library or my own living room?

I've never seen the prairie. Nor a rolling cornfield. Never made apple pie out of a pumpkin, nor bed-shoes out of an old blanket, but that's a different subject. I clicked on a few of the links that *Almanzoor* posted with his announcement and looked at the sites.

One trip was set for mid-September. "America's favorite pioneer girl..." Look-alike contests, a kids' costume parade, a worship service, Ozark music, and a parade. That was in Missouri. In De Smet, South Dakota (*Dakota Territory*, I always said in my head), there was a summer festival that we'd miss, but that was okay because on the website it looked pretty hokey.

But the Ingalls home, the schoolhouse, the Brewster school! I wanted to see the main street where Royal Wilder's feed store had been. I wanted to see the tree claim and the pink screen doors that Tay Pay Pryor, who was drunk, had kicked through. I wanted to see where Gerald Fuller the grocer had done his clog dance, and the Big Slough. Oh, the Big Slough—which I pronounced "SLAW" as a child. The Big Slaw, where Pa cut the heavy grass that they burned to keep warm through that hard Long Winter. Where Carrie and Laura walked around and around, lost, until they peeped out at the Wilder brothers, little rabbits in the undergrowth, and Laura saw Manly's blue eyes for the first time.

I think that's when I first fell in love. Who wouldn't love a guy named Manly?

I think that's why I have never loved any other man. He was never Manly enough.

I typed a short reply to *Almanzoor* that maybe I was interested and to send me more details. I wouldn't go, of course. It was fun to pretend, though. I scrolled through a few more pages, and then I went to the kitchen and pulled a pot pie out of the freezer. It wasn't made of blackbird. It was chicken, though. And that would have to be good enough. I cracked open a brown bottle of locally brewed ale and went back to my desk.

Mail and bills to pay, and a new budget to make, since I was going to be on pioneer provisions in the near future. I could do it. If Ma could make a lamp out of axle grease, a rag and a button, I could figure out how to survive on unemployment. And if Laura could teach school at age 15, by the Great Horn Spoon, I was certainly going to be able to find another introverted nerd job.

I found my old resume in a file and started to work on a new version that was about fifteen years closer to reality than the former.

* * *

In my dream, I was wearing a white dress. In a golden wheat field. Huge blue empty sky overhead. Huge sky. Blue. Empty. Waving wheat. Dress blowing. My loose hair blowing. I kept pushing strands of my hair from my face. No sunbonnet. I left it in the little house, where Ma and Mary were sewing.

Ma says I'll be brown as— No. I won't say it. There's nothing wrong with being brown, Ma. The hatred in her eyes. Hate and fear. Maybe I didn't know the massacres that Ma had heard of and feared. Maybe they happened or maybe they didn't. But in my dream, I know it's racist and despicable, and when I awoke,

I knew Ma was wrong. I lay in the dark, tears dripping down my face because Ma was so wrong about so many things.

I checked the clock. It was 2:25 a.m. and I still had hours of dark ahead of me. And I was crying over what? Not Ma and her fierce hatred. But because I had lost my job and was alone and scared, and I had to do it all myself. Figure it out. Boil the beans or sew on a button or clean up the cat puke and get my oil changed and declutter my hard drive and things like that.

I lay in my own puddle of tears for a little while until I fell asleep again, cats draped across me like a rich lady's furs.

CHAPTER 3

I was young when I discovered Laura and the world of her little houses, as I said, and at first did not know that the books were a series or in any sort of order. I couldn't even pronounce her name correctly.

"I'm reading a book by Laura Ig-NALL-iss Wilder," I told my mother after that trip to the library.

She corrected me. "Ingalls," and I repeated it once, aloud.

But forever, in my head, it's been "Laura Ignalliss." I taught myself to read and often found that my pronunciation of words did not match the rest of the world's. Pagoda was "PADJ-ah-duh," for example. Sounding out words on my own gave me the *Big SLAW*, but it also gave me a running start on figuring things for myself. I sometimes looked up information, like the city of Gen-OH-a, in the at-LAS. And when I said my special words aloud, I was IN-uh-VEET-a-BLEE teased, tormented, and humiliated. Best to read in silence, I found.

Silence was a safe corner under the kitchen desk, with the chair pulled in. Behind a living room chair was also good. Under the tall stool in the kitchen was a one-foot square space I could sit in with crossed legs. I loved to tuck in a blanket along the top bunk, so that my bottom bunkbed was a magical chamber, a tented caravan, a secret cave where I ate a stack of Oreos and chewed on my thumb-skin while I read and read and read. Noises went away. Raised voices disappeared. Scares were not scary.

Homework and school were never difficult because I could read. I could read faster and better and further ahead than anyone else. I found myself in a special reading class with blue- and aqua- and tan- and orange-coded readers, and a light box that increased my reading speed one highlighted line at a time. Mr. Matthews was the teacher of this class, and I remember his ginger curly hair and his yellow tie, and the stack of readers that I worked through until I had read the last one, every last one. All the books in the world awaited.

Silence was a place where words did not disturb the surface, the unrippled rim of things we didn't say. The way the neighbor next door had lifted me to his kitchen table and fondled my knee. Stroked my arm. Books were the portal, the clichéd secret passage to elsewhere that wasn't here, that wasn't now, that was far and away more interesting.

In the pages of the library books, I found a friend who wasn't good as gold, who got into trouble and thought selfish thoughts and wished she could climb trees and wear copper-toed boots. I could climb trees, and I didn't know what copper-toed boots were because I wore blue round-toed Keds. But I loved the books enough that I checked them out, over and over, until for Christmas the yellow box appeared, and I owned my own set of the nine *Little House* books, including the mysteriously dark and dreary *The First Four Years*. I wrote my name in cursive on the box, and I read those books, absorbed them as scripture, chapter and verse.

From *Little House in the Big Woods* I learned that Cousin Charley was a jerk, that Mary was a priss, and that Jack would be ever at Laura's side. I knew I could wipe dishes (whatever that was) and help make cheese or butter, and that cousins for Christmas were a delight. I learned that Pa could do anything. He could bring home a bear or a wagonload of fish; he could avoid bees[8] and bring home honey, too. Pa could tell stories and Pa could play. Ma was gentle, yet creative, making paper dolls and circles in the frosty windows, and she made Charlotte the rag doll, too.

From *Little House on the Prairie*, I learned that houses and neighbors changed. Wheels rolled away with families and possessions, and later, when we moved houses for the first time, I understood what that really meant. But I knew it better because of Laura. I learned that Native Americans, like all people, were complex—sometimes threatening, to Ma's eyes, sometimes generous, to Pa's. I learned about building something from nothing, and then walking away from it all—in a way I (again) didn't understand until adulthood. But when it happened to me then (a roommate from college suddenly booting me out), I recognized it. This is what Pa and Ma Ingalls felt, what they did to preserve the family. Government rules were sometimes the hardest to accept. And sometimes, just being a good neighbor was harder.

By the time the Ingalls family reached *The Banks of Plum Creek*, I got to know Laura's naughty side. She disobeyed, sassed, slapped, and almost drowned herself by being willful and independent. She hadn't yet learned to tame those parts of herself, to channel that independence into something bigger than mere self-indulgence. She also learned about other cultures—Johnny the cow-tender who couldn't speak a word of English. About Swedes and Norwegians[9], about going to school and church, about the bleak weather of the Midwest. About real-life drama and fear, like a bully at school. Like a grasshopper plague. Like Pa failing to arrive in a blizzard and trying to get through the

---

[8] Bees don't sting me, he said.
[9] They're so *clean*, the folks said. As if it were a shock, to people who bathed just once a week.

next few days till they could learn his whereabouts. Of hearing that Santa Claus might not be real.

And then, *On the Shores of Silver Lake*, tragedy. Mary's blindness, the crushing debt, the illness of half the family, while Laura and Pa endeavored to carry on. Jack, her beloved dog, dying[10] as they set out for new horizons again. Laura, shouldering the yoke of caring for her sisters and helping Ma when Pa went away. And then, the excitement of a railroad town, and the surveyors' house, and being the only visible souls on the prairie. Silence again, outside, with the icy lakes and the wolves.

A new town. A new start, a new life. I've been there (me, lost after college, until I found my way to the library).

Baby Grace, lost on the prairie, found in a violet-filled fairy ring.

And suddenly—a cold winter ahead. A long winter. A *hard* winter. Starvation loomed. It was a real thing. The family's perseverance, their faith, their dogged determination to survive— lessons in making do. A button lamp, sourdough wheat bread, sticks of hay, made-do Christmas gifts and the risk, every few days, of Pa sledding out to the homestead to load more "slaw" grass. Banker Ruth, capitalist, buying up all the lumber for fuel. Storekeeper Loftus trying to gouge the starving townspeople. The blind orders of the ignorant train supervisor to ram a wall of ice, and then to cut off all train service to the outlying towns until spring out of petty revenge. That was an eye-opener for me.

I re-read those chapters in an era of political unease in Washington D.C., and heard bits of commentary on the radio and television. Was government an entity you could trust? Was

---

[10] I will never forgive Rose for jerking me around with the nonsense tale about Jack, the bulldog who actually went away with the ponies and the wagon at the start of Plum Creek; the story about "Jack" who clung to the family until he dies peacefully at home? A brutal melodrama played upon sensitive children—not cool, Rose.

there anyone in control, and whose welfare did they have in mind? Perhaps these family stories helped seed Rose's latent Libertarianism.

The Ingalls family emerged after that Hard Winter and entered society again, into a *Little Town on the Prairie*, a crocus in the snow, a beam of light ahead. Better times for everyone, and for Mary, a miracle that turned those thoughts on their head: a government college for the blind. Laura said goodbye to her uncomplaining disabled sister, and then, in a genius move, gets busy. *Stop shilly-shallying*, she tells herself, and proceeds to clean the entire house, top to bottom, to please her Ma[11]. Even around Grace, who is not helping. Many times, so many times, I have been miserable, sad, brokenhearted, alone, and made it through my feelings by getting *busy*. Laura and Ma taught me that.

The Wilder boys had appeared by that time. First in *Silver Lake*, in a horse race that seemed unfair, but Almanzo won anyway. In *The Long Winter*, Almanzo and Cap Garland saved the nascent town with their cheerfully grim ride into the winter sky to bring back wheat. By the time Laura is a teenager in *Little Town*, Almanzo escorts her home from a church revival meeting and she begins to learn a little about men. Cigars versus pipe tobacco, for example. Making small talk. Being teased by her friends.

Royal Wilder ran a feed store in De Smet and appeared once in a while in the pages to give depth and character to the grown-up farmer boys. Sister Eliza Jane makes her villainous appearance on scene as the teacher, Lazy Lousy Lizzy Jane, and mercilessly bullies Laura and Carrie in class. All Laura can think is *not to slap* old classmate nasty Nellie, and perhaps someday Laura would get a ride behind those Wilder horses.

And she did.

---

[11] I learned the lesson about keeping busy from the Ingalls women, but I still haven't learned that there is no pleasing a narcissist, no matter how many times you try.

Now tell me: Is there anything as satisfying as seeing Nellie Oleson turn red and look away? Not in this Nelly's eyes. Nellie Oleson was a bitch. I think we can be clear about that.

Then we sweep into *These Happy Golden Years*, which is not how I felt about high school myself, but I consider this my first romance read. With gothic overtones at the Brewster place, including the Victorian madwoman rocking by the fire, doom, gloom, wailing and gnashing of teeth, the Brewsters offered Laura a terrifying first venture away from home. Awakening to screams and a knife in the dark, to long hours in the cold schoolroom with belligerent teen boys and no teaching experience, Laura faces the bitter reality that not every family is loving, and not every morning is good. It's only when Almanzo sweeps into the settlement with his Morgan horses and carries her back to her family, a white knight with jingle bells on his steeds, that she feels safe again.

Almanzo proved to be her knight in shining armor again and again—choosing Laura over Nellie, marrying in haste to sidestep the unwelcome Wilder wedding party, planting a tree claim to settle into a new generation of pioneering the tamed prairie. The golden glow of Almanzo loving Laura has overlaid every imagined relationship I ever thought about, and is it any wonder? He asks her if she will have him for her husband, and brings a pearl and garnet ring, and Laura grants him his wish: "You may kiss me goodnight."[12]

Laura gives him permission to love her. He doesn't take it from her without asking. He isn't that kind of man. How much stronger a role model could a girl have?

How much more, then, did I long for a man who would ask permission instead of take what had been mine, and ruin what

---

[12] This line made me blush and giggle so hard as a tween. I skipped past it as a teen. As an adult, I swoon over it every time.

might ever be for me? What broke before I understood. What lay damaged inside for so many years.

Manly[13]. Almanzo. Where are you for me?

---

[13] I never understood the nickname *Manly*. Manzo was Royal's nickname for Almanzo, and it's perfect. Almanzo, Manzo. Manly? It's a little cringey. And also: There is apparently no truth to the story about a Crusader named El Manzoor, and the likelihood of the Wilder family carrying that name for ages is slim, given that their genealogy does not bear even the slightest witness to the so-called generational tradition. So one wonders why his staid New Englander folks dubbed him such "an outlandish name," as Almanzo himself puts it (in Little Town). Could it have been the romantic influence of the Victorians?

CHAPTER 4

You noticed that I did not speak of *Farmer Boy*, that third but the only not-Laura piece of the canon. If *Little House in the Big Woods* is Laura's paean to her father, *Farmer Boy* is her love letter to her husband. This is how Almanzo lived in his upstate New York youth, New England to the core, apples and onions fried together, wintergreen berries in brandy, Malone Academy and more.

"Manzo, be you sick?" The colonial-esque manner of speaking felt foreign when I first read it, and I could not help but compare the portraits of two families so juxtaposed by the same author (or authors, since Rose also wove these pages).

Laura's Pa loved progress and automation. It was a great age for mechanizing, and when Charles could afford to hire threshers or buy a machine, he did. A sewing machine, a parlor organ—he brought machines into the house as well, beyond the ones he could make with his bare hands[14]. Pa looked to the future, in organizing a county and sitting on the school board. He looked far across the horizon, leaving the bunched old woods of Wisconsin for the open prairies of the Dakotas, for Minnesota, toward Oregon, if he could have gone. He loved the far shore and the high plains—but heading for progress, not escape. Industry and thrift, those great virtues of the Scots, were his and his family's.

---

[14] From the carrot-grating old bucket to the china shepherdess's carved stand, from the rocking chair, doors, hinges, and windows Charles made in Kansas's Indian Territory, to the many little houses he built, Charles was a whiz with his hands.

In contrast, Almanzo's Father looked back to his English forefathers, to work the land slowly and lovingly, to peel corn or shave a shingle by hand, so that none was wasted. He threshed the wheat with care, and handled the wool of his Merinos, the melons, the pumpkins; he hand-reared his horseflesh as well. James Wilder did not want to mechanize; he gathered in rich harvest and put money in the bank. Look backward, look to tradition; sit quietly on Sundays and obey, always obey. Use your head, learn what a potato costs, what a nickel will buy. At least that was Father's philosophy as a middle-aged man. Somewhere along the line he failed himself, and trusted his youngest son, Perley, who lost all Father's money in a stock scheme. Father died in penury, some sources say. A great pity.

That story's not in the books, but if you're a literary nerd like I am, you'll keep reading till you learn more and more, until your head is full of useless tidbits like this and you'll bore friends and family alike with your trivia-laden conversation. Trust me. You will.

One of my college professors warned me in front of the whole class, "Nobody likes a pedant." [15]

Laura and her sisters learned at home with Ma, who had herself taught school, and then attended the one-room schoolhouse in whatever town they were in. The Wilder children went to the local school, and then to the Malone Academy, where Royal learned not to be a farmer but a capitalist, and Alice and Eliza Jane learned how to dance, embroider and fuss about Father's table manners. All in all, not the education I assume James had planned for them. Only Almanzo seemed to escape

---

[15] Apparently, this is true, which is why I'm still single and, indeed, still a virgin.

that fate—by staying on the farm[16] with Father and learning the tricks of horse-breeding, of raising cattle and sheep, of tilling the land for a good harvest.

What I learned from *Farmer Boy* was that simple food is the best, homemade, lovingly prepared, and eaten in gratitude. The boy stuffed himself with sliced ham, turkey, mashed potatoes, mashed turnips, apples and onions, gravy and cranberry jelly[17], sliced bread with creamy farm butter[18], stewed squash, apple pie, fruit cake, pumpkin pie, and a tall glass of milk. And he had room for nuts and apples and apple cider[19] after a game of snow fort. With some fluffy hot popcorn to follow. No shame in eating his fill; body dysmorphia for any gender wasn't an issue back then[20].

Almanzo loosened his belt and crammed in another few bites, with fruitcake in his pocket as he headed out the door. Cookies, doughnuts, pound cake, watermelon, ice cream, almost every grain of the white sugar—into the bottomless pit that was a nine-year-old boy.

I've fried apples and onions together, and it's delicious. When I read *Farmer Boy*, I want to cook, I want to bake, I want to black the stove and curry a horse and have my foot on the steps of the church by 9 a.m. on a Sunday. I want to be Mother's hands, flying at whatever she does: shuttling sheep's gray back and forth in her

---

[16] If I were Pa, I would burst into an appropriate song here about staying home on the farm, boys.

[17] Not the kind that comes in a metal can with ridges down the side. Homemade, of course. With real cranberries.

[18] The best butter the buyer had ever seen, and people in New York City ate Mother's butter and wondered at who had made such wonderful stuff.

[19] Was it alcoholic? I presume it was, but low in proof.

[20] As Aunty Em says to her farmhands in *The Wizard of Oz,* "You can't work on an empty stomach! Have a cruller."

loom, to make a suit for Royal. Cutting crusts with her sharp knife and shaping bread. Filling the kerosene lamp or making a plate of scraps for a lonesome dog. Providence, she called him.

Reading of their industry made me ashamed—that my hands were idle, that I wasn't feeding a tableful, that I was that Austenian abomination—a single woman in want of a husband. And yet, out of this same household came Eliza Jane, a single woman with a quarter-section claim[21] in De Smet, just like her brothers. She took the train out West on her own, had a claim shanty built (probably by her brothers), lived alone and taught school. We never witness it in the text, but one can only assume that she badgered the bejeesus out of Almanzo and Royal in De Smet just as she had done in Malone.

Eliza Jane, that castrating bitch. Any redeeming values here? Hard to say; again, none in the canon, as far as I can tell, but in the Talmud of Laura, the spinoffs about Rocky Ridge—all the books started by Rose's foster grandson Roger Lea McBride and finished by *his* daughter—if they can be trusted, tell us that Eliza Jane, or EJ, as she was sometimes called, moved to New Orleans. Rose went to live with EJ to be further educated. How that must have galled Laura, no? To have her only precious daughter entrusted to the clutches of *that woman*—that tormenter[22]. What a legacy to share—the strong woman who Rose became was surely influenced by Eliza Jane as much as by Laura, for better or worse.

---

[21] A quarter section is 160 acres. *By herself!*

[22] Or was any of that De Smet nonsense even true? Did Rose make it all up for dramatic tension? Poetic license? Didn't it bother Almanzo to have his sister (whom he admired and loved in *Farmer Boy*) pilloried as a bitch in the pages of a children's story? Why didn't EJ herself ever toss a defamation suit at Laura and Rose? Because she died in 1930 and never saw the offending text.

* * *

Early Saturday morning, needled by idle hands and an empty agenda, I baked a loaf of bread from scratch[23]. I didn't use the bread machine, either, choosing Father's methods over Pa's this time—needing the soothing feel and scent of wheat and yeast and a hot oven to think over my options. I filled out my paperwork for unemployment and looked at job openings online for a while, as the dough rose. I kept my stapled booboo finger out of the dough.

It had been twelve hours since I last checked the website and, by golly, things were happening in the world of *LauraLand*. There was an Exquisite Corpse game going on where different members added a line or two to a story and then passed it on. So far the story had Alice Wilder in a three-way with Mary Powers and Cap Garland. It was pretty ridiculous, so I eschewed participating and clicked through to the bulletin board.

Almanzoor had been answering questions about the proposed trip to De Smet, and it looked like about a dozen people had RSVP'd the invitation. That should be a manageable-size group. I clicked "maybe" again as my response on the questionnaire, because I couldn't go anywhere with zero income, but I wanted to be kept informed of what was going on, and a "maybe" would get me copies of the announcements.

Someone from the Chicago branch had uploaded photos from their Dime Sociable, a costumed re-creation of the Ladies Society for the Church in De Smet back in Laura's day. Laura and Mary Powers went together, paid their dimes, and sat primly, only to be bored to death. The photos seemed to show

---

[23] Wash on Monday...Bake on Saturday.

that more fun was had in the reenactment. The fellow who often portrayed Dr. Brown, the minister, was there in his dark suit and white beard. And I couldn't be sure from the photos, but it looked like the original menu—white cake and custard—had been faithfully recreated, too.

Such is what passes for entertainment for Laura-lovers.

* * *

My phone buzzed at about 10 o'clock, when my mother usually rings. I'd like to be able to say I called her Ma but that had never passed my lips. She wouldn't have appreciated the old-fashioned charm. She would have thought I was mocking her. She greeted me but did not ask about my layoff, which suited me fine because I was still pretending it hadn't happened. Somehow, she would indicate that it was my fault. I must have done *something* or they would have kept me. Getting hired last was such a sin.

"I was talking with Trudy and she says that old Dr. Felzman died. *Killed* himself. Too bad, poor man."

"Poor man?" I choked this out.

"Yes, poor thing. She said he had cancer—inoperable—and so he shut himself in the garage and turned the engine on. Gassed himself. Sickening."

Dead.

"Are you still there? Hello?"

"Yeah—I'm here. I can't believe he's dead."

"Such a tragedy."

"No, Mom. It's not. Good riddance."

"How can you say that? It's a disgusting thing to say—"

"How can you say it's a tragedy, after what he did to me? How can you just act as if that never happened?"

"Are you still going on about that? It was a long time ago. Everyone else has forgotten it. Why can't you?"

"Because he fucked my whole life up."

"If you're going to talk like that, then this conversation is over. For heaven's sake, Nelly, why do you have to get so excited? Why can't you just let bygones be bygones?"

I sat in silence, my heart pounding in my ears, my mind whirling.

"Penelope?"

"I have to go, Mom."

"Well, don't go and sulk now. You always do this. Come along, let's move on. You're fine, it's all fine, we're fine. Come on now."

I did it then—I hung up on my mother. I was shaking. I wanted to vomit, to expel everything in my stomach and my gut, both ways. Sick, sick, sick man. Sick mother. Sick world. I could run screaming down the road, I could drink an entire bottle of wine, I could go jump in front of a moving truck if I thought it would stop the pain. It wouldn't. This kind of anguish is deeper than skin, breath, memory, death. So much deeper.

I quickly pulled a book from the shelf—*On The Banks of Plum Creek*—and submerged. Like the frog in the pond, I went down underneath where only my eyes showed, where my feelings were blocked by bloodwarm pondwater. I felt, tasted, smelled, heard nothing but the story in my mind. My eyes saw only words.

Sixty years ago when your grandma and grandpa were children, a little girl lived in the Big Woods, and she wasn't afraid of anything because Pa had his gun and the walls were thick, and when the wind blew, she was warm and safe.

Hours later, I closed the back cover, knowing that Laura and Mary and Baby Carrie were tucked into bed and safe as houses.

I love Laura. The Laura of the stories. The Laura of the books who was also a real girl and woman named Laura who wrote children's books about her life—even if she took liberties. It's what we all do, isn't it? Take liberties with our own stories?

My own story, for example. If you asked my mother, she'd tell you that it was misremembered, head-in-the-clouds, much ado about a little thing from long ago. Rainbows and waterfalls. If you asked me, I wouldn't tell you anything. The truth is somewhere in between.

Saturday was mostly gone and I hadn't eaten a thing. I got up to fetch myself a glass of milk[24] and an apple, because I didn't have popcorn at hand, and I couldn't think any more than that. At the end of the book, Pa was home, safe and sound, from the snowbank where he'd been lost. I was home, but I still felt lost.

Why not go to the *Little Town on the Prairie*? I mused, drinking my milk. Why not get out of this town, throw my stick and bindle over my shoulder like a hobo and just—go? An apple in my pocket, a dime in my shoe. No one, literally no one, was the boss of me now.

So I went.

---

[24] An equal amount of popcorn would go into a glass of milk and the milk would never run over the edge, a science experiment thought up by one Almanzo James Wilder. But Mother didn't like the milk pans disturbed at night.

CHAPTER 5

I said yes.

I made a reservation for the cross-country train to get from here to De Smet, or close enough. I don't like to fly, and it seemed more fitting that I should travel there by train, since I couldn't get a covered wagon. I'd have to rent a car for the last bit. I had no job, but I had a credit card. So I was going on the private tour.

I'm not one of *them,* of course. I mean, the ComicCon-Trekkie-Janeite-uberfangirl-starfuckers. I'm not writing fanfic. I don't do steampunk with pioneer flair. I didn't name my cats Charles and Almanzo. Or Plum and Silver. I don't wear gingham. I don't own a sunbonnet. I use my real name in the LIW forum: Nelly. Everyone thinks I'm playing.

I'm not playing.

I'm a word nerd. A dissociating bookworm. I love the Laura world in real life—the history, the harsh reality. What was it like to get your period out on the prairie, when the wolves could smell your menses? What the hell is salt pork, anyway? It's not bacon. Did they have to roast their own coffee beans as well as grind them? How could she stand being that sweaty every day, stomping down the hay in the back of the wagon in a high-necked, long-sleeved dress in a prairie summer, and no bath till Saturday night? No deodorant, either. Dress shields, maybe?

I don't have any doubts about living without the internet, without electricity—I could do that, and it's obvious how they filled their hours—with work, more work, Pa's fiddle and study, no idle hands; maybe singing or crochet or something in the dark. But what about having a headache? And what about things like toothbrushes, and backaches without benefit of yoga and chiropractors, and what about bladder infections? If I don't drink cranberry juice often enough, I get that burning sensation and I'm weeping to my doctor. What did the Ingalls women do out on the prairie, out on the homestead, in these situations?

What about toilet paper? What about dental floss? What about moldy food and cleaning things without rubber gloves? Horrible things like chamber pots or diapers, vomit and mouse poop and all the other kinds of dung present on a farm? What were Laura's feet like, if she went without shoes all spring and summer? What were her hands like after scrubbing the floor with sand and a rag? What was her skin like after years of drudgery and no sunscreen (she hated to wear her sunbonnet). Did she ever wash her knee-length hair? Did they have a compost pile? Did they recycle[25]?

What about the facts of life? Is that what was happening when Ma spoke to them "seriously," in the tiny shanty on Silver Lake, surrounded by railroad men? Did she explain how babies were made and that's why "being free" with the men was not allowed? Did Laura know what to expect on that first beautiful night in the little gray home in the west? Did she freak out when she saw *her* pillows, *her* Dove in the Window quilt on a bed for two—that they would sleep *together* in that bed? Did Almanzo help Laura with her corset strings, since her sisters were no longer at hand? Did she enjoy the act of love?

Did Laura want to stay down in the cool cellar when Manly came looking for her that first afternoon—did she want to stay down there and cry? Was she crying? She grew up with just girls;

---

[25] By that I mean, reuse empty cans and newspapers and glass jars, if they had them?

little brother Freddy died as a toddler. Was Laura afraid of what "Manly" really meant[26]?

Those are the questions that I like to research. I like to know facts. Solid, dependable, bricked against the nonsense of not knowing. Knowing makes you safe. Knowing gives you power.

Some LIW fans are *aficionados*. They read the books; they watched the show; they pray for a(nother) reboot. They read the books again to their kids. Some people kick it up a notch: They name their children Laura and Mary and Carrie and Grace (not Nellie, though; that would be outré). They play recordings of Pa's fiddle tunes and sing the hymns that Ma loved. They join fan groups and meet regularly, visit the historic sites en masse, wear the clothes. They taste the goodies, roast a pig's tail, make vanity cakes and bake cornbread in a spider[27] over the coals. They make cheese and twist doughnuts and go all Martha Stewart with pinking shears and string. It's fine—just a little bit—much.

And then there are the *vampires*: The child-stars who played Laura or Nellie or Albert or Willie[28]. These child stars never seemed to move on and do anything else, so they continue to ride the coattails of their meager success or stay locked in the prison of bad 1970s television. They make a career out of "being" Laura, of "being" bad Nellie. There are authors spinning out what little information there was about Ma, a.k.a. Caroline Quiner, and telling her stories. And her mother's stories. And *her* mother's stories. HarperCollins and Scholastic have made a killing on retelling the tales of Laura's extended family. Rose, too, came in for such spinoffs.

---

[26] *I guess you'll be frying my breakfast pancakes in the autumn,* he said, laying down the gendered future before them.

[27] Don't freak out. It's not a real spider. It's a frying pan with legs.

[28] Who the hell is Albert? The dead brother, whose name was Charles Frederick, aka Freddie? Fakery! I call shenanigans!

Other followers write fan fiction, spinning the spinoff to create "historical" stories that never happened—such as Pa visiting Laura at Rocky Ridge Farm, years after the real Charles Ingalls had already died, for example. Websites dedicated to the idol worship of Laura. Tales of Mary at the College for the Blind. Of Nellie getting even with the world at last. So. Many. Stories. Marginally true. Maybe literally true, some—but emotionally? I don't know.

Best of all, in my view, are the scholars: Ann Romines, William Anderson, Fred Erisman and Anita Clair Fellman. The serious nerds writing papers and presenting at academic conferences on "Western American Literature" and "The Women's West." Romines shook up and offended *LauraLand* with her discussion of seduction, incestuous longing and secret bonding between Pa and Laura. I'll admit that it offended me at first. Like spitting on the Bible. But Romines was right—in viewing the father-daughter relationship though a feminist prism, the bond between the two is the strongest in the series. And the sexualization of that, though it doesn't come to fruition, still lingers beneath the surface, still bubbles up when necessary.

Now that's what I'm talking about. That's my kinda party. I love looking sideways at literature, and in my graduate school days I felt sated every day as I consumed these theories and volumes of words. I ended up with a useless master's degree in children's literature, useless, that is, until I got the library job, and was able to feed my habit on a daily basis. I can expound on topics that will make you hate kid-lit—put it right in front of you so you can't read another page of JK Rowling[29] without seeing anti-Catholicism and prejudice against the Irish in every volume. You won't be able to enjoy *Little Women* without understanding the thwarting of women's anger. You'll be afraid

---

[29] Not to even mention her anti-trans crusade. Cancelled!

to take your kid on the *Peter Pan* ride in Disney World because you know that Wendy is Peter's surrogate mother and the object of his base Oedipal complex. You'll read *Lord of the Rings* as a Jesus allegory, and anything written between 1840 and 1910 as churning with sexual angst. Have you seen the grotesques in Edward Lear's poetry? Paging Dr. Freud!

The Victorians—sheesh.

But I digress. Clearly, I love lit-crit, I do hermeneutics, I exegete like an academic. Specifically, I'm a historicist.[30] What do the times say about the literature, and what does the literature say about the times? And how did Laura manage to break through the glass ceiling that her mother and grandmothers had laid upon her? How did she get away with it? And how come I haven't done anything like that?

Also, I'm alone. Which shows you just how sexy all this book-learning is to the opposite—or even the same gender.

I made my reservation on the cross-country train, a roomette for privacy rather than the cheapo coach car, and at the small hotel where *Almanzoor* had arranged a group rate, the Cottage Inn. I got organized, ate or froze all the groceries that would spoil in my absence, and arranged with my vet for kenneling the boys.

I packed a big T-shirt for sleeping, lots of comfy academic attire[31], a cardigan or two, and a black dress for evening dinner. Black Converse sneakers and my alternate pair of cat-eye glasses (red ones, these). I brought my most prairie-style tiered skirt and some pull-on boots because I didn't do well with pointy toes, like the ones Laura wears on the cover of *The First Four Years*. But if I could find them in green? That would be worth buying. Of course, my mother hated my clothes, quibbled about everything I

---

[30] As well as a single middle-aged virgin cat lady.

[31] I love a tight neckline, buttoned to the top, with a bowtie or a brooch. Just try and see my cleavage. I dare you.

wore, and how I did my hair (usually in a single braid, but often in a claw or clip on my head, for ease). I could do a serviceable bun *a la* ballerina if I had to for the library. I packed some black tights in case we had to dress up, but otherwise, I would stick to my little socks and Converse, if it didn't rain.

The night before I left for Dakota Territory, I texted my mom to let her know of my plans. When Mom called back, I didn't pick up. She left me a sharp message but I didn't listen to it. Not then, nor the several other times that followed. I wanted this adventure, and I was going, no matter what she said. And I'm sure she said plenty.

I didn't know what else to take. It'll be early fall on the prairie. What should I expect? Tornadoes? Green hail? Early blizzards? Indian summer[32]? A hissy fit from my mother[33]? A begging call back from Dave? Dead silence?

No matter what I took to this event or left behind, it was very clear that, as they say, I had too much baggage.

---

[32] Sorry, not sorry, Ma.
[33] Sorry, not sorry, Mom.

CHAPTER 6

The first time Laura takes a train (headed toward Silver Lake),
she is fascinated by the red velvet seats, the slanting sunshine
on polished wood paneling, the dear little spigot for water and
the communal tin cup at the end of the car. A boy sells candy
onboard and Ma forgives herself for paying *ten cents*[34] for a box
to celebrate their first train journey. The train is taking them to a
new life in Dakota Territory, and they go as far as the train goes,
and then by wagon to join Pa at the rail camp.

I've always had a hankering for a rail voyage but haven't ridden anywhere of note (the Bay Area BART system doesn't count).
It wasn't the Ritz[35], but I liked my little sleeper cabin roomette,
and the view. The train pulled into the station before 8 a.m. with
deep rumbles and a few shrieks on the tracks. I hauled my rolling
bag behind me to the open door. I was bound for Omaha, then
driving a rented car north to De Smet. It would take me two days
on the train, each way, but I was unemployed. I had all the time
in the world, right? It had taken the Ingallses weeks to get where
they were going, always. And the Wilders, too. So what the heck?
Who cared how long this variety of transportation took?

---

[34] Valued at $2.91 today, which seems about right for a box of 12 pieces of candy.

[35] We always say this, but I literally know no one who has ever stayed at the Ritz. So how
would we even know? Maybe the Ritz is shit now.

I had dropped my cats at the vet the night before for kenneling[36]. It would cost a fortune, but I have a credit card, and I did not want to ask my mom or my neighbors for anything. I also did not want my space invaded while I was gone. I was feeling too raw and vulnerable, too judged, these days.

I settled my luggage in the rack and hung up my coat, then took myself and my laptop and headphones to the viewing lounge car where I could write and yet see the scenery a bit better. We were headed east across California, from the Bay Area up through the Sierras, across Nevada to Utah, Colorado, Nebraska, almost to Iowa—making the Donner Party wagon migration backward to older cities. Once I left the train in Omaha, I'd be following the ghosts of Laura.

Knowing the route beforehand was a comfort. If I know where I am going, I know what to expect. No surprises for me, thanks. There is something freeing about leaving your world behind and heading into the great unknown—provided, that is, you know exactly where you're going and what you intend to happen. That's not what others might call freedom, but it works.

By the time I caught up on email, the daily news, and what passed for news in *LauraLand*, we were already chugging across the Carquinez Strait and heading into the Sacramento Valley. The attendant made a lunch reservation in the dining car for me, and I enjoyed the bottomless cup of coffee in an official Amtrak mug.

Although I had my earphones and some gentle Satie piano queued up, I could still hear much of what was going on around me. My eyes were on the screen, but I muted the music for a minute to listen in.

---

[36] Ridiculous how much I missed them already.

"Will you look at that!" The woman's voice had a particular pitch to it that probably shrivels testicles. "Look, it's some kind of bird. Larry, look. Look!"

I heard Larry, whoever he is, murmur in apparent agreement.

"Get the book. Larry! Look it up!" Book-lookery commenced and the bird was duly identified as a Great Blue Heron.

Yeesh. Sorry for your troubles, Larry. Have fun with her, whatever her name was. I unmuted the music and swiveled the chair a little to see who else was in the viewing lounge. One table was occupied by newspaper-reading elders. Several folks read books, magazines, one was doing a crossword; some younger adults scrolled tablets or video game screens. A lady knitting. There's always some cleverfingers, isn't there, making something out of yarn? I've knitted, crocheted, hooked rugs and needle-pointed pillowtops in the last decade or so. But I moved on to embroidery and needle-felting, and had a brief fling with burlap and white stencil paint earlier this year. I was thinking of taking up tole-painting next, as one of the last bastions of complete nerdwhizzery for defective spinsters. And what the hell? I might as well take up wool-spinning, too. Long winter nights being what they are.

The lounge was quiet enough for now, with California farmland rolling past and the Sierras in view already. There was snow on the high slopes, and I wondered how cold we'd be. And if there was enough food for the crossing. And if we got stuck in the snow, who'd be the first one to get eaten.

Laura took this trip once, by train. She came out to California to visit Rose in San Francisco in 1915; Rose who was still married to Gillette Lane, or faking it for her mother. Laura came all this way, and walked where I walk. She described getting off the train to eat or stay a night with a friend along the way. The first time Laura rode the train in about 1876, she noted that the train could travel as far in an hour as a team of horses could go in a day—10 miles with a wagon to pull, twenty without. They rode that train for several hours, ending up somewhere in Dakota Territory. They all got out at the station, heard a rail worker singing a blasphemous song that shocked Ma, and went to dinner (lunch) at the hotel.

We passed Sacramento and began the long chug into the foothills, rounding corners and bends and curves dimpled with the refuse of strip-mining, with the tawny veldt grass of a California autumn. It hadn't snowed yet in the foothills, and the trees were reddened, browned, picture-perfect for autumn, until we reached the rocks and the evergreens. It was my turn for lunch in the dining car; first I took my laptop back to my sleeper, then passed through swaying corridors and the precarious terror in between cars stuck together with accordion pleats and steel flaps[37].

The dining car attendants had no time to mess with impatient diners. "Please wait at the end of the car until you are seated." His tone was like a teacher's—you wouldn't dare to contradict him.

An attendant in a blue vest with brass buttons beckoned me and pointed to a table with two people already seated. "Please scoot all the way in. All tables are community-shared." He handed me a menu and a ball-point pen.

A minute later, a middle-aged guy in jeans and a golf shirt and cap plumped in next to me and the party was complete. I took a breath, my introvert self shrinking, and forced myself to look across the table at my companions, who were, thankfully, not Larry and his bird-watcher wife. An elderly couple of men faced

---

[37] *Yikes*, always a terror for me, because *of course* I visualize the train cars uncoupling, or smashing together with me in the middle. Of course, I imagine that *vividly*. Every time. Don't you?

me, murmuring to each other about the specials. The gentleman across looked at me and smiled.

"Hello." His shirt had the logo of some engineering firm.

"Hello."

His partner looked up from his menu and chimed in, "Hi, there." He wore an identical logo shirt, and I noticed they had identical wedding rings. Do married couples turn into twins?

The attendant with the shiny buttons came back with warm dinner rolls and butter pats and took our orders. He asked us to sign our order to our roomettes, then leaned way over the table as another passed behind the rocking narrow center aisle with a laden tray of plates.

"Whoops," said our attendant, or was he our waiter now? "Almost got me."

I wished I could have worn my earbuds. I could have eaten from the snack bar, but dining car meals are part of the ticket I bought, and it looked like every meal through to Omaha would be shared with strangers. Intimately. I got kicked under the table by one of the elders, and Mr. Golf next to me was dangerously close. I was cornered at a table with three men, and though it wasn't exactly a panic situation, I felt nonetheless discomfited. I yearned for escape. It was only a matter of time before the questions began, questions like—

"And where are you headed?" Elder Number One asked Mr. Golf. Golf Guy told some boring story about visiting relatives and retirement looming.

Elder Number Two helped the conversation along with a marked "Oh!" and "Well, now." And soon it will be—

"And you?" they asked. My turn.

"I'm on business," I said with a quick little smile. "Omaha."

They looked expectant, waiting for more details, but the attendant/waiter arrived with sodas and iced tea, and I became very, very busy with the squeezing of my lemon wedge and the stirring in of my sugar. By the time I slowly crumbled my straw wrapper into a little ball, our salads had arrived, and we got to offer one another the basket of salad dressings and crouton packets and pass the pepper.

The mechanics and niceties of sharing a meal with strangers was so exactly not what I wanted to do on this journey. I wanted to bliss out in the oblivion of having to be nowhere, and simply dissolve into the ecstasy of a topic I love dearly. I wanted to go deep enough into the Laura world so that I didn't have to think about tomorrow.

All her yesterdays are enough for me.

Outside, the rugged granite dropped away and the South Fork of the American River swirled alongside, a sinuous companion. The train slowed from the speed of the flatlands in the valley, and we were definitely chugging upward. With a sudden jolt, Golf Guy's iced tea spilled across the table, and so did the drinks on other tables. The Elders whooped in surprise and flailed at the approaching liquid in alarm. Golf Guy apologized and threw his napkin into the fray. Attendants swooped down the aisle with towels and fresh paper placemats, napkins, retaking drink orders, and I was trapped by the hullabloo.

If wishes were horses, I'd be on a black pony racing with Cousin Lena under the stars[38]. Too much people. I don't mean too many—*too much* with the bumping elbows and the senseless chit-chat. I hated them and loathed myself[39].

At last, the mess was cleared and the meal was over. I scribbled my name and cabin number on the receipt and excused myself. I headed out through the end of the diner toward the parlor car, and had taken a few steps into the new car before realizing

---

[38] *In the starlight, we will wander, gay and free.*
[39] Same as it ever was.

that I'd gone the wrong way. This was the snack bar and lounge for coach passengers. There were newspapers and magazines in this car, too, and a young woman reading the familiar yellow volume—*Little Town on the Prairie*, it looked like. Next to her, another woman, older, reading *The First Four Years*. Next to them, a child, with *Farmer Boy* in her lap and a doll dressed in an apron and sunbonnet. Apparently, the party was traveling in Coach, if they were in this lounge.

A couple of young men played their video games, and another pair of men played a travel set of chess at a small side table. The bumps and rattles didn't disturb the magnetic game. Beyond them all, I saw the intense blue of Donner Lake flash in the distance. Blue lakes, silver lakes, Twin Lakes, Spirit Lake. I couldn't believe I was going to see these things, to walk along her trail. Some thousands of lakes in this world, and the ones Laura immortalized were about to become real to me. I wasn't sure I could stand the suspense much longer.

I went back through the dining car, the lounge car, through another sleeper back to my own little roomette, and slid the door shut. Outside, granite boulders, like a giant toddler's playthings, lay in jumbled profusion up to snowy heights.

What was I doing? Why was I here? I didn't know. I was just—going.

* * *

At 4 o'clock we rolled into Reno and the train paused for twenty minutes, so I got off to get some fresh air. The air was scented with pine and cedar and woodsmoke, plus diesel exhaust. Seemed like everyone in Reno had a big truck or an SUV, grinding and growling up the wide highways and the mountain roads. From the train station you could see a couple of large parking structures, Harrah's Hotel and casino up the street, and a lot of sky. I could also see my breath and feel the chill of the late afternoon at altitude.

I walked along the length of the train, toward the back of the train, past the lounge car, the dining car, the snack bar, three coaches and the baggage car behind all. It felt good to stretch my legs and roll my shoulders a bit. Attendants dropped off trash bags and brought in stacks of canned drinks and bags of ice. New passengers hoisted their suitcases aboard, with a baby in a carrier, a foldable stroller, a set of skis, a snowboard or two. Backpacks and duffel bags, boxes and, delightfully, a set of stilts and a unicycle.

About twenty feet back, along the fence, the smokers kicked the dirt and smoked and gave each other lights. At the end of the track, I turned and walked back the length of the train, beginning to recognize fellow travelers. The girl had her doll on her arm and was jumping on and off the car, singing to herself. Her mother sucked a butt a dozen feet away. The chess players detrained and I didn't see them again. One of the magazine readers from the parlor car, standing with hands in his corduroy coat pockets, caught my eye and smiled.

I nodded in recognition[40] and kept walking, past all the same cars and passengers milling about; along the lengthy train toward the front, three red engines rumbling idle. The front had no kind of cow catcher, not what I expected, just a block of machinery on iron wheels revving for the next leg through the high desert. I took deep breaths of the mountain air tinged with diesel, then turned back and headed to my car again.

Like something out of a movie, the conductor called out, "All aboard," and though I wasn't at my sleeper yet, I hopped on, a little fearful of being left behind.

---

[40] Don't recognize me! Don't see me! Ack!

The magazine reader got on right after me. He was handsome, perhaps Hispanic, with brown hair, brown eyes with a strong Aztec brow, tan skin, a polite smile. He didn't say anything, which I appreciated. *Don't talk to me.* I liked him for that.

The train blew its horn and began to glide forth. I went upstairs from the exit and luggage storage toward the roomettes, the magazine guy behind me. I turned right into my compartment and he passed behind me. I shut the door with a pneumatic click and drew the curtain. I didn't want lookers-in. The door and curtain closed out the inner world of the train, and the outside world slid by a little faster until we were steadily on the rails again, heading eastward, through the high desert and in and out of tunnels through stony mountains too high to climb over or too steep to roll around, even if you left Independence by early summer.

I kept my laptop open and took notes about my journey, and when we approached somewhere near civilization the internet sprang back to life. I surfed the web for news, stories, and things that caught my eye. I was drifting, with no job, no family, no purpose. I fell into a funk, it seemed, like Laura after she lost her unnamed boy-baby[41]. She lay in bed and heard the hired girl speak sharply to toddler Rose, and knew she must get well and get up. She had to come back to life, come out of the bleak landscape of loss. Even if that landscape felt familiar.

The land outside was beige, tan, buff, not drab, but neither was it vibrant. It was a lot like my life had been. The shades were muted but varied. How could I step outside of the armor I'd grown around me? What useful work was there for me outside of the library? How would I elevate, motivate, expand my tiny horizon? I was on a train, heading east. Why was I there? Was

---

[41] How do you go for three or four weeks without naming your first son? Didn't they want another Almanzo? Neither Charles nor James? I still don't get it.

heading east going backward, and was that a bad thing? What could I hope to find?

What if *eastward ho* was my way out? What if what I needed to find, or escape, was where I was going? Would I find what I need? And would I know it when I found it?

The rocking of the train lulled me into a nap.

Dinner could be somewhere between 5:30 and 7:45, depending when I got a reservation for the dining car. The attendant came through the cars again with his notebook, taking names and numbers for dinner. He knocked on my glass door, startling me out of a deeper sleep than I expected. Disoriented, I pushed my glasses up and clutched at myself for a second, then answered, while flipping back the curtain. "Yes?"

"Dinner reservations, Miss?"

"Yes, 7:30?"

"I've got 7:45 and that's the last seating."

"Wonderful, thank you."

That was perfect, actually. Late seating, fewer faces. And I'm a coward, I guess. Not able to talk to new people. Except about books, across the counter, my library reference desk fortress, lost to me now. Books. As cliché as it is, they are my refuge.

The little house in the woods, on the prairie, in the bank of the creek, on the shore of the lake—a little house where I could bake bread and grow violets and rock the churn and string buttons. The black bear comes into the cow's yard, the panther screams up among the trees, and Pa's rifle is above the door. I am safe. The plank bridge keeps the water from the door. A shim of wood slipped in the door handle keeps the bad men from the attic. A biracial free spirit on horseback keeps the Ingallses from being robbed on the high prairie. *Deus ex machina* appears in the form of money or a job or the Chinook, just in the nick of time. Something happens to keep them safe. There is no more sadness, danger. There are happy endings. There must be.

Laura didn't like to feel so many eyes looking at her. She felt faint at the thought of her first classroom, of giving her first talk at the school exhibition. She knew what I felt. We were simpatico.

But—

Sassy. She was a little bit impudent, wasn't she? Laura dragged Mary behind her, over the woodpile, when Pa's mad-dog game got too real. Laura fought back—at the bullying tactics by Miss Eliza Jane Wilder, schoolmarm. She scolded bully Clarence Brewster in her first teaching assignment at age 16. Later, Laura slapped the Native man who allegedly grabbed her arm in the first year of her marriage, who spoke in Rose's cartoonish attempt at pidgin. *"How!"*

How[42] indeed?

In a story that didn't make the novels, during the Silver Lake years, obnoxious Cousin Charley had grown up and was working a man's job on the railroad. He cornered Laura in one of the little shanties, and tried to make her kiss him. She held him off with a kitchen knife, and eventually the scene was deleted from the narrative.

Rose, co-writing with her mother, said, "You can't make her a gamine fighting for her virginity." But that's what Laura *was*—a young girl, barely 13, assaulted by her own double cousin[43].

Was it for just a kiss? Did he get the kiss? Was there more to it before or after? The shadow of this incestuous assault underlies

---

[42] The caricature of an "Indian" saying "How" in the movies and in Rose Wilder Lane's fiction comes from the Anglicization of the Lakota word *háu*, which was used by men to greet other men. Rose used this false pidgin language in scenes in *Little House on the Prairie* as well as *The Long Winter*. "Heap big" and "Great Spirit," stuff and nonsense. Racist-Libertarian-government-aid-denying-self-dramatizing-bipolar Rose took many liberties with the truth, in fiction and in life.

[43] Laura had many double cousins, because her father's siblings married her mother's siblings. Peter Ingalls married Eliza Quiner, and Henry Quiner married Polly Ingalls. Cousin Charley Quiner was as much kin as if her were her own brother.

the scene where Ma "talks seriously to her girls," and explains that "rough men" and rough times lie ahead of them in this wild railroad camp. Mary and Carrie are terrified of the thought, and Laura feels curious, but realizes that Ma knows best. Did Charley's attempted assault come before or after this? Did that serious talk even happen at all? How much of Laura's young world was colored by the shattered boundary? She remembered it enough to try and include it in the story, and Rose, ever the story-shaper, overrode and excised the scene. A palimpsest of this fear remained in Laura—until she met Almanzo[44].

I thought about this unpublished story as the sun slid behind the western hills, the mountains purpling and the sandy wastes staying light even in darkness. By nighttime, the sand looked like snow, and as we crossed the eastern Nevada desert, the air grew colder. The window was chilly against my forehead, and the vent blew cool from the ceiling. I sat in my seat, hurtling across the desert wastes, and watched the sky alight with stars.

The dining car manager called dinner reservations on the intercom throughout the evening, and when she finally announced 7:45 reservations, I worked my way back through the swaying cars. The dining car was not full, I was glad to see; in fact, there were a few folks still eating and just one or two waiting at either end to be seated. Rather than seat folks alone at tables, they filled each table to conserve their efforts in the narrow car. The attendant beckoned me, pointing to a table with a man seated on one side. Luckily, I got to sit facing forward, toward the front of the train. It's hard on my stomach eating backward, as it were.

"Oh, hello." The magazine guy. Nice smile. Deeply tanned face, clean-shaven. Clean but callused hands, too, holding his menu. My age, late forties, early fifties, I imagined.

---

[44] I get it. Wondering if/when this palimpsest vanishes for good.

"Hi." I couldn't think of another word to say. Why bother? I picked up the menu and studied it. A steak[45] sounded good, with a baked potato, but I didn't want to eat a slab of meat in front of a stranger. I would probably choke. Then I'd need the Heimlich and mouth-to-mouth and that was just not cool. Seemed like pasta might be easier to manage.

The server came around with water and warm rolls and gave us salad and the basket of dressing packets, took our orders and swept back down the car. There was a mysterious dungeon below us, it seemed, where food was cooked to order despite the narrow width and the swaying along at 70 miles per hour.

And suddenly I was sick of my own same self, shy and scarred and stupid, and looked across to see this man looking at his silverware, placing his napkin in his lap. He looked at me.

"Hi, again," I said, and gave him a fake smile. What the hell, right? I'd never even see him again. *Just be cheerful, will you?*

"Hello again," he said, just a guy saying hello. No knives, no guns, no agenda. He smiled back. "Where are you heading?"

"Omaha."

"Omaha," he nodded. "Ever been there?"

"Never."

"Visiting family?"

"Business," I said, though I was unemployed, and technically this was for giggles and grins.

"Ah. Well, good luck with that—we get there at the crack of dawn."

"Five a.m. Just my luck. Oh, well." I shrugged. "I'll get breakfast there, anyway, before I get going."

---

[45] Amtrak's Signature flat-iron steak has been praised by foodies as unexpectedly delicious. In *Business Insider, The Times and the Wall Street Journal,* travel writers describe Amtrak's signature dining-car steak as "better than expected," "custom-cooked," and "the perfect meal." So why not try it?

He nodded and, since he was, so far, non-threatening, I ventured to make conversation. "Where are you headed?"

"I'm getting off at Des Moines. I'm meeting some friends for a road trip, and that's the closest the train goes."

"What time is that?"

"About two hours after Omaha. Seven a.m. So not much better than your exit." He laughed suddenly, something the very essence of cheerful. The sound made me smile, spontaneously, something I don't do. Because—hello—my life sucks. And that made him smile back.

I looked down at my salad, its three little beans perched atop a mound of lettuce, and felt a wave of inhibition roll back again. Nice guy. Nice smile. Nice laugh. *Now eat, stupid.*

He ordered a beer and I, in my new attempt at recklessness, ordered a glass of red wine. If I'm gonna dine on the train, I might as well dine in style. Soon, my pasta, his steak and baked potato arrived. And no one else was seated with us. In fact, the servers were already filling sugar packets and saltshakers and pulling the tablecloths off to set up for breakfast. About three tables were still full when we started eating, and just one other was left when I finished my rigatoni.

Somehow I found myself telling him about the library, but not that I was laid off, and how I wanted to write a novel someday, and he said he loved books, too, but that he had always wanted to be a farmer.

"Not a farm worker," he said, with a grimace. "My parents were farm workers. I want to be a real farmer. With my own land and grow corn and beans and tomatoes and all that kind of good food," he said. "But I can't compete with these big industrial farming operations. So I want to specialize. I have been taking classes in sustainable practice and organic farming methods, and I want a truck garden that I can sell from at farmers' markets. And I think Asian vegetables and herbs are the way to go. It's still an expanding market, and no one is really doing that organically in the Western states. So much of those veggies are imported from Mexico. I'm just looking for the right place and the right time to get going. Maybe not next year—but soon."

"Where would you do that?" Where, I wondered, is this idyllic space, where these dreams can come true?

"Not sure yet. Some place where there's still good land that hasn't been poisoned, where there's a water source, a place for some ducks—the Asian market is crazy about ducks. And chickens and maybe some goats, and room to grow. To expand. A little house[46]. You know, all that good stuff."

"For your family?" I wasn't fishing. I was just asking.

"No family yet. Not married."

I must have grimaced.

"What, you don't believe me?" He wiggled his fingers. "No ring."

"No, solidarity. I'm not married, either."

"It's not so bad, being single."

"No, it's not." I didn't say "*but—*."

"But it would be nice to be married."

"A relationship, then marriage. Kids. Step-kids, I mean. The whole package." It was easier to talk about this than I thought. I felt lighter, having admitted out loud that getting married and having a family unit were actually important to me. Not being alone forever, just me and the cats avoiding or suffering my mother. I liked this non-threatening guy, this magazine-reading man. And I didn't even know his name.

Suddenly that seemed wrong. "I'm Nell," I said, feeling a bit like a liar.

---

[46] Squee! The magic words.

"I'm Al." He reached across the dirty dishes and offered his hand to shake. I took it. Two shakes. Released and back into my lap, warmed by the touch of another human being.

"What kind of books do you like to read?" He leaned on his elbow, ready to listen.

But just then the server dude came back and said, "I'm sorry, folks, but we need to clear up and get ready for breakfast. Would you mind signing off on these tickets so we can close up?"

We signed our names, paid for our drinks in cash and left tips—his more than mine, both together a nice sum for the server.

"It was nice chatting, Nell," he said, and gestured for me to pass ahead of him up the aisle. I went ahead up the rocking train and pushed the button for the pneumatic door at the end of the car. The door opened and I turned to hold it, but he had gone the other way, to the other end of the car and was already passing through the other door.

I walked to my little roomette alone.

CHAPTER 7

We drew into Elko at 9:30 that night and it was just a short stop. No time to get out and stretch. But I had to leave my little compartment anyway because Ronald, the bow-tied Black sleeping car attendant, wanted to make up my bed. I found myself wondering how long he had worked for Amtrak and if he had a family history of being a porter. But it was racist to presume, and none of my business, so I quietly mused on the Pullman porters[47] while I waited.

Ronald swung back up the stairs as the train started again and tapped on my window. "Are you ready now?"

"Yes, I'll just go to the lounge for a few minutes."

"It won't take but five. Come back whenever you want to."

I stepped around him into the narrow hall. I supposed this was when someone would pull the old switcheroo and murder me or be murdered themselves. This was no Orient Express, but we were surely heading east. Would I come back and find Ronald with a knife in his back?

---

[47] Don't make me explain this to you. George Pullman hired formerly enslaved Black men to work on the railroads, beginning in about 1866; Pullman porters existed through 1968; thereafter, porters became sleeping-car attendants on Amtrak. Pullman porters had their own union, the first all-Black union, The Brotherhood of Sleeping Car Porters, which they formed to get a living wage instead of relying only on tips, and in hopes of being called by their own first names instead of being known as the generic "George" after George Pullman.

The train was on its way across the high flat, more or less along Highway 80 for some time now, and we were headed out of Nevada. I expected we'd be climbing soon, over the ridge of the Goshute Mountains past Elko, and onto the dry moonscape of Utah. Out the window, there were a few lights, far off, and we clanged across an interchange with a car or two waiting patiently for us, gates down but rising as soon as we passed.

Would I sleep tonight? I didn't know. I often fought for sleep and didn't get it. Too tightly wound. Too full of thoughts and unending replays of all my mistakes. Maybe if I had another glass of wine I could relax and get a decent night's sleep. I also knew from experience that it wouldn't help, but with nothing else to do while Ronald tucked in the sheets, I decided to follow that urge. I trekked down the rattling, rocking train to the snack bar, the lower level of the lounge car, where one can buy a small split of wine and a plastic cup and take it back to Coach or First Class with no judgment.

The parlor car was dimly lit, about half-full with assorted readers and knitters, and a new pair of chess players quietly engaged in the business under an overhead lamp. I didn't see my new friend Al, which was vaguely disappointing, but not really. That would mean talking. I spied the grandmother of the LIW-reading trio I had seen before, reading a wrinkled copy of *Woman's Day* with a Jack-o-lantern on the cover. The mother and the little girl must be asleep. The games cabinet by the door to the car displayed a number of old favorites in it, as well as gently read, dog-eared magazines. Maybe on the way back, I would grab a women's mag[48].

I pushed through the accordion connector between the parlor and the dining car; it was dark and set for breakfast.

---

[48] I'm a sucker for "47 Ways to Reuse your Paper Bags!" and "Make Curtains out of Bedsheets!" and the like. Give me a numbered list of crafty how-tos and I'm a reader for life. At least I used to be, at the library. Now I'd have to settle for second-hand copies.

The lounge car with the lower-level snack bar lay ahead, and it was also rather quiet. I went down the circular stairs, hanging on the slightly greasy metal handrail while the train swayed and jerked.

The snack bar was still open until 10, according to signage. The smell of microwaved White Castle burgers and butter-flavored popcorn made the air taste salty, oily, like a college chow hall. Bags of chips, candy, pepperoni sticks, and super-processed baked goods hung on clips all around, accompanied by a refrigerator for cold drinks, pre-made sandwiches tightly wrapped in plastic, and a freezer for pizzas and burritos, all shining with fluorescent enticement.

Behind the counter, a white woman of my age sat on a tall stool, one leg on the floor and the other hitched up on a rung, tapping at the register and taking money. Her uniform trousers had shifted up to reveal red socks. I wondered if she were a rule-breaker or if those were regulation-wear socks. Her hair was a very dark brown or black, hard to tell in the fluorescent lighting, with white streaks, brushed back into a tortoiseshell clip. She looked at the wall clock as I came to the register with my cash card in hand.

"Can I get a red wine?"

"Cabernet, Zinfandel, or rosé?"

Tsk. Rosé isn't red wine. "Zinfandel, please."

"I like anything that begins with a Z," she said.

Like *zebra*? I observed her hair. "I'm partial to the letter Q myself. It looks like a cat[49] when you draw it just right."

"You're a cat lady." She seemed to recognize her own kind.

---

[49] An idea stolen, of course, from plucky Ramona Quimby in *Ramona the Pest*, by Beverly Cleary, erstwhile children's librarian of Portland, Oregon. Draw ears and whiskers on your upper-case Q and there you have it. Or maybe it looks like Black Susan, with a long tail and whiskers, sign of a good mouser.

I shrugged. No sense in showing my hand. I'm enough of a freak without trumpeting it aloud in the snack bar. "I like cats."

I paid with a swipe of my card, adding a tip for her curious Z fetish. As I returned the way I came, there at one of the tables was Al, with a bottle of beer, reading a book whose cover I couldn't see. He had, in fact, covered the book with newspaper. I hadn't seen a book cover like that since high school. Whatever it was, it must be embarrassing?

I was faced with the everyday dilemma of my life—stop and say hello, pretend I didn't see him, ignore him, or what? Why was I always beset with this anxiety? Why did I fear[50] the experience of a standard greeting? *Stupid, stupid Nelly.*

But what would Laura do? She'd pick up the baseball and throw it back. She'd call out, "You all sound like a bunch of prairie chickens!" She'd march to the front and say her piece, regardless of Nellie Oleson, Miss Wilder, or Clarence Brewster. I was a prairie-chickenshit next to Laura.

This monologue/exercise in self-shaming was taken from my hands as Al looked up, smiled, and nodded a greeting. I said hey and kept walking. He might have had something more to say, but I kept moving, because I was a frozen-solid heart with legs, a prairie gopher afraid of the shadow of a hawk, a small girl in a log cabin hearing wolves on the other side of the wall. I was afraid[51], I had no Pa to comfort me, and I was going back to my little compartment to hide.

Ronald had made my fold-down bed. I locked myself into the tiny cabin. A foil-wrapped chocolate rested on the pillow—what a nice way to end my last few minutes of self-doubt and loneliness. I ate it, then undressed, slipped into the cool, tight sheets, and

---

[50] Of course, I knew why, but I couldn't get over it.

[51] Of everything and nothing.

watched the lights of the occasional crossing or tiny town pass by. It was mostly dark. I pulled the window-curtain closed except for a few inches of sky I could see from my pillow, and I watched a million stars stare back at me.

Somewhere in the night, we crossed into Utah, and I felt the train leaning left and then right, and getting louder as we passed through tunnels. I slept fitfully. The wine made me sleepy at first, and I fell asleep, but then the rocking car awakened me. The night seemed to go on forever. According to my phone, we pulled into Salt Lake City around 3 a.m. I heard doors slam and some feet passing in the hallway. Eventually, the doors slammed one last time, and the train moved again on into the rocky flats and red caverns of that part of the world.

The sound of a door sliding or slamming is one of my worst triggers. A silent door opening—and I am trapped. I cannot speak. Sometimes it slams. Sometimes not. The sounds of slamming doors on the train brought me to full consciousness, heart pounding.

My eyelids were stinging, longing to sleep away the rest of this long blackness, but my mind was a squirrel on a wheel, a waterfall of forgotten memories or nightmares, imagined conversations I was too stuck to have. I'm not broken. I'm wounded. Not everything is frightening, but some things—they get me. They just do. What would Laura have done?

I don't know what she *could* have done but live how she lived—taking on whatever was handed to her—making it work. She didn't have the benefit of therapy or taking a vacation. Of turning off social media. Getting a pedicure instead. Tossing back a glass of wine.

She just dealt with it. Maybe that's what I ought to do. Just deal.

In my little berth, before dawn, I at last found deep, dreamless sleep. Or it found me.

* * *

We hove into Green River in the morning, as I was eating a breakfast sandwich in the snack bar. I felt too little rested to face a breakfast table of perky travelers in the dining car. The train turned south, and the light of the sun was in my eyes, slanting across the Formica table. I sipped my coffee with gratitude of an intensity unbeaten by any fervor I had ever shown in church. I felt I should whisper "Amen" before each sip. My eyes squinted, gritty and stung by sunlight, but by Jove, I was awake and a day closer to my adventure. I couldn't stop yawning, though.

The new set of chess players hunched in another booth with paper coffee cups and no conversation, but to their credit, no clock. It was a serious game but not a competition. Across the aisle, an older white man read the newspaper; a brown teen girl fiddled with an e-reader at a different table. I heard music coming from her earphones, not the tune, but the *bzz-bzz, bzz-bzz* beat emanating from her tiny personal symphony. It seemed no one wanted to break the morning's meditation. But as soon as the train stopped at the next station, the car came to life. People looked out windows and started chatting, the attendants heaved bags of trash from the side doors and loaded up more boxes of goods: napkins, linens, bottles of water, sacks of ice.

So much coming and going on a train.

I'm no child of the nineteenth century like Laura, but even I, twenty-first-century, university educated, well read, city-born, found it a bit mesmerizing. The well-oiled machine and the synchronized actions of the ground crew, the train crew; their cheerful camaraderie, and their badinage with passengers. Laura had stood in abject fascination at the making of the railroad grade, how the valleys were raised high and mountains laid low, leveling the path of the trains from coast to coast. It felt like a piece of history to be on the train that crossed the Golden West—or took the forlorn and dejected folk[52] back east, back home, admitting defeat.

And today, when everyone's in a hurry, when I coulda-shoulda gone by air, woulda gotten there sooner, could have tagged base and turned around and gone home just as fast—I didn't need to hurry. No reason to get back. Nothing waiting for me there, just my fur-boys, safe with the vet.

So why not enjoy the ride?

Because this is me. And the ride was always bumpy. I knew enough to laugh at myself when I say these little peppy epigrams. "Silver lining," I'd say—but the tarnished edge is right there. *There is no great loss without some small gain*, Ma said. The chickens got free food when the grasshoppers ate the crops. Why not be ready for it? A step ahead?

Fiddlesticks. I guess I should tattoo that on my arm. And on such a bright morning.

Today, I vowed instead, *I will step outside my comfort zone, I will.* I'd say hello to two new people and if anyone asked what I do, I would tell them I'm a book reviewer. Better yet, a book critic[53]. I'd been wanting to do just that. I had contacts at the library journals. My local paper, now online, always wants reviewers, for books, movies, theater. I could start a book blog, make videos about it, and write about books all day, every day, if I want. Why not start my new career right now? I only needed to figure out how to make it pay.[54]

With this nugget of hope in my pocket, I carried my paper coffee cup back toward my sleeper car and rounded a narrow corridor too fast, right into Al. Coffee spilled out of my cup-lid

---

[52] Heh. Like me.
[53] Why not go for the $10 title instead of the ten-cent one?
[54] Insert maniacal laughter here. This is always the catch.

and onto my hand, but it wasn't that hot anymore, just warm enough to still drink, not to burn. It didn't splash onto him, but we both jumped back.

"Are you all right?" he asked as I stammered, "I'm sorry, I'm so, so sorry!"

"I'm fine," he said. "Did you burn yourself?"

Coffee dripped down my hand and trailed my arm toward my elbow. "No, it's not hot. It's fine, it's okay. No biggie."

But Al persevered. We were near the bathrooms; he tried a door, opened it, grabbed a few paper towels. "Here. That should help."

He held my cup while I patted the coffee trail from my elbow and hand, and looked at his shoes: athletic shoes, not ostentatious and gleaming white for show, but the kind a real runner wears when he's not running. Jeans that were neither ragged nor flashy, basic Levis with enough wear to tell me he was a casual guy, not a slob, not a fop[55]. You can tell a lot about a person from his shoes and his jeans.

"Thank you," I said, thinking I should have said it earlier. The train blasted its horn, and the doors slammed below us. "I'm sorry about that. I just had breakfast. I thought I'd get some fresh air, but I guess I missed it."

"I was just going to get some coffee. Let me buy you a fresh cup."

I'd rather say no; I preferred to back away. Instead, I said, "Okay," because I had promised to break out of my comfort zone. And what the heck—my coffee was all but cold anyway.

"After you, then."

"Thank you," and I led the way back to the snack bar. When we each had a cup of fresh hot coffee, we headed to the parlor car; we found two swivel armchairs and turned them to face the

---

[55] Nobody ever says the word *fop* anymore. It's a perfectly serviceable word.

windows. Outside, we were heading up again, winding around mountains of increasing height, into the Rockies. Aspen was ahead of us, and the foliage was a mass of yellow outside, of bright yellow and shades of gold and red.

"Tell me more about your farm." I made the opening gambit like a real human being.

"I don't have a farm. Yet." He swiveled his chair toward me. A half-smile quirked his mouth. "I'm going to have one, one of these days. Still looking for the right place. I was thinking about raising Asian vegetables for restaurants."

"That's what you were saying last night."

"Oh, sorry, I did say that already. I suppose I should grow native—I mean, stick with heirloom tomatoes and peppers for the Mexican restaurants, but I'm kind of tired of that," he said. "I was raised on it, but I'm looking for a change. I'm kind of over the taco-truck scene. I want some cross-cultural flow."

"I like tacos." I said it with all sincerity, knowing it sounded like a complete and utter lie. "More than Chinese food."

"Eh, I like Chinese and Thai and Vietnamese and all those Asian cuisines. It's all delicious. Why not throw it all onto a tortilla?" He smiled, a little self-deprecation in his sincerity. I liked it.

"Mmm," was my brilliant reply. And then I could not think of a single other thing to say. I was boring him to death. He would turn gray and petrify and then fall into a dust heap as I spoke to him about my fondness for burritos and other take-out food, and I had nothing to add because I was a spinster with cats and no fricking job.

The trees rolled by outside. Off in the distance, I saw a flash of blue-gray, a mountain lake, a cluster of cabins or houses, a dock extending into the cattails at the edge. A white egret stood like a lawn ornament knee-deep in the lake.

And yet, my cavalier persevered.

"You know, everyone thinks that Mexican food is so spicy, but the hottest naturally occurring chile in the world is the Trinidad Moruga, from the Caribbean. It might have come from Africa before that, but it's definitely not Mexican. The second hottest is from Bangladesh, and there are so many chiles in India—and then there's Thailand, China, and Peru. All those chiles, and Mexico doesn't even have a chile in the top ten."

I couldn't tell if he was proud or dejected by the fact, but I found this level of nerdery absolutely, pardon the pun, to my taste.

"What about Habaneros?" I inserted this tiny advance.

"From Havana. And from Peru, before then. But Cuba's proximity to the Yucatan is how it came to Mexico."

"Are you a cilantro fan?" I asked, thinking about the genetic link to soapy or fragrant cilantro, which I loved in Thai spring rolls as well as fresh fish tacos.

And away he went. "Ah, I love it!" He rolled his eyes and smacked his lips just once, not enough to disgust me, just enough to emphasize his delight. A fine line, but I'd allow it. "Cilantro"—he rolled the R a little—"is a bridge between cultures, just like basil and lime—even cabbage! Did you know that—"

Meanwhile, the desert bloomed pink, palest violet, peach, taupe, brown, and an indescribable color somewhere between pink-gray and white as the morning rose up.

Mysterious industrial complexes—beige-painted silos and tanks, power stations, rusted cars and trucks moldered off the tracks. A veritable graveyard of trailers and RVs, slag heaps, the hideous detritus of modern human life, discarded out of sight of local residents, but in plain view of the train as we rolled along.

Wires on pylons, swooping—*one, swoop, two, swoop*—like Laura said. You could see how fast the train was going.

Al had been waxing poetic, but he stopped. "That's enough of me. Too much."

I liked hearing him talk. There's nothing more attractive than enthusiasm—and competence. I felt soothed and relaxed into my swivel armchair, almost sleepy despite the two cups of coffee I'd had. I wanted him to go on, to keep talking, while the mountains rose around us.

I smiled sleepily at him, cat-like. Blinked in the brightness. Stretched a bit. *Purr.*

"What about you?" he persisted.

"What about me?"

"Where are you going?" He had asked me this before.

"Omaha, on this train. Otherwise, not so sure."

"What's in Omaha?"

"A rental car. I have some business to attend to," I said, because I think of Laura like a joyful secret, not an open passion to be shared. It's children's lit, for one thing, and there might be something abnormal or socially unacceptable about a grown woman enjoying children's books. There might be something wrong with it. *Cat lady.*

"And how long will you be there?"

"A few days. Then home again."

"Where is home?"

"A little suburb in the Bay Area. Identical houses. Identical lawns. *Little houses*, all the same," I said, hiding the code word in the middle of an old song lyric[56].

"Hmmm." He nodded a little. "I know that kind of town. I like little houses. Just not too many of them all together." Just like Pa.

Was this a test? He passed it—or it was too simple.

We watched the outside world go by for a while. An Amish girl in a blue dress and a bearded young white man in a basic shirt

---

[56] *Little boxes on the hillside, and they all look just the same.* — Malvina Reynolds

and tie walked past, swaying, grabbing at the seats for balance. Her hair was twisted up under her black linen cap. Her face was plain as a rice cake, no makeup, no smile. His face was just as plain, no smile, not much fire or curiosity in those blue eyes. I wonder where they were going and what they thought of this modern world.

Al watched her, too. "What do you think?" he said softly, pointing with his pursed lips, a nod of the head. "Where are they going? Why are they on the train?"

"I was wondering, too. Maybe they are going to a funeral?"

"No, maybe they are on their honeymoon?" He winked.

Nope, a black cap meant unmarried. Were they running away? The thought cracked me up, and I laughed right out despite myself.

Al turned his swivel chair toward me again and laughed, too. "Wow," he said. "I didn't know you had it in you."

I wiped my eyes, still giggling, and felt a blush—yes, a tender little girl's blush, because I think I understood—*he's into me, he was flirting with me, and I'm still here.* I kind of liked him, I thought, and it was all very middle school for a dame of my advanced years, but it felt good, and I liked it.

Say hello to two new people today. So far, I had said hello to a semi-new person, and there I was in conversation, if not outright flirting. So far, so good.

The higher we climbed, the sunshine slipped away, and we rose into mist. Smoky blue fog hung like a cloak around the pylons, which looked like gray skeleton-queens preparing for court. Arms akimbo. Dripping with diamonds. The pine and cedar trees were bejeweled with raindrops[57]. They splattered against the glass.

Where the cloud thinned, the single God-beam shined through.

---

[57] But Mary didn't care for such fanciful language. Killjoy.

We sat in what felt, to me, like a comfortable silence, despite the other conversations and the rattling train. Along the ridge of one mountain, with gray tumbled stones, down into oblivion, went a deep ravine. A glimpse of a stream. A downed tree. There must be wildlife in these trees, among the rocks. We sliced through that place too fast to recognize anything, anyone. Going, going, gone.

I swallowed, and my ears popped, popped again. Going up, up, and over the Continental Divide. I wonder if those folks in covered wagons long ago had felt their ears pop, or if it was too gradual to notice?

Now a lake appeared, not too far from the tracks, and we traveled around it. Ducks, mallards and grebes, cranes and such, massed on the surface, near the shores. They would be leaving soon, should perhaps have gone already. Time to fly.

I was silently appalled at so much trash by the sides of the tracks. Here a mattress, there a sheet of plastic, rotten tires, an abandoned rowboat. What a mess people leave behind.

When we went through a town, we didn't pass through the city's portals, no red carpet for us. No warm welcome, no ambassadors with oversized scissors. The train always comes to the back door, through the armpit of town. More trash, rusty leftovers, the backside of beyond, just graffiti on billboards, overcrossings, and sound walls behind houses.

I could see over their back fences, into the yard with the swingset, the plastic kiddie car, the dog-run. Bicycles against the back of the house, a laundry line. Picnic table. *Swoop, swoop*, moving past us, behind us like a ribbon on a kite. I saw into the back room sometimes—a kitchen window with a person at the sink, a silhouetted head in a window with the light shining out.

I see your back door, your choice of curtains. I see your trash cans, your basketball hoop, the way the ivy creeps over the wall, the bougainvillea clinging to the chimney. Your sawhorses. Your treehouse. Your rope swing. Your doghouse. Your stepping stones. Your dying lawn. I see them all from the train. No secrets, no matter how hidden they seemed from the front yard.

The town passed, and we swooped into the trees again. People, no people. Trees, more trees. And telephone wires. *One, swoop, two, swoop.*

The clouds came even lower, or we were higher, and we saw more houses and buildings at the outskirts of Aspen. We talked[58] until the conductor called out the station over the speaker, and by then I was socially spent. I'd said my say, whatever it was, and knew some quiet time in my little snug harbor was called for. We introverts have an hourglass in our heads, and when it's time for quiet, go we must.

"Well, take care," I said, and he stood like a gentleman when I got up, but he stayed at the seat.

"You, too."

I didn't see him again the rest of the day. I ate a snack in the early afternoon in my roomette, read *West from Home*, Laura's letters to Almanzo from her visit to San Francisco in 1915, since it was a train journey like mine, and I dozed, still sleepy from the night before. I got a 6:15 reservation for dinner. The server seated me with a chipper senior couple heading down to Albuquerque, after the switch at Galesburg; they didn't press their names upon me nor beg for mine but made funny quips about the shaking of the train and the passing of the salt and pepper. I felt my assignment was complete. I had spoken to two complete strangers and did not bleed from my eyes nor grow a second head. My faculties were intact.

I am no monster, despite my mother's voice in my head.

---

[58] Of shoes and ships and sealing wax, of cabbages and kings. About everything and nothing. But not about Laura. Shh. My little secret.

I felt as if I'd seen every corporate work yard for the past thousand miles. Giant spools of wire and cable, piles of logs, phone poles, gravel, brick. The mountains went up and up, and down, and up. Piles of rocks that were moved from this place to that. More rocks. The mountains look almost dead, but they were alive with history—memories—relics of efforts that didn't pan out. And along the creeks and riverbeds, the yellow treetops peeked over the rim, a yellow chain of dying leaves.

Then *whoosh*—a freight train blasted past. My view was occluded, blocked by the staccato, colorful flashes from the rust-red, mustard-yellow, faded kelly-green of the freight cars as they passed. They sounded horns, exchanging hellos; silver stock cars with sheep; cattle; the next one with new cars inside. It passed doubly fast, heading the other way.

We slowed to pass through a town, paused at the station, and were gone with less than two minutes there. Can I say I've been to a place where I've never set foot? Can I say I know what a place looks like or smells like when I've never stepped on the ground?

Inside a fenced yard, a black dog and a white dog trotted along the fence, digging at a brush pile. Black pipe, a foot or two in diameter, lay alongside the track, following us with its fuel or water or waste, whatever it carried, for some time. We cut through small hills, the sides graded and shaped, some hillsides cemented in place. Thoughtful graffiti decorated those walls: strange names slashed in defiant paint, daubs of an argument over who had been here: *Herk*, apparently, had been there first.

Inexplicably, in the middle of a slope of scree perched an abandoned floral sofa. Wisps of cloud looked combed across the sky. We made it to Denver for dinner and passed into Nebraska by midnight.

Again, I found sleep elusive. I wanted to close my eyes and drift, but the action made my mind speed up instead of slow down. I would get off in Omaha at 5 a.m., and I was anxious about missing the stop. I could feel the train descending, descending the mountains, and my ears popped, creaked, built pressure, and then released with a yawn or a swallow.

How will I manage my own little house without a new job soon? How would I feed Fergus and Sammy? I missed their warm pressure against the backs of my knees at night. I missed the rituals of morning feeding and evening snuggles. Hoped they were being fed and petted and cleaned up after by my vet's staffers.

I kept checking my phone to see where we were, what time it was, how much farther, how long I had left to sleep, as if dreading the first day of school. My mom had called and texted me, but I continued to ignore her all-caps *CALL ME IMMEDIATELY* texts. She was not the boss of me on this trip. But it was hard to actually ignore her. Years of training left me struggling with guilt and the malaise of feeling like a bad person.

I finally fell into the bizarreness of dreamscapes, with boulders perched on high cliffs in a Fred Flintstone landscape that looked a lot like the Arizona desert. I was near the edge, my white apron flapping in the incessant wind.

They say the prairie wind will snap your mind if you're not careful. Some pioneers couldn't take it and hanged themselves in their little dugouts or blew out their brains in the middle of summer, when the prairie wind wouldn't stop. And the winters were worse.

I'd never been in a blizzard. But in my dream, the blizzard came up out of the northwest, and I had to run for the sod house. I was almost there, just past the clothesline, when the blizzard hit. I clawed for the door, tried to find the solid mass of my safe little house. I swung my hands in the flurry of snowflakes, the bludgeoning wind, and felt my legs entwined in my flapping skirt. I tried to get there, I tried, when my hand hit something, and I woke up.

I had smacked the back of my hand into the window, and my legs were indeed tangled in the sheet.

I was awake. No blizzard. I checked the time. 4 a.m.

I lay back until my heartbeat slowed. The train rocked and jiggled, and I felt a wave of sleepiness coming over me, but it was too late. I was getting off in Omaha. An hour to go. I slowly, slowly got dressed and ready to detrain, and when Ronald came up the corridor and tapped my door, I pulled back the curtain to show him I was ready.

"Ten minutes," he said.

I was desperate for coffee. Ten minutes later, he handed me and my suitcase off the train. I slipped him a tip and said farewell. But before I had walked the length of the train into the station, the cars began to move off, and soon I was one of a few lonely souls awake in Omaha. My hands were freezing, my coat flapping open. I had gloves in my suitcase to look for as soon as I got indoors.

A stiff wind blew and the skies were still dark. It's not this cold in California in September. At least not where I was from[59]. Maybe in the high Sierras, but this wind, this cold? The station was warm, though. A few patrons waited for who knows what, dozing on their benches.

It was far too early for the rental car place, next to the train station, to be open. I looked, just in case, but the sign said it opened at 8 a.m., so I had three hours to kill. I did not want to look at my phone for three hours. The station dude at the counter, a mustached guy about forty or so with tattoos peeking out of his shirt-wrists, an Amtrak ball cap with the brim tilted up, said I could check my bags until 9 a.m. but then he closed for the rest of

---

[59] The Bay Area is famous for its delightful late summer heatwaves in September and even into October.

the day. Trains passed through only at night in these parts, he said. He directed me up the street to a little gravy and biscuit diner.

"Is it safe? I mean—to walk alone?" I don't know *these parts*.

He laughed. "Safe as candy," he said. "Go on. You'll be all right."

Funny how all the heads swiveled when I walked into that diner.[60] They all knew each other, but they didn't know me. *Stranger danger!* I sat in a booth that seated just one on each side, the tiniest booth in the history of all diners, and gladly slipped my hands around the thick white mug. Coffee warmed me, and I read the local newspaper so I wouldn't have to chit-chat with locals; I turned the phone to silent so I wouldn't have to deal with my mom on the phone. Nothing personal, I was just not ready for my next challenge of the day.

★ ★ ★

The coffee at breakfast had done me good, and so had the eggs, grits, and sausage. After that, I was ready to make the drive north and even set myself the goal again of speaking with two new people. Really *speaking*, I mean. Not just muttering and nodding, per my usual.

Soon enough, I was picking up my car keys and adjusting the seat and mirrors, ready to cross the prairies in my own little wagon. I liked the car—a basic four-door Nissan Sentra. Silver. About as ordinary as you can get.

But this one had more get-up-and-go than my old beast at home. There was a better stereo, seat warmers and better lumbar support. I rather enjoyed stepping on the gas, and as soon as I got myself out of the downtown area, I merged onto Highway

---

[60] <Insert record scratch>

29. From there, it was basic: due north, straight, hardly a turn or variation[61] for four hours toward Brookings[62].

On the road, I slipped into that mesmerizing mental place where you think about all kinds of things, and then realize you've been driving blindly for many miles. Al-from-the-train was a nice dude, and I had successfully talked vegetables with him and my head hadn't shriveled like an apple doll. It was nice to know I could do such a thing, and maybe my mom was wrong. Maybe I wasn't terrible at everything.

I saw farmland through my windows: fields and more fields with plow marks, with the scrape and contour of the harrow or the mower. Laura was a simple woman at heart, and she wrote her books without embellishment—nothing too fancy. She turned in the manuscript of *On the Banks of Plum Creek* with the story of Pa's new *plow* and was disgusted to find the printed pages bearing the word *plough* throughout at the whim of some highbrow editor[63]. It infuriated Laura from the beginning and has remained in every edition since. I don't suppose there was a thing she could do about it, either—how do you go back and fix such an egregious mistake[64]—or editor's presumption?

Alongside the highway, vegetable farms and solar farms, fields that smelled like an open jar of dried onion powder. Globby green things that looked like broccoli (I'll bet my train boyfriend Al

---

[61] And for this, we thank the surveyor team of 1860 or thenabouts.

[62] Brookings? Brookins? They used to say it both ways. They also spelled it both ways.

[63] A burden that women writers everywhere often face or faced. Just ask Emily Dickinson's editor—he changed all of her long dashes into periods. The very nerve! See also: Rebecca Solnit, *Men Explain Things to Me.*

[64] It wasn't her—or Rose's—worst mistake, or misstep. The 1935 edition of *Little House on the Prairie* said that there were "no people" out on the prairies, although there were, in fact, tens of thousands of Indigenous folk living there in both settled and nomadic fashion. No people, however, obscured the fact that Pa jumped the gate and tried to steal land from Indian Territory and its inhabitants. Nobody, huh? "No people" was fixed in subsequent editions, however.

could have named them). Vineyards, nut trees, and then cornfields. Or what would have been vast fields of corn if it were the growing season. In autumn, the fields were down to the last scrappy stubble of where corn had grown all summer long. The fields were vast, wide, combed surfaces that varied little in shade or tone.

I had to stop in Sioux Falls for the surprisingly clean restroom and a gas station doughnut, but then I was on the last leg of this journey toward De Smet. When I hit Brookings[65] I knew I had only half an hour farther to the final destination, and I was already in a place that Laura had known.

De Smet: Home of Laura Ingalls Wilder
and the Little Town on the Prairie.
Population 2010 Elevation 1726

I made it. I'm here.
At last, I'm her.

---

[65] Squee!

PART TWO

LITTLE TOWN ON THE PRAIRIE

CHAPTER 8

I drove around and found the little bed and breakfast place where *Almanzoor* the tour planner had reserved a dozen rooms for us private tourists. I wanted to go out, right away, right that very second, and start lapping up the sights, but I needed to check in first. The weather was still gray and windy, and any time I stepped out of the car, the wind whipped through me. Perhaps it would snow—I hoped not, because I couldn't drive in the snow.[66] But it was too early for snowfall.[67] Rain, perhaps, was coming.

The dumpy white woman, older than me by a good ten years, at the front desk wore a name badge that read *Liz*. Her brown hair was pulled back into a ponytail, held in place by a white satin clip-in bow. It could have been elegant in other circumstances, like a ballroom, maybe, but here, in De Smet, her white bow seemed dorky and out of fashion. Her smile was genuine and friendly, however, so I swallowed my prejudice about small-towners in the Midwest.

"I'm here for the *LauraLand* tour?"

"Oh, yes, we've been expecting you all."

Indeed, a room was reserved in my name, even though I arrived earlier than the posted check-in time.

---

[66] Remember? California-born?

[67] Let us not speak of the Hard Winter, with blizzards October through April.

The key to my room was a metal key, but modern, not a skeleton key, which I had imagined. They hadn't quite advanced to electronic passkeys—or perhaps Liz just liked the jangle of keys? I mentally kicked myself, because I was judging again, and who was I, some genius or movie star? Nope. *Just enjoy yourself. Stop fussing.*

I went up to my room on the second floor of this Victorian house, with its carpeted staircase and a couple of hallways with paneled doors and crystal doorknobs. I was not surprised to see a quilt on the iron bedstead, a sampler on the wall, a wooden rocking horse in the corner, and an old-fashioned standing mirror. Gingham curtains and an imitation kerosene lamp, wired for electricity, completed the look. The bookcase held leather-bound copies of the Little House series, and a framed sepia portrait, the one of Laura at age 18 with her curled bangs and sober mien, hung on the wall.

I hoped to high heavens that there wasn't a Disney version of this fantasy ahead of me.

It seemed like I'd just eaten, but I was hungry after the four-hour drive with only a sugared doughnut and water to sustain me. I thought I might as well stretch my legs after the two-day train trip.[68] The party of *LauraLand* tourists was supposed to meet in the parlor downstairs at 5 p.m. for a get-acquainted glass of sherry and then troop by foot to a local restaurant for supper. Liz had tourist brochures, a cartoonish map of De Smet, and answers to any question about Laura you could pose to her, probably. I expect all of the townies spoke Laura Ingalls Wilder very well.

---

[68] Who am I kidding? I wanted to see it all on my own, without having to mingle and chitchat and share our experience. I wanted it just for seven-year-old me, and for myself now.

The schedule said that tomorrow we *LauraLanders* would visit Pa's store building and the Surveyor's House in the morning, with a pioneer "dinner" (lunch) at the one-room schoolhouse, and then take a van to the homestead in the afternoon. The day after, we'd go out to the tree claim that Almanzo and Laura had farmed, with a natural history lecture in the afternoon about the Big Slough, wetland reclamation and lakes Henry and Thompson, or "free time for shopping" in De Smet. There was a farewell supper that evening, with departures planned for the next morning.

Our tour was a scant few days, but the sites were near enough that we could see them all and be ready to leave thereafter. And after my homebound train, book reviews, and a new resume for me.

I bundled up in my winter coat with a woolly scarf and gloves and pulled up the hood of my coat against the wind. I wore my sunglasses even though it wasn't sunny, because my eyes kept tearing up from the bitter wind. I looked like a terrorist. Or a movie star at Sundance, I wasn't sure which.

I asked Liz at the desk which way to the nearest café, and she laughed.

"We don't have cafés here," she said, turning to look out the front window. "We got the diner 'cross the street." She pointed. "Or you can go up to the main street 'round the corner. There's an Arby's up there, a Pizza Hut, and another diner, the Steel Trap. Then there's the Garden—aren't you going to some fancy supper there?"

"Yes, I believe so—the Garden Inn?"

"Yes, that's very fancy there. Tablecloths and candles. And there's the Wagon Wheel."

"Oh, my." I already was taking on her cadence and folksy interjections in the five minutes I had been there.

I closed the heavy wooden door behind me and started up the street to the right, and, sure enough, there was a diner at the crossroads, across the street, with an out-of-business trailer home sales and a shuttered feed store.[69] That felt a bit depressing, so I continued along the same road and turned up Calumet,[70] the main street in De Smet, the sites of Mead's Hotel and Gerald Fuller's general store, Power's Tailor shop and Royal Wilder's feed store site, and—right before me—Loftus' General Store.[71] It was still there, generations of folks who had kept the name and the store—where Laura had shopped for Pa's suspenders, and Pa had bought the last two cans of oysters for their Christmas supper that Hard Winter.

I had kind of an epiphany moment then—the reality of walking in her footsteps really hit me. *Laura walked this street*, once upon a time, and went through *these* doors to spend her nickels and dimes at Loftus' General Store. I felt as if angels were suddenly singing a harmonic note and a rainbow had appeared over my head. I had no choice but to enter that hallowed ground.

Inside, all the LIW tchotchkes in the world held pride of place in rows of metal shelving—shot glasses and socks, tin mugs and sunbonnets, the whole selection of books plus the spinoffs: *The Caroline Years, The Martha Years, The Rose Years.* Spoon-rests and potholders. *I'm a Prairie Girl* pink T-shirts and *Farmer Boy*

---

[69] Not Royal's feed store

[70] I knew this only as a brand of baking powder for the first forty years of my life. It was only upon employment at the library that I learned about the various native tribes and what horrible things had happened to them in Wilder's day. I was from California, and we "don't have Indians here." Wrong, wrong, wrong.

[71] Yeah, the capitalist dude who jacked up the cost of the wheat that Almanzo and Cap Garland had brought back from way out on the wide prairie, risking life and limb to save the townspeople from starvation. And then this dude, Mr. Loftus, tried to leverage the townsfolk until they threatened to blacklist him after the winter. He relented. He doesn't come out looking too sharp in the novel. Perhaps he redeemed himself later in life.

tractor caps. All of it, made in China and priced above what I'd pay for socks or shot glasses or a T-shirt anywhere else. It *is* Disneyland, I guess, for average Little House fans[72]. And also the inevitable chips and sodas, plus horehound candy and other such treats that Laura and Mary and Carrie might have enjoyed. Meticulously reproduced for the masses.

I felt a little dirty then, a little tainted. This was not why I had come, nor what I was looking for. I came for relics[73], for a shrine. It seems I had found schlock, touts, and hucksters. I wanted a piece of horehound[74] candy just for the sake of it, but I didn't want to put money on the pickle barrel just yet. I would come back before the end of the tour. I sniffed deeply. I wanted to remember the smell of a general store, but it smelled like a drugstore or a Target. Plastic and made-in-China.

I finally left the store and went a little farther up the street to the Pizza Hut and bought a personal pan pizza and a Coke. It helped me feel a bit more normal, more grounded in the 21st century. I could find myself in the time-space continuum with fast food and plastic straws. It was the anachronisms in modern times, or vice versa, that hurt my brain. I wondered if Laura ever ate pizza; I assumed that she did not. What would she have liked on her pizza, I wonder? Probably the delightful mix of Canadian bacon (ham) and pineapple[75], as pineapple was still a rare treat in the middle of the undeveloped nation in her day.

---

[72] Not I. I'm not *the average fan.* Laura is a part of me, and she lives in my heart.

[73] Catholic hagiography has delineated three degrees of saints' relics: First-degree relics are literal pieces of the body—bones or teeth or hair. Second-degree relics are possessions that were owned by the person while they were alive. Third-degree relics have been touched to the saint, or to the saint's belongings, or to what the saint had blessed. Everything else is just schlock for sale. I wanted all of it from Laura. Well, second-degree relics, anyway. She could keep her teeth and bones.

[74] And I can't help laughing at the homonym: *whore hound. I'd never been that. Not yet.*

[75] Don't come at me. It's a reasonable choice. Chicken on a pizza, however, is an abomination before the Lord.

I quickly checked for messages (Mom, Mom, Mom) and email (Mom, library layoff stuff) on my phone while I ate and decided to go back to the inn for a nap before tonight. If seeing the fanaticism rife in Loftus' Store made me antsy, imagine what a roomful of *LauraLanders* was gonna do? I ought to catch a few Zs, with apologies to the snack bar attendant, before the crazy began.

★ ★ ★

At 5 o'clock, I assessed myself in the long mirror and rubbed a stick of pink-tinted gloss on my lips. I'm not a big makeup person, but I needed some color. Traveling for two and a half days straight is a little wearing, and it was starting to show in my face (hello, eye-bags). Otherwise, I looked casual-chic for a cocktail party and dinner among fellow and sister *LauraLanders*—my black jersey dress with patterned tights and my boots, a textured scarf in gray-white. Less dark-academia than I usually wore to work, and a little more of the "I'm a writer" arty vibe. My hair was simply brushed back from my face, nothing fancy. As confident as I have ever felt, I felt it.

And believe me or not, I was excited to meet my comrades-in-Laura, face to face, for the first time[76].

I descended the staircase to the parlor, where I heard a buzz of voices as I grew closer, and a burst of laughter.

Liz stood at the front desk and said across the counter, "Go right in. They're just getting started in there."

So in I went.

My eyes were drawn immediately to a petite, beautiful woman in a paisley skirt and blouse that had just enough pin-tucks and touches of lace at its neck to recall a calico dress—with

---

[76] Please don't be too freakish. Please let me not be the only normie, or the only super-freak. Let me be right in the middle, unremarkably remarkable.

contemporary flair. She wore ankle boots with a sharp point at the toe, and a lengthwise purse that crossed her shoulder and chest like a trapper's pouch. Her hair was dark brown and her eyes coal-black in her lovely face; she wore her hair up in a twist at the back, with short-chopped Betty bangs. She was glamorous. And not just to me. Who was she? Most of the people in the room—a dozen or so, including, no surprise, the three-generation LIW readers from the train—were also gazing upon her, whoever she was. Magnetic Mary? Fabulous Fannie? Who was she?

The little girl from the train had her history doll with her, and they wore matching red calico dresses with sunbonnets. Never mind that pioneer girls didn't wear sunbonnets indoors, in the winter, but on the little girl, it was adorable. Not so much on her mother, who wore the same outfit in a brown color scheme. I suspected a sewing marathon in the not-too-distant past. Grandmother came dressed in a black dress with a crest of lace at her breast and a cameo pin. It was very elegant and era-appropriate, but had I not received the memo? No one had said to dress in costume—and though I despised such a cornball assumption, I felt left out.

When I stepped into the room, someone approached from the side, while I was looking over the brunette bombshell and the rest of the room. A tray of tiny glasses was proffered, which I saw peripherally. I looked down.

A tray of sherry, offered by my railroad friend, Al.

"Hello!" His face was bright with pleasure.

"Hi—what are you doing here?" Not the politest of replies, but it was true to my heart.

"I arranged this gathering. *Nell*—You must be—Nelly Wainwright?" I nodded.

"Al. *Almanzoor?*" I was blown away. "I can't believe we talked all that time and didn't—"

"I know!" He laughed. "You got off in Omaha!"

"And you went to—?"

"Des Moines," we both said.

"To meet friends." He laughed again.

Fabulous Fannie, the brunette bombshell, glided across the room. "What's this?"

"Lorena," Al said, rolling the R in her name like a purr. "Nelly and I traveled on the same train but didn't realize we were going to the same place."

She flashed pearly teeth and held out her hand. "Nelly, a pleasure to meet you."

I shook her slim, firm hand and felt the graze of her nails as she withdrew. I didn't know her from the website. She was beautiful, as lovely as the mean girls at a table in the cafeteria in middle school; perfect as a homecoming queen who had eyes only for the other cheerleaders, not for invisible Nelly the Ninny. Her nails were purple shells, her lips, a cupid's bow of glossy color; her perfect smoky eye and her Betty bangs made her cooler than any Rockabilly artist. The suggestion of tattoos peeked from the lace cuffs of her costume. Lorena, the opposite of Nelly: hip, pretty, magnetic.

She terrified me.

Al cleared his throat a little ostentatiously. "As the crazy guy who started this adventure, I'd like to thank you for coming all the many distances." He flashed his smile around the parlor. "I know we all have different reasons for being here, and for loving Laura Ingalls Wilder and the Little House books, but I would like to welcome you to De Smet. I've never been here, but this is one of my lifelong dreams—so thank you for helping to make it come true."

He raised his tiny glass and said, "To Laura."

Lorena stepped in close and clinked her glass to his. "*Salud,*" she said to him. I turned to the little trio of females nearby and touched my glass to theirs, and gestured around the room. Lorena seemed to have fastened herself to Al, but he looked over her shoulder and saw me.

He raised his glass to me. "Nell."

"To Laura," I said again to him. Lorena's eyes were cool and so dark they seemed empty of iris, only pupil, and she held her glass level, neither raising nor lifting it to me. Remembering my vow to push out, try harder, I raised my tiny glass while looking right at her. Not a blink.

Okay. So that's where we are. Great.

Al said over general conversation that we should bundle up and prepare to walk up the street to the restaurant, and so we fetched our wraps, as Ma would say, and did as he asked. Good thing, too. It was bitterly chilly outside now, still no moisture in the air, but the wind blew right through. My legs were shivering, even though my body was warm. I should have worn thicker tights. Or snowpants. Perhaps a buffalo robe.

I fell in with two New Jersey schoolteachers and heard about their car journey west, and how they had stopped in Minnesota to look up the Ingalls house at Walnut Grove, also known as "The Wonderful House" in the chapter of *Plum Creek*. Their brassy travelers' tales were punctuated with snorts and guffaws as they made jokes about the adventure and mocked the Minnesota accents along the way[77].

The sky was clouded over still, so I wasn't able to visualize Laura sitting in the carriage out under the stars, singing, "In the Starlight." I wasn't able to picture Almanzo holding her hand and asking her to sing. I didn't know which way was northwest to look for a blizzard cloud rising. But I felt it under my ribcage, the dark cloud rising. I already felt on the outs, and we had just begun this adventure. I'd come a long way to feel like a useless

---

[77] Trust me—you haven't lived until you've heard two Jersey girls trying to do a Minnesota accent. It is to laugh.

tool. I could have stayed home and felt that way for free if I'd known about Lorena.

But perhaps I was getting ahead of myself. So far, no overt offense had been made. True, I felt judged by her beauty and her raking eyes. But feelings are not necessary reality. A lifetime with my gaslighting mom surely had taught me that. I was beginning to make friends with the Jersey girls, and who knows, they could be a lot of fun. I mentally bit my tongue and tried not to be a freak.

As a group, we retraced the route I had taken earlier in the day on my way to Loftus's store, but turned in at a family-style restaurant that had a Westward Ho theme to it (wagon wheels lining the front walkway, mounted cattle long-horns, and a rusty plow up on the wall). Cattle branding jazzed up the menus and curtains, and gentle Western music played over the sound system. It wasn't quite Disney's Country Bear Jamboree, but it threatened to go there.

I didn't expect to sit next to Al[78], but found the women racing to take his neighboring seat a little amusing. And no surprise, Lorena won. She was two steps short of cooing, "Oh, Cappy, I love candy!" and clutching his arm while the horses reared[79]. I rather relished the thought.

She spoke softly to him, and although I wasn't listening, I could hear that she was speaking Spanish and both of them were chuckling. I almost felt like leading Lorena to the watering hole where the leeches lurk.

I ended up seated between Dan, a high school history teacher from Philadelphia, and one of three Japanese women in the tour group. She was adorable, even tinier than Lorena, and attentive

---

[78] I didn't own him. We were two people on a train, that's all.

[79] A mixed set of scenes, I know. Nellie Oleson tried to steal Mary Power's beau, Cap, and later she clutched at Almanzo when he was trying to control the horses. Cut me some slack. This is what passes for humor in *LauraLand*.

to every bit of information and Laura trivia. I asked her name, and she replied so softly that I had to ask her to repeat it twice.

"Please call me Mary."

Her sister-travelers watched from across the table, and when I caught their eyes, they boldly introduced themselves as Grace and Carrie. When I said my name was Nelly, they burst into peals of tiny, sparkly laughter like Tinkerbell flying across the sky.

"No, it's really my name," I said, with my fake smile[80] across my face. "Really, really." More laughter.

So much more laughter tinkled from the Japanese contingent that even Lorena was compelled to stop her deep conversation with Al and look in our direction. Her smile—well, let's just say it was not as real as mine.

I told myself that I did not have a broken heart and I was not jealous. I was not in middle school. I was just hungry. I was a nervous, crotchety, perimenopausal cat woman trying to order food in a western-themed restaurant, and nobody in a pin-tucked paisley skirt was going to keep me from my vittles. When the waiter came around, I ordered the roast beef dinner. Gravy and mashed potatoes make everything better.

At the other end of the group Lorena had roped in someone from another table, one of the local tour guides, an expert on all things Laura and De Smet, it seemed. Lorena monopolized his time and we never heard a word he said down at our end of the board. *Rude.* Was it going to be like this all week?

When the meal finished, Al paid with a credit card (we had all paid in advance when we registered). I left an extra tip anyway. My occasional foray into waitressing had made me very aware of the low salaries of waitstaff. Somehow on the way back out the door Lorena took Mr. Expert to her side and kept chatting

---

[80] You cannot imagine how long I have parried this question and this laughter. I am so tired of being Nelly, "like on Little House?"

with him—but she couldn't also hold onto Al. Her attention was fully engaged elsewhere.

We headed out the door into the wind, en masse, but along the two-block route, we spread out again. I found myself walking alone among the crowd and liking it, to my surprise. I felt myself among friends, mostly, or at least among fellow freaks (except for *Lorrrena*). The weather felt frosty, cold enough to see your breath and make the sparse grass along the edge of the sidewalk crunch underfoot. My toes were numb inside my boots, and I knew I'd need to add a layer or two just to warm up to sleep. I'm from California. We don't get cold winters, nor long ones. It rains a little, we sometimes get a frosty night or two and have to put a tarp over the Meyer lemon, and bring the begonias inside. But this cold in October? It was all part of this dream.

The cold night seemed to make the skies brighter. Maybe it was the clarity of the air, or the surrounding farmland and wetlands, fewer city lights lighting the darkness. It seemed cleaner here in South Dakota[81], less, I don't know, fraught with hustle and hurry and worry. I think the backsides of all those train towns had left me feeling filthy. I would take a hot bath when I got to my room.

"Penny for your thoughts?" Al's voice right next to me brought me back to the present time and place with a shiver.

"Nobody says that anymore." I looked over at him. "Are you an old-fashioned guy?"

He laughed a little. "Maybe."

"You're not from here, are you?" I joked. Of course, he wasn't; we'd been on the train from California.

---

[81] "These prairies are so clean!" Laura gushed to Mary when the blind woman feared eating a bug. But I think she was correct—the prairies were clean.

"Not at all. I was born in Mexico City. *Can't you tell by my accent?*" He exaggerated a cartoonish South of the Border accent on the last line.

"No, not much. Once in a while it shows up." I gave him a sideways look. "It keeps one guessing. I wondered but wasn't sure. Your English is perfect."

"It should be. I worked my tail off getting it right."

"In school?"

"In the library. In school. Tutoring. Practicing. You know what was the first book I read in English, all the way through?"

"*Farmer Boy?*"

"*Farmer Boy.* I had read all of them in Spanish in school. That made me want to go north, to the Great Plains, to the land of *Laura Ingalls Wilder*," he said, heavily accenting her name in Spanish. "I studied and practiced my English, because I wanted to be Almanzo. I loved his Spanish name, his name's history, and I wanted to be a farmer boy." He looked up at the sky and around at the little town. He chuckled. "I still do."

"I'm excited to see the houses tomorrow, and the homestead."

"So am I—it'll be like touching a dream."

"I know. A dream come true, maybe."

We walked along in company, breathing deep lungfuls of cold night air, our footsteps matching. The Japanese girls giggled together right behind us.

"Nelly's walking with Almanzo!" said Kellie in her overloud Jersey voice. "Laura would be so pissed off!"

"She'd put out a hit on Nelly. Wham, bam, Nelly's sleepin' wit' da fishes!" Amanda squealed with laughter.

Lorena glanced over her shoulder at us and released the arm of Mr. Local Expert. She said, "My, aren't we cozy back there?"[82]

---

[82] My god. She was so Nellie!

Well, we had been, but it was clearly over. Lorena waited until we caught up with her and then fixed herself on Al's other arm. I guess she couldn't walk without hanging onto someone. Poor thing.

"Did you hear what David was telling me?[83] He said—"

Al looked down into her perfect face and replied. Lorena was beautiful. She sounded intelligent. She knew her stuff. But she had dismissed me, pressed me back as with a hand. I fell back a few steps and walked with my New Jersey homies. Kellie planned on jogging in the early morning, but Amanda and I agreed to meet for breakfast at eight at the diner across the road.

We stamped our feet against the cold and rubbed our chilled hands as we went up the walk. The Jersey girls were used to cold weather, but Roxie from Sarasota was freezing, like me. We went in and found that Liz had made the woodstove toasty in the parlor and had brewed some cinnamon-ginger tea. The warm inn smelled delicious.

I wanted to make a quip about asking for cambric tea[84], but I was afraid it would be lost upon my traveling companions. I don't know why—wouldn't these smart *LauraLanders* get me? I was so accustomed to being misunderstood.

The parlor held a few photo albums from past Little House Days celebrations, so we looked through those and enjoyed our tea, talking about our journeys and why we were here. Eventually, Lorena and Al came in from outside. I wondered why they had stayed back and imagined that they were connecting under the stars on a celestial level while I sat playing Tea Party with the other nerds. I don't know who I hated more, *Lorrrena* or myself.

---

[83] "My tongue's made to go flippety-flop!"
[84] Weak tea with milk and sugar, for children.

Liz had plenty of hot water ready for another pot of tea. It was true, what Laura discovered that first long winter—the scent of ginger can really chirk you up when you're cold and tired. We all began to call out our favorite *Little House* novels, going around the room in a disorganized but entertaining way like a party game. If we approved, we cheered, or we argued back over the reasoning.

"*Big Woods* for me," Kellie took her stand. "I like how Pa and Ma can make anything from scratch. I felt like I could make a straw hat or a bullet after reading that book."

"But what about the romance? What about *Golden Years*?" Roxie held her hands to her heart. "So romantic!"

"No, wait, *Farmer Boy*—"

"We know—because of the food!"

"*Silver Lake!*"

"*The First Four Years*[85]," grandmother Marian said when we turned to her. "It's the most realistic. Not fluffy."

Her adult daughter, Sandy, rallied for *Big Woods*, for the storytelling. Little June, the 9-year-old aficionado who was as much a part of the tour as any scholar, took a stand for *On the Banks of Plum Creek*, "Because Laura is so naughty!"

Although it was spontaneous, we were suddenly in the throes of Getting to Know You activities. All we needed was a Trust Fall and a Myers-Briggs assessment, and we'd be ready for committee assignments.[86] Whatever *moment* I'd had on the walk home with Al, if it could even be called that, seemed to be over. Perhaps Lorena was nicer than she seemed, if Al liked her. Perhaps I had misjudged her. Perhaps.

---

[85] Marian goes to the wall with this choice—*The First Four Years* was untouched by Rose, and it is pure Laura: stark, humorless, and bleak as an empty wallet. No nonsense is maybe a better descriptor, but also, no fairy tales.

[86] Is my city government experience showing?

I waited for a turn to say my own favorite book, when Lorena popped out with it: "*The Long Winter.*"

Damn! She stole my opinion!

"Why, Lorena?" Al asked her.

"Perseverance," she said at once. "It was so long and cold and miserable, and they just kept clinging to life. They survived it despite being down to rags and a single potato and a cup of tea, and with the grinding wheat and twisting hay? It was almost unbearable. I don't know—I just feel it in my bones," she added.

Damn. That's why I like it best, too.

Al turned to me and nudged, "How about you, Nelly?" He was still handsome, but now that I kind of liked him, more than I had on the train, I was a little lost in his deep brown eyes.

I wanted to be glib and clever, but the early train arrival and long drive to De Smet had finally caught up with me. "Mine's the same—*The Long Winter.* It reads like a bout of seasonal depression to me." I half-laughed but no one else did. Awkwardly, I added, "It was just so dark and cold and precarious. Their perseverance, as Lorena[87] said." I had to give her credit, and I hated myself for it.

I said my goodnights and went up to my room. I sat on the edge of the bed to undress and looked at the paneled walls and sprigged calico curtains. Part of me was still in a state of shocked delight, of, "This is crazy. I can't believe I'm really here!"

And the rest of me was thinking, "What am I doing here? What am I doing with my life? Why am I such a dork-ass fool?"

I ran a hot bath and stepped into the water, extending my full length of five feet into the tub, then slipping down to my chin. If I could only be Mary Powers, slender yet well-shaped, a lovely face and many admirers, I'd have the ability to wear a hair switch and

---

[87] I just said *Lorena,* without rolling the R.

get away with it. If I could be jolly Irish Ida Brown, with curly black hair and laughing eyes, and a sweetheart named Elmer who would walk with me by the lake. If I even had half an ounce of the moxie displayed by Laura's nemesis, Nellie, in the books—the nerve to take what I wanted like candy from a suitor's hand, to dress grandly from a charity barrel and suck up to people like Miss Wilder, and the scheming to do Laura out of her beau or her birthday party or her velocipede or whatever, who would I be?

I didn't even have the guts of Laura, wheedling Nellie into the shallows toward the crab under the rock, or where the leeches lurked.

I was probably more like the leech anyway, ugly and mud-colored, clinging where I was not wanted. Leaving a bloody mark when pulled away.

The noises of De Smet at night were far fewer than in my California suburb. We'd have barking dogs, cars, buses, occasional sirens, with the whoosh of the freeway a half mile or so away. But here, it was positively still. An occasional pickup truck went by with its big motor. I hadn't seen anyone walking a dog, though I supposed people out here had dogs. Maybe out on the farms. I guess only city people have to *exercise* their pups. I let the water go and stepped out of the tub, warmed from the soak.

I could hear the soft sounds of the inn, of doors gently closing, of footsteps in the hallways. Voices behind doors, through walls, but soft, muffled. Water running in pipes, maybe. A soft ticking from the baseboard heaters. Gentle sounds of a house shutting down for the night.

I turned off the overhead light and got into my long, warm T-shirt. Socks, too. It was not sexy, but no one was looking. Why should I care?

The sheets were fresh, white, and crisp, the way hotel sheets should be, and tucked in tightly, but it was an icy envelope into which I slid, despite space heaters and insulation. I put my head under the covers and blew on my hands, creating a warming chamber in my dark little tent. It was cold in South Dakota in October, and I pitied Laura, Mary, and Carrie in their uninsulated attic bedroom, with the frosty white teeth of nails in the boards over their heads. I knew now why Ma wrapped a brick with flannel for their feet, and why Mary put her cold feet onto Laura. I felt the sensation of warmth beneath and icy cold above the blankets, but not as much as Laura had known it.

I'm not sure I could have lived like that. I'm not actually sure I *am* living like this, whatever this is. It's 140 years after Laura and Mary clung to each other for body heat, and I'm supposed to have evolved, but I wondered if people had. If I were any more innovative or advanced? I don't think so. These pioneer girls had it all over me in relationships, in family bonds, in making the most of what they had, and in keeping a stiff upper lip. Somehow, despite plagues of locusts, scarlet fever, child death, and a river of tears, Laura got through it all.

What was so wrong with me that I couldn't get through a day, an hour, without hating myself? Without having the ability to live a life where there is hope? Was it just—choice?

I thought about Al and his face, his jasper brown eyes, brown-black hair, his slight, just a trace, accent. His passion for the land. His friendliness. His strength, and his kindness to others. He was a born leader. No one even questioned his plans or what he had arranged for us. My admiration for him had grown since we met again this evening, and I drifted to sleep thinking of a smile, a laugh, an invitation, a chair pulled out, a glance.

In the night come the dreams. The door cracks open. I hear it and pretend to be asleep. If I keep my eyes closed very tightly, I will be sleeping and no one will bother me. The toy box I put in front of the door is not heavy enough to keep the monster out, and I hear the door push open, and the box slide across the floor with a low scrape. The hall light slices in like a wedge of orange cheese. The footsteps. A presence over me. The sound of breathing. Waiting for the touch. The touch.

CHAPTER 9

The morning opened up like a gift with cold sunshine, high wispy clouds across the sky. There might be rain later. There would be wind.

Out on the plains, there's always wind. Ma's clothesline flapped incessantly, and their skirts blew around their legs, aprons lifted as if an unseen hand were playing tricks, strings from bonnets and aprons and pinafores twisted and fluttered. Delicate ostrich feathers whisked away by the western winds, caught by her fingertips at the last second. Dust stirred and raised mini devils on the road. The grass of the Slaw folded and bent under waves of the invisible. Clouds blew in and passed over. Rain blew sideways. Trees bent and undulated.

Pioneers lost their minds on the open prairie. The winds that never ceased. The sound of the air crying. Easterners came out to the prairies in shirt sleeves and took walks; the weather changed, and they froze to death. Pa told such stories, and Laura relayed them. They must be true.

I wrapped a pashmina around my neck and tucked my jeans into my boots, pulled up over an extra pair of socks. Gloves in my coat pocket instead of baked potatoes, but perhaps I'd pick up a few hot potatoes[88] later in the day. Just to see if it worked[89].

---

[88] Literally, or maybe just socially.

[89] True confession: I fully expect the hot potato to explode in my face, like poor young Almanzo's did.

I jogged down the stairs lightly and slipped my sunglasses on against the bright glare. I was glad I had the pashy. I might go back for a warm hat later. I could feel the nip of autumn here. In California there were still heirloom tomatoes on the vine, and the grape harvest for next year's wine was in full swing. Apples falling to the ground in luscious profusion.

Amanda was seated at the café, I mean *diner,* already, and enjoying her coffee. The waitress brought me some as I settled in, and I went ahead and ordered an omelet. I assumed they ate omelets here in the Midwest. No one stopped me from ordering. I poured dairy cream, or what I hoped was cream in this land of rolling prairie and farmsteads, and asked Amanda how she'd slept.

"Horrible. Too quiet. Much too quiet! Where's the city noise? I miss Jersey already. Honk some horns already!"

With her boisterous attitude and cheerful disposition in my face, I couldn't feel too bad about missing California. California was our own Garden State. I didn't mention my dreams. No one liked to hear that kind of thing.

A few of the others drifted in and had their breakfasts at the counter or other tables. I didn't see Al or Lorena. Kellie rolled in after having taken her morning run and told a funny story about jogging past some cows and stepping in poop. She called them *bulls,* and it went downhill from there, made all the funnier with a Jersey accent. Especially when she learned that there's a breed of cows known as Jerseys.

"I'm up to my ankles here in this Jersey *boolshit!*" she said to whomever would listen.

After breakfast, I ran back up to my room, thinking I might need that hat after all, but up at the top of the stairs, I saw Lorena coming out of Al's room, turning back to talk to him about something, but I didn't hear what. She laughed and they spoke in Spanish to each other. I turned and rushed down the stairs and outside. I should have known. They spoke the same language. My shame bubbled inside me. It had been too good to be true, a cool guy just being friendly with me, that's all. Nothing more.

★ ★ ★

We were to meet at 9:30 at the Discover Laura Learning Center at the Surveyors' House for a private tour, and when we walked over, Al was already there, speaking with the education director. Lorena walked with us, but I couldn't hear what she said to her nearest companions[90]. I couldn't hear eyes rolling, either, but mine were spinning. I was awash with Mean Girl jealousy. Of all the names in the world, why couldn't hers have been Nelly and mine Lorena, or Lorelei, or Laura?

"Good morning, everyone, and a very warm welcome to the Laura Ingalls Wilder Surveyor's House. I'm Rob Reynolds, Education Director, and I'm so pleased to see so many bright and eager faces here today." A middle-aged thinning-hair white guy in a sweater vest and bow tie over a white button-down shirt, some teacher-like dark slacks and loafers, he spoke as if we were schoolchildren. But I suppose that was nine-tenths of his job. Probably all the kids in surrounding counties came to visit De Smet and all the Ingalls hotspots by sometime in middle school.

I had hoped to find some hidden depths here. The morning would reveal whether that was the case or if I was in for a visit to Disneyland.

"We're especially delighted to welcome this group of *LauraLand* scholars and enthusiasts who have dedicated their time and expertise to exploring the life and works of Laura Ingalls Wilder. Your presence here in De Smet, where Laura spent some of her most formative years, is truly inspiring."

---

[90] I was getting the strongest *Lazy Lousy Lizzie Jane* vibes I've ever had in my life.

I stood up straight. I enjoyed the flattery. He was right. I had studied my topic for many years, and I was, as it so happened, an expert.

"This house, the Surveyors' House, holds a unique place in Laura's story. It was here, in this very house, that the Ingalls family briefly resided while Charles Ingalls worked as a bookkeeper and paymaster for the railroad. Imagine the conversations that took place within these walls, the dreams that were shared, and the experiences that would later shape Laura's writing?"

I had spent portions of my life doing just that—imagining Laura and the conversations around her.

"If these walls could speak," I half-whispered.

Roxie next to me, who was also a librarian, murmured, "I know, right?"

"Your research and insights are invaluable to our understanding of Laura Ingalls Wilder's contributions to literature and our appreciation for the pioneer experience. We hope that your time here in De Smet, and specifically at the Surveyors' House, will provide you with new perspectives, spark fresh ideas, and deepen your connection to Laura's world.

"Imagine the Ingalls family within these rooms, consider the challenges and triumphs they faced, and reflect on how this environment might have influenced Laura's writing. We encourage you to examine the artifacts, study the architecture, and immerse yourselves in the atmosphere of this historic home. Our volunteers are passionate about preserving Laura Ingalls Wilder's legacy and are eager to assist you in any way possible. We are all here to learn from each other."

Okay, buddy, we get it. Can we commence the exploration now? I was getting antsy. I had heard this kind of greeting in so many museums. I wanted meat, juice, blood, and sinew. I wanted tissue samples. I wanted to inhale Laura and absorb her into my pores and cells.

"We are confident that your time here will be both productive and enriching. We look forward to hearing about your research and the insights you gain during your stay. So, once again, welcome to the Laura Ingalls Wilder Surveyors' House. And thank you to Alberto Escano for leading this group so far into the heart of America!"

It was the first time I'd heard his full name. I had been thinking of him only as Al, my train crush, or *Almanzoor,* my *LauraLand* dude, all this time. *Alberto*, like the shampoo[91]. I liked the heft of it. It was a real man's name. Even if it wasn't *my man's* name.

Then Rob Reynolds opened the door to the Surveyors' House, stepped back to hold it open, and let us in.

My first sensation as I stepped into the very house, the place where Laura and her kin spent the winter of 1879, was a rush of tears to my eyes. I took a deep sniff of the air: It smelled dry, wooden, maybe a little like straw or dry grass? Or was I imagining sticks of hay from another book? My hands were shaking. I was in her footsteps, in her very presence. Laura, as alive to me as my own self, had lived here. I could almost feel her hand in mine, leading me forward.

Antique surveying equipment hung on the walls. I hadn't been sure what surveyors were when I first read the books, and had scant more familiarity now. Surveyors look around and make marks on trees and write things down, I guess. Make the crooked way straight[92]. Some kind of compass and measuring chains, with a wooden tripod that was clearly very old, and some

---

[91] Cheaper than store brands, Alberto VO5, of course. Or did your grandma use Head and Shoulders?

[92] There's nothing like seeing colonial deer paths (used by Native folk), made into cow paths made into wagon roads made into curving, twisted streets paved for today's vehicles, versus the long straight and narrow that surveyors made on the highways of the middle west. Folks say in England, the curved roads are Anglo-Saxon, and the straight roads are Roman. Here, it's the deer paths vs. the surveyors. Nature vs. progress, writ large.

clipboards hung on square nails pounded into the plank walls. I had thought of clipboards as modern; your coach or tour director uses them, but no reason why they should not have been used back in Laura's day. A surveyor's brass instrument[93], still shiny, stood on the desk, with its wooden and felt-lined traveling box. These technologies must have thrilled Charles Ingalls and his thirst for modern progress[94].

The storage room had wonderful antiques, jugs and dishes, even a washtub with a mangle. The pantry shelves bore all kinds of foodstuffs—canned goods (in glass jars, not metal cans), crocks and sacks, probably full of Styrofoam pellets or rocks rather than beans. A fake loaf of bread waited to be sliced, an apron hung by its strings, a knife on the board looked as if Ma had just walked away to tend the fire and left her work unfinished.[95]

I remember reading about the delight of canned peaches for the Ingalls family, and the full barrels of flour and sugar, cornmeal, and salt pork. There were soda crackers and salted fish, dried apples, potatoes, and dry beans. Sometimes I buy canned peach halves, or can them myself.[96] I, too, savor every golden bite and lick the spoon of the delicious, heavy syrup. Little things like this—the sensuous nature of pioneer living, I guess—still exist in my mind.

---

[93] A *theodolite*, the sign said.

[94] Wouldn't he have loved to have a smartphone? Able to see a blizzard coming days in advance? Know when to plant the corn with advance warning on out-of-season frost? Keep an eye on the political news instead of waiting for the *Chicago Inter-Ocean* to arrive in the mail? Set up a website or a FAQ as a member of the county board and school board?

[95] As if! Ma never left her work unfinished, which is why Pa insisting that they leave immediately, the plow still in the furrow, in *Little House on the Prairie,* was such a shock.

[96] One year, I picked and canned peaches, but I could not get them to cut in perfect halves, and the resulting chunks looked like a kindergartener had attacked a peach. But they tasted delicious.

The pantry offered a couple of hand-worked meat-grinders, vise-gripped to the counter or shelf or whatever that was. Old pioneer kitchens didn't have slate countertops and cherrywood cabinets, stainless steel trash compactors, garbage disposals nor appliance garages. But that's what I'd call it—a countertop, the wide shelf under all the other shelves in that marvelous pantry. It even smelled old, in a good way. Like onions and coffee, like a small-town grocery store, not like my grandma's basement[97] smelled old.

I looked upon the wooden potato masher, the rolling pin, the iron trivet, and the twisted wire frying fork. They were old, or *vintage*, as we'd say on Pinterest or Etsy, meaning quaint, trendy, but not remotely usable today. But to me, they were absolutely perfect. I loved the tools that Ma and Laura and Mrs. Boast would have used, if not these exact ones, and thought not about Pa's fascination with technology, but how technology helped women, even as it added to their workloads.[98]

I wished I could move into this house right now, and have the thrill of a loaded pantry, the excitement of Pa bringing home a goose or a jackrabbit for supper, the fun of sliding on the lake in my shoes, holding hands with Carrie until we saw the wolves on the opposite shore. I wanted all of it except the misogyny. Oh, well. I suppose they were inextricably entwined.

A recreation of the famous Silver Lake "what-not" (the trinket shelf) was in the corner, with little china items that recalled

---

[97] Mildew, urine, and old perfume. An olfactory time-bomb.

[98] Experts say that for every home appliance or device, you could eliminate the job of one servant in old England. Flush toilet? No need to empty chamber pots or clean the privy. Running water? No need to haul buckets from the creek. Hot water heater? No need to gather/burn wood/coal. Dishwasher/garbage disposal? No need for the scullery maid. But also: A vacuum cleaner meant the woman no longer had to pull up carpet tacks and beat the rug; but she had to do it every week instead of twice a year. White clothing meant she had to wash clothes much more often. Every raised standard of cleanliness added to her workload, while Daddio sat in his chair and smoked his pipe.

Carrie's china bulldog and the porcelain box with the wee cup and saucer on the lid[99]. I wanted to see the mythical china shepherdess but she wasn't here. A similar tchotchke was nearby, in Keystone, at the house of Carrie Ingalls, but that wasn't the real one either.[100] I almost didn't care where it was—what I wanted was continuity, familiarity. What was real, and what was imaginary? These icons weren't there. It upset me a little, just a smidge. Happily, for me, in the smallish main room (the room Laura remembered as so large), there was a chest of drawers that Pa had made. That Charles Ingalls had touched it made it *real*.

The tablecloth with red checks against the wall between the doors, just as Laura described it, yes! But the organ in the corner—not right. They didn't have the organ until they added on the extra room out at the claim, when Laura was teaching school and working in town, and could afford to help buy it for Mary. But Mary's organ is lost to time. No one knows where it is, either, any more than the china shepherdess who guided Laura's sense of home. And the checkered tablecloth—I had one just like it from Home Goods.

For some reason, this outraged me. I looked up the narrow stairs to the loft and remembered the drawing in *Silver Lake* by Garth Williams, the one where Ma gives Laura a piece of wood to lock the door from the *rough men* passing through, sleeping on the floor, who sometimes had their liquor. A sliver of wood for defense. Thanks a lot, Ma. A strong kick would blast the door down, and someone would get through. Maybe it happened, but Laura didn't write about it. Maybe she couldn't speak of it.

I found that I was shaking again—with rage this time. I stepped back and let two others in front of me, stepped back

---

[99] And, although perfect in their own way, nothing like I had imagined for the past forty years.

[100] In fact, no one knows what happened to the original china shepherdess.

again, until I was in the back of the group, and turning away from the tour guide. I was so angry. I stepped outside. I was missing the tour. Our personal guided tour. But I can't—I just couldn't bear it.

A piece of wood to keep her daughters safe. Is that the best they could do?

★ ★ ★

I wasn't alone. Sandy, the little girl's mother, was outside, tears on her cheeks. She looked at me and said, "I'm sorry. I just can't—"

In sympathy, or solidarity, I walked over to her, put my hand awkwardly on her shoulder. I felt like a dog offering a paw to shake. I don't have friends. No one hugs me.

"I don't know," she said. "It's just so small, and—wrong and—not what I was thinking."

"Disappointing?"

"I don't know, maybe." She drew a deep breath and sobbed a little. "It's not what I expected. It's too—*real*." She pulled a ratty tissue from her pocket and blew her nose. "I have been reading these books since I was a kid and they were always just *perfect* in my mind. But then to see such rickety walls, such rattly furniture—it destroys the dream. It makes them these hardscrabble people who struggled, just like us." A fresh wave of tears spilled out of her eyes. Her tissue was a sodden ball.

She mopped at her cheeks. "Stupid." She said it to herself.

I thought I was the only one who talked to myself like that.

"Look at me." I held out my shaking hands. "I took one look at that staircase and had a panic attack."

Sandy started to laugh and put her arm around my shoulder, and then we were both crying and hugging at the same time. About that time, Al looked out the door and started to come over, saw us weeping like a couple of ninnies, thought better of it, and went back in.

"Let's take a look at the house together, then," I said. "I want to look at everything, but I don't want to be told what to look at. I want to kind of feel it and be here without hearing them say the same thing for the hundredth time."

"That would be nice. Perfect, in fact," Sandy said, sniffling and wiping her last tears.

As the others began to leave the Surveyors' House through the back door, Sandy and I went back in the front door and looked again at the scarred kitchen table, the old cook stove, the wondrous pantry. I ran my fingers across the wooden smoothness of the chest of drawers that Pa had built. All real. Not too real. But very, very real.

We could hear June calling her mother from outside. Sandy and I rejoined the group just as they crossed the street to the old schoolhouse, now the *Discover Laura* Center. Inside, exhibits on how to read Braille, treadle a non-electric sewing machine, and practice using a drop-spindle to spin wool held captive the various lookers. I skipped those activities and sat at a desk at the back of the room, closed my eyes and ears. Submerged like a crocodile up to my eyes. The schoolhouse wasn't large, and once again, it didn't take long until I felt closed in, claustrophobic, with our group, and then a class of fourth-graders arrived, chattering. I was glad Sandy and I'd had a little quiet time in the Surveyors' House, but I feared it was the only quiet time we would get.

We were scheduled for a "pioneer picnic" somewhere nearby at noon, weather permitting.[101] I saw Al talking with a docent and nodding. I decided not to worry about things I couldn't control, for at least five minutes, anyway. I had already shared intimacy

---

[101] So far, it permitted.

with a stranger and I felt flattened enough. I didn't realize how draining it is to feel emotions right out loud and everything.

Al raised his hand above his head with a yellow placard in his hand that said *"LauraLand"* on it in stark black letters, and we left the schoolhouse.

"We're going up to Calumet Street," he said, to see the original store sites. "And we'll end up at the Ingalls home on Third. The picnic is taking place there."

Sandy glanced at me. "I wonder why they moved the party?"

"Too many people here, I guess." We followed Al out the door and, as we had done last night, we straggled along First Street in a bunch toward Calumet Avenue, Laura's "Main Street," where we could see the original town site.

The streets are wider in De Smet than most residential streets in my California suburb. I mentioned it to Al, and he didn't know why. Roxie, Florida beachcomber, also didn't know, but then the Jersey girls overheard.

"Snowplows," Kellie spoke with certainty. "Don't forget that it snows here."[102]

"A lot," chimed Amanda. "Trust me, we know from snow."

At the corner of Calumet, we stopped and looked around. To the right was the town library, the museum in the old depot[103], and the schoolhouse museum. But in Laura's day,

---

[102] That ain't it. It turns out that streets are wider in many little (or big) towns that were planned in the West and Midwest were given streets wide enough so that a large wagon with horses could turn around easily. Brigham Young is famously said to have wanted a street wide enough that he didn't have to curse while turning. However, if you come across a wide street in a city with mostly narrow streets, you've come across a former streetcar line (see if the rails are still there — there would have likely been two sets, heading in either direction). As well, there's some indication that health and welfare were a concern. European (and then East Coast) cities that were densely packed had terrible rat and flea infestations that led to infection and pandemic, the Black Plague, and so on. So wide streets became a thing.

[103] Where the Woodworth boys lived.

there had been only the empty prairie off to the right. The depot used to be farther behind us; it had been moved to its current location. If it was snowing here, if there was a blizzard, without electric lights or even with them—a person could get lost. Quickly.

First building on the street in Laura's day would have been the Mead Hotel with the saloon next to it, then Wilder's Feed, where Pa went to borrow seed wheat to feed the family, and Barker's Grocery. The Beardsley Hotel was next, and Hartham's grocery store, with Couse's Hardware on the corner. On the other side of the street, Laura would have known Wilmarth Grocery and Clancy's dry goods store, where she sewed shirts by hand one hot summer.

Fuller's Hardware was next—it seems strange to me now that there were three grocers and two hardware stores within spitting distance of each other. Bradley's Drugstore, then Power's Tailor Shop, where Laura often met Mary Power and her Irish parents[104]. Tinkham's Furniture, where Laura went to the Dime Social. And Loftus' General Store, still there. Pa's store building was across the street from Fuller's Hardware and had had Pa's stables behind. Behind that would have been the stables and home of the Garlands, Laura's teacher Florence and the handsomest boy in town, Cap.

Gorgeous blond Cap Garland, he of the dangerous winter wheat adventure, he who tossed a baseball at Laura on her first day of school. Cap with a cold temper so powerful he'd made teamsters back away from a fight. Cap of the striped bags of candy. He died a few years after school ended, in a threshing accident.

---

[104] Mrs. Power came along with Ma when Laura gave birth to Rose, and dear friend Mary Power died in childbirth after marrying. So young. Sigh.

The Welcome Center is now in the space that had been the shop of Gerald Fuller, who could clog dance and spoke in his English way, "I say, old chap!" Time is a strange human construct. It's like I'm in the past and the present at once.

On we walked, not really talking, looking at each of the sites and reading the map, the guidebooks, the placards on the walls. Each of us a little lost in our own inner prairies.

One thing was certain: There was still a local grocery store in that block, albeit a modern one. "Some things don't change," someone joked. On the other side, the east side, was a catering business, a cute little bar and grill. Where Laura had worked setting collars on men's shirts in the humid summer heat, watching drunks carouse up the street, you could now order barbecue with coleslaw, a biscuit, and a beer. A brick building took up the next corner at Second and Calumet, with a lawyer, an accountant and a real estate office inside. A blue fabric banner with gold writing on every other lamppost proclaimed De Smet "The Little Town on the Prairie."

Across the street, we also passed the little post office, with pride of place held for the Laura Ingalls Wilder stamp and a ZIP code of its own: 57231. There was no ZIP code when Laura was here[105]. I just wanted to sigh. There was also a saloon—in a building that may be as old as 1900, in brick and stone, keeping that old timey Wild West feeling alive. A PBR beer sign flashed in the window.

We stepped off the curb and crossed Second Street—and there we were at Pa's store building location: where the family spent their winters, where they survived that long, hard winter. When the snow was up to the second floor, Laura could see the dainty brown hooves of Almanzo's Morgan horses trip past at eye-level. It was like being rabbits, the girls had thought. And from this

---

[105] ZIP codes were not used until 1963.

corner, they tried to keep watch on the northwestern sky, seeking the dark cloud, harbinger of yet another storm.

I still couldn't tell you which way was northwest. I asked, and Al came behind me and physically turned me kitty-corner, to face the saloon opposite. You couldn't see the sky with the buildings there, I mean, not far enough to be helpful. Perhaps it had felt the same to Laura. We looked at the northwest, and back to the space that was their town home those years.

My shoulders tingled, and I felt his touch like molten lava. I had not felt this kind of heat, and—was it *desire*? If ever I had. I didn't want the closeness to end. It was so high school to have a crush. So juvenile to know he liked someone else, and yet to still burn for him.

But the original wooden store building was gone. The big heater and the big desk and the curtains that blocked prying eyes from looking inside at Laura, gone. The people who had built it and lived here were dead and gone. I knew it was just a midcentury brick building, just somebody's law office, but I put my hand on the corner and said aloud, "Oh, Laura. You were really something."

Then everyone else copied me and put their hands on the building like some kind of ritual blessing, and in a minute, I could see the people in the office looking out at us and shaking their heads.

Yes, we're freaks. So what?

There was still a little alley behind the building, and that's where the stable would have been, where Pa would have held onto the clothesline to get to the stable in whiteout conditions. Where the lean-to and a pile of straw for making sticks of hay used to stand.

It was so strange walking in Laura's footsteps. I can't explain it—just a sense of bridging history and the present day, of crossing a time between the centuries, being one with an imagined life that was as real as mine or yours. It felt a little like being in church. Of being awake and asleep at the same time. I was strobing in two timelines, it felt like.

I had walked up that street myself yesterday and went into Loftus's Store, and I hadn't really thought enough to look at my map and really envision where we were. I declined crossing the street to go in again. I was still raw from my earlier cry-fest at the Surveyors' House. I peeked into the florist shop and wondered about the age of the buildings there. The Loftus store had been standing since the 1880s. And the other few stores nearby looked as old. Were these the very doors?

We walked a bit farther along, and there was city hall and the *De Smet News*, where Carrie had later worked and where Laura had kept in contact with old friends. "Have we all become so old and gray?" she wondered. Other typical stores of the modern century lined the street—medical offices, an appliance store, a bank. Everyone and everything seemed to have the stamp of Little House on it—and the people seemed weary as all get-out of their role as tourist attraction. They'd look up, and then get back to what they were doing. We'd peek in, and keep walking. Hard to live, I imagined, in some kind of fishbowl.

We turned up Third Street and headed west toward the Ingalls' last home.

"How fitting that we're heading west," Lorena said, echoing my own thoughts. *Damn, did she read my mind again?*

We strolled through a lovely, quiet suburban-style neighborhood with green lawns and neat sidewalks, and suddenly there we were at a white clapboard house that wouldn't stand out from the others unless it had that standing sign in front proclaiming it, "The House That Pa Built."

Corny? Yes.

I was simultaneously embarrassed and exhilarated to be there. I could see a pop-up canopy set up around the back, along with some tables for food. Al went around the back to check on the arrangements, and we went to the front door and awaited our docent.

This tour-leader gave us much the same speech as we'd heard earlier in the day, with the same cadence and pauses. Perhaps they all trained together. It was a little annoying to hear the wonders proclaimed again, when obviously the Laura artifacts and sacred spaces are why we came. But so it goes. A group tour is a group tour. The guidebooks all say that volunteer historians would "interpret" the displays and artifacts for us, but I felt fully capable of interpreting what I saw with my own eyes and my own mind.

There was a kitchen, parlor, three bedrooms, and a porch, and none of it described in any detail in Laura's books—it was her parents' place, never her own. I was not attuned to any nuances of her footstep here. The walls were a riot of faded wallpaper in the style of the Victorian era, which had come and gone, leaving shadows of itself behind in homes like that. The Modernist era never came near there. Blind Mary had her own bedroom, styled in tones of pink, with her big Braille book at the foot, in a special glass case. An organ, though again not Mary's, stood vigil in the parlor. Baby Grace's room was sweetly staged[106] with a pink quilt as well.[107]

Ma and Pa's bedroom was similarly arrayed, with a patchwork quilt and embroidered towels and pillowcases. An ewer and basin sat atop the dresser, and underneath the bed—a chamber pot. For some reason, this chilled me. Pa Ingalls pissing in the

---

[106] Can we call it staged or styled, when this is how these folks truly lived? Or do we even know the truth? Perhaps they never made their beds, and perhaps Mary hated pink? Or did she even care what color it was, being blind? One wonders.

[107] It's hard to picture Grace as an adult woman, or even a teenager, although Rose called her Aunt Grace "a jolly girl." Grace married but didn't have children. She was a spoiled toddler, but who was Grace as a woman? Laura left De Smet without telling us more.

chamber pot is not a picture I can make in my mind. I might need this to be "interpreted" for me.

And then there were the shoes. Whose shoes were those, white kid curling with age and browning at all the seams? Ma's? Mary's? Carrie or Grace, the eternal children of my mind? Or mere antiques from some donor?

Once again, I felt I was trespassing on hallowed ground—with a tawdry gift shop at my elbow. I wanted to drive the money-changers from the temple. It all felt so wrong, so sacrilegious, so unlike my daydreams of the Real Laura—but I'm one of the gawkers, too. The looking and touching of this family's things, this having made relics and saints of them.

Again and again, I wondered, *what am I doing here?* Why are we chasing this ghost? I needed a job. I had bills to pay. Laura is dead. What difference does it all make, anyway?

I pulled my coat around me and stepped outside again for fresh air. My phone said it was time for lunch, besides the many messages I was ignoring. My usual ploy to pass the time was to check into *LauraLand* and see what was new or happening. But with some of the main contributors in this tour group, I doubted that I would see anything of interest online. Perhaps I should snap a few photos and post them. Show what we're up to. Make a move and be the first instead of the follower.

I waited at the back of the house near the tent until the rest of our party came out.

Al came over to me. He slid his phone into his back pocket and zipped his jacket. The wind tousled his brown hair. "I saw you duck out again. Are you okay?"

"Yeah, I'm fine."

"You're not feeling sick or anything?" He seemed genuinely concerned. I was surprised by how that felt inside. He wasn't fishing for a way to turn it back on himself (hello, Mom!) or trying to pull the rug from under me (bub-bye, Dave). What was this? Actual interest? At the very least, I was flattered. But it also felt like a little more, as if he was already on a different level of friendship with me, beyond the small talk on the train and the chit-chat between events. His greeting was—dare I say it? *Intimate?*

Damn. I liked it.

"No, I'm not *physically* ill—it's, I don't know. Psychological? I have dreamed of coming here for so long that actually seeing Laura's places, her family's home, all of this? It's so real it almost hurts. I don't know whether to cry, laugh, or vomit." I made a face. "Crazy-making. Seriously."

"I know what you mean. Walking in the footsteps of giants, and then they turn out to be like five feet tall. They're tiny." Al laughed. "Do you realize how tiny they were? Laura was under five feet tall, and Almanzo was just a few inches taller. Five foot four, he was. Little leprechaun people."

"Probably malnutrition."

"Probably." He cleared his throat. "Speaking of which, it's time for our lunch, out in back." Al gestured toward the house, while others filed around through the gate.

The wind was held at bay by six-foot fences, although the tent-canopy overhead flapped, as did the pastel pennants someone had hung for decoration.

Each of us received a lunchpail bucket of metal, some brightly painted, some original silver. The lunchpails contained slices of dried apples and peaches, rustic bread and butter, a hard-boiled egg, a wedge of local farm cheese, and a still-warm apple hand-pie. The pies smelled so good, I took a bite as soon as I saw it. Delicious cinnamon and spice filled my mouth. On the table were pitchers of lemonade and milk, and carafes of coffee and tea. The drinks were served in speckled enamel cups. I couldn't think of a meal that would serve me better just then. I needed simplicity to work out my tangled thoughts[108].

I ate and listened to the laughter, the badinage. I rather liked everyone, or at minimal, didn't hate and fear them, at the moment. (I still had my reservations about *Lorrrena*. Why was she so freaking pretty? Why were all her opinions the same that I held?) I was able to eat and chuckle along when someone said something funny. I had been a meticulous observer for so long that speaking up and out was not my strength. I'm the cyclone within. I felt wind tearing up my insides, strong enough to spit out two young boys and a broken mule. Or a wooden door right back to its original house[109].

I loved drinking our coffee in tin mugs, like Ma and Pa on the long road to Kansas and then back to Plum Creek. The mug warmed my hands. I clasped the heat close, then pressed my hands to my cold face. We sat under the canopy, but the sun shone through. The air was chilly, despite the high fence and sunshine, and it seemed colder than when we had started.

As we finished, Sandy and I helped clean up after our al fresco meal. It always felt better when I kept busy, helping or doing busywork. Whatever it is to keep me from small talk, face to face. *Intimacy*. (There's that word again[110].)

Sandy said as much. "I don't want to just stand around. I need to keep busy, even if it's mom-work!"

Two white vans with rows of seats and the *Little House* logo on the sides pulled to the curb and waited for us to gather

---

[108] And why I couldn't just let it all wash over me is part of the tangle. Just relax and enjoy it—or anything. Hyper-vigilance, I guess. You know. Trauma.

[109] These are tornado references from *These Happy Golden Years,* if that seems too random. Trust me, nothing in this story is random.

[110] Some people say *intimacy* = "Into me you see."

and climb in. We had a very short journey ahead of us to the homestead—the actual Ingalls homestead. My childhood stories were coming to life, my escape hatch exposed.

Laura and Carrie had walked that distance to school every day. Almanzo drove out from town every Sunday to take Laura riding in his carriage, with his horses to be trained. Laura and Pa walked home from work one summer evening, carrying a basket of newly hatched chicks between them. By car, it was six minutes, a mile and a half. We didn't walk it. We took the modern route, on paved roads, with GPS. I expect the Ingallses walked it as the shortest distance between two points, not taking any turns.

I was awash with nerves, for no reason. Just seeing my lifetime idol and her sacred grounds *in situ*—no reason to get so excited. I felt my stomach lurch. We clambered into the vans, Al taking the shotgun seat, and I took a different row than *Lorrrena*, behind her, where I could admire, envy, and detest her at the same time.

By and by, we were on our way.

CHAPTER 10

The landscape flowed away from us like an empty scroll of paper, awaiting the pen. Stubble here and there, empty dirt fields that had been groomed by the plow and rake, the patchwork of tilled and fallow lands that brought the harvest. From the air, I know they are circles of green fields with brown edges to make up the square. But at ground level, it's either green or brown.

We were crossing wetlands before I realized that it was the Slough, and I said "The Big Slaw" aloud without thinking. Lorena started to laugh in the seat in front of me in the van, turned to look at me, and laughed some more.

"I know," she said. "I know."

Finally, she was able to gasp out, "I always said it that way, too. And *JIN-jam* for *gingham*." Which blew my mind because Lorena was perfect. I assumed she had come naked from the seashell when God took her ivory hand and blew the East Wind into her lungs, knowing how to read and speak before mere mortals. I was a little startled to find her with feet of clay and lips of putty like me.

When the laughter subsided, we were already rumbling down the rougher side road, Homestead, and crossing Rose and the Avenue. We pull into the dusty parking area with a swirl of white-gray dust and the crunch of gravel underneath. *I am the bloody finger and I'm in your driveway.*

There was already a school bus and a couple of family cars[111] parked there, but the site was not packed. It was less busy than a mall on a Saturday. We stood looking around at the flat prairie, waiting for a docent to join us. He or she would "interpret" for us the tallgrass prairie and the shortness of the beds and the doorways, the difficulties of mowing, twisting, stirring, or cranking, and the cheer and gratitude with which the Ingallses surely went about their way.

The Visitors' Center awaited, and we crossed the dusty lot to meet our docent. A lanky white dude about 25, he was far younger than I expected, and though Brandon wore a long-sleeved shirt and a bandana tied around his neck, I could see tattoos peeking out at his neck, a snake or scorpion's tail. I also spied a divot at his nose that was surely a nose ring in his off-work hours. He sounded like a normal dude, not a hick. He was surprisingly[112] nice.

"You can start here at the lookout tower to see everything before you decide which way to go," he gestured to the structure not far off. "Or you could circle the place clockwise, starting here with the visitors' center, then the dugout and the shanty, then on to Ma's little house, the livestock barn and the garage, the church, the wheat fields, and take the walking trail around."

He paused and added, "Just watch out in the marshy area out there—also known as the Big Slough. It's pronounced *slough*, like *blue*." He laughed. "But when I was a kid, I thought the word was *sluff*."

---

[111] *Baby on board. My Middle Schooler is on the HONOR ROLL.* Car seats in the back. That's how I knew.

[112] I'm so judgy. I know, I know.

Lorena and I exchanged a glance. Who invented that word, anyway? Why was English so weird? And how did I suddenly become friends with *Lorrrena*?

Brandon pointed out various directions and areas we might like to explore.

"We have about four hours here," Al announced. "So prioritize your time, but you should be able to see everything you want to."

Then Brandon sent us on our way. I was so glad that we were not going to shuffle around in a group tour and be talked at like as if we were children or newbies. We were all scholars of some sort, *aficionados* at the very least. If we had questions, we would ask. I was also glad there was a child among us: June, with her doll. I overheard June confess her longing to camp out, and I shared that same longing. What must it have been to camp here under the stars, until the claim was built? But Laura never did that—she was in town with Ma and the girls, running the boarding house while Pa got his claim shanty built, and then they rode out into the prairie when the surveyors wanted their house back.

June understood that it was too late in the year for the covered wagon campout, but she intended to make a corncob doll and twist some hay and grind some wheat in a coffee mill if it was the last thing she ever did. Off she went with Sandy and Marian, and Addie the doll, to try on a sunbonnet and apron and begin her *Little House* adventure.

The Japanese women headed straight for the memorial grove. They had brought along onion-skin paper to make rubbings of the marker. Roxie and Lorena made a beeline for Ma's little house and the wildflower patch, and the Jersey girls wanted to ride behind a horse on a wagon to the schoolhouse. I watched them disperse, including Al walking slowly toward the croplands laid out mid-property. The Homestead Association sows corn, wheat, and oats there every year, so visitors can see the rising green, the gold of wheat, the gray-green oats; hear the rustle of corn leaves and contemplate the struggle against crows and gophers. *Four don't go'fer.*

I wanted to see the Little House relics, touch them if I could (though they wouldn't let me), and breathe upon the glass. But the real Little House on this prairie is gone. The little house here is a reproduction of the right size, in the right place, and it would have to do. I imagined it like the *Balclutha*, a rigged sailing vessel in San Francisco I had visited as a fourth-grader, but no, that had been an actual cargo ship. I was so afraid that the homestead would feel like a Disneyland version, like Main Street USA plopped into the prairie. What if it failed to pass muster, in my own starry eyes? What if—.[113]

At least the cottonwood trees were truly Pa's. I strolled on the dirt road toward the distant schoolhouse—about a mile circle around the center of the property, perhaps where Laura took Mary walking 120 years ago[114]. I could see the wetlands to the northeast, then I looked northwest to try to see ominous gray clouds, if any. I saw the Slaw off to the east, but there was rough slough grass right here on Pa's place. I bent and picked a few blades of the coarse grass for a memory album, a tactile memento of this place, but after a few minutes, I dropped them. Slough grass, slaw grass—it's a weed at home. Acres of it would be strange to count as a bonus, and I wondered why Pa selected this bit of land after all. Maybe, if he was the last to file, it was the last place left. Maybe it wasn't his *first* pick, but his *only* choice, and Laura (and Rose) spun it to seem like he got just what he wanted.

---

[113] What indeed? Why am I so anxious to make these childhood dreams a reality?

[114] *Are there such things as fairies? Great hairy brutes*—it hurt me when Pa told Laura her fairies were buffalos, and the fairy ring a buffalo wallow. Couldn't they have let her dream?

I think I might have spotted a chink in Pa's shining armor[115].
I didn't like it.

There were more wetlands as I kept walking the dirt road. I
wondered how bad the mosquitoes were in the spring and summer, and what birdwatching was like in the warmer months.
There might be bats if there were mosquitoes. Did they ever get
malaria (what they called *fever and ague*) again[116] after their bout
in Kansas?

Before long, I heard horse hooves clopping and a rattling,
squeaking wagon, and happy voices coming behind me. I stepped
off the dirt and into the brown grass to let the wagon pass. June,
Sandy, and Marian waved at me. They were all wearing *JIN-jam*
sunbonnets now. Mary, Carrie, and Grace were also onboard,
grinning and giggling into their hands.

"Want a ride?" The woman docent, dressed in her own calico
get-up, on the front seat, asked, ready to whoa the horses. A child
sat on either side of her, one of whom was "driving" the horses.

"No, thank you. I'm walking." But I was suddenly Laura,
suddenly Nellie, offered a ride by a passing neighbor. I could take
it. Why not? I could be brave, friendly. A good sport.

But on they went, and I didn't stop them. I kept walking until
I saw the little shack out on the far side of the land, built as a rest
area. I didn't need to rest. I wanted to think.

Although the prairie looks flat, it's not, exactly. If you look out
in any direction, there are no hills. No mountains. It's all horizon.

---

[115] And oh, there are many chinks, when you start looking. Various websites describe him
as a wandering troubadour, a dreamer, an itinerant carpenter, a jack of all trades with a
fiddle on his chin. He must have had some magnetism for Caroline Quiner to have fallen
in love and let him drag her (pregnant!) into the wilderness, or into life as a landlady,
among other lapses.

[116] Malaria is known to make repeat relapses if not fully cured when it appears. It can
cause some spooky long-term consequences. One wonders if this is what happened
to Mary, with her early teens stroke and blindness a scant few years after their Kansas
sojourn.

Dizzying, in a way, like the sea. You always know which way is up, with the huge dome of sky, a cupped hand held over us. I felt small and insignificant. The wagon, and an airplane overhead, moved from my line of sight as I walked, curving away at the edge of my sightline as the earth spun. The other houses and buildings seemed small, too. And the wind.

Always the wind.

I was quite alone. I closed my eyes against the autumn sun that was not warm enough, not as warm as I'm used to back in the Golden State. I turned around once or twice, listening to distant voices, to the wind, the rustle of grasses, an occasional bird. They've all flown away, the geese and ducks, and the muskrats have built thick shelter. The harvest is in, and the hay is stacked. Plenty down cellar in a teacup. Plenty more in the stores, on the train, coming from afar, if we get hungry. I am there, almost—in *her* world, in *her* story. Almost.

I opened my eyes to the sun, the wind, and the awareness that someone was approaching. Al. Smiling a little. Not laughing at me. He approached, and seeing my face, my eyes open, he spoke.

"I don't want to disturb you."

"You're not."

"Are you communing?"

"I am, rather. Meditating, I guess. Trying to be one with the spirit of this place. With Laura. If that's even possible." I made a fruitless gesture. I couldn't explain it any better.

"I want to run into the wind, ride a horse, harvest the wheat." He shrugged a little. "I want to be Pa. Or work alongside him. Or Almanzo, maybe. Help him when he couldn't do the work anymore, after diphtheria."

I looked at him with a kind of awe. No one had ever spoken to me like that. My love language. The way I feel. About this kind of thing. Just a fluke, I'm sure.

"I get it."

He half-laughed. Said something in Spanish under his breath. "Do you?"

"I think so." A boldness seized me. "Try this," I said. "Close your eyes and turn around twice." He looked back for a second, and then he did it. "Now stand there and listen. Feel it."

I did the same. Stood in silence. Felt the earth spin. The wind blew. Sky-bowl over us. A cupped hand.

"Is it this place—here? Or is it us?" His voice was soft.

"Both."

"Explain that to me."

I blew out a breath. "I don't believe in ghosts or spooks or spirits."

"No?"

"No. Not at all. But the feeling of this place—."

"Yes."

"You could call it the spirit of the prairies if you want to. It's the openness, the way it makes you feel small, and, I don't know, *needful* of your family or your neighbor. It makes you feel both completely alone and yet one with the Earth. Awake and alive, and asleep."

He didn't answer right away, chewing that over. Nodding his head in slow agreement. "Okay. And what about us?"

"That's easier, I think. We're open to—this spirit. We've studied, prepared the ground, so to speak. We're ready to feel this. We've been taught. We know the feeling and can grasp it when it comes." That wasn't quite right, but it was a work in progress. It was all I could think of. "Maybe. I don't know. What do you think?"

"Something like that." Al smiled. "Mine is a little more mixed up in my Catholic and my Mexican heritage—a little of the conquistador coming to the Americas and claiming it. A little of the *grita* of the native being vanquished. A little of the blood of Christ. I'm here to fulfill something in myself, maybe something that my ancestors set out to do 400 years ago, I don't know. Or to appease it, atone for it. I know that I need the land—I need to get my hands dirty, and by doing that, I cleanse—I can try to cleanse—."

He stopped. Crouched down and dug a little at the soil with his fingers. "I don't know how they did it, without electricity or hospitals, or anything but guts and brawn, and faith, maybe. But I want that, too."

Al stood and squeezed the soil together in a fist, then opened it and looked at the doughy soil, crumbling like cake in his hand. He brought his hand to his nose and sniffed it lightly. He smiled at me. "Smell that?"

I leaned over and breathed in the scent—it smelled like clean dirt to me, with a whiff of hay or dry-smelling grass, and whatever aftershave Al had used. I smelled that, too. I made an "I don't know" face at him and he laughed at me, dropping the dirt on the ground.

"Do you have any brothers?" he asked.

"No. Just me."

"That explains it. You should never smell something when a guy asks you to 'smell this.'"

I cracked up and said, "No, I suppose not."

We walked again. I could see the schoolhouse ahead of us, and I didn't want to go there. I've seen one-room schoolhouses, and I knew this wasn't Laura's anyway. "I think I'm going to check out the hay-roof barn."

He turned and walked with me, and we fell into conversation about green-roof buildings and how the soddies, that is, the sodbusting pioneers who built and lived in homes of earth like the Ingallses, were the original sustainable-living hipsters. We saw the barn and the cows and horses inside, and the little sod dugout with its damp gloom and dirt floor that smelled like an open grave.

The shanty they had built for size comparison was a scant 140 square feet, and trying to squeeze a family of six into that space could not have been easy. Laura wrote of how they arranged the beds and the table and Mary's rocking chair, with essentially no room left to breathe. Life in a rough railroad camp kept the girls close to the house, and except for Laura getting water and running errands, the rest of the girls were virtual prisoners in that tiny space. I felt claustrophobic again when I was inside, and had to step out for air and light, even if it meant the wind cut through my coat and made my hands as cold as last week's leftovers in the fridge.

We had another hour before the van was scheduled to take us back to town. And all this time, I'd been walking and talking with Al.

"You want to go up in the lookout tower, or over to the memorial?" He gestured at each as he spoke. It seemed like a test, almost—look out and ahead, or look back and mourn. Which would it be?

"The lookout," I said, and finally took out my gloves and stopped trying to brave the wind. "If we have time, we can go look at the memorial."

We crossed the mown grasses again and joined others climbing the stairs up and around to the second story of the outdoor viewing platform. The wind was keener up here, and that same sense of dizzying flatness, the endless horizon around, the cup of the sky leaning over us. Higher up, I felt even smaller, and I unconsciously stepped back from the rail, bumping into whoever was behind me.

"Whoa," Al caught my shoulders. "Easy there." He rested his hands on my shoulders for an instant. My back against his chest. I felt his chest move with a breath and wanted to lean into him. I started to turn toward him, my shoulder again grazing him, and he smiled down at me.

"It's so big," he said. "So much land. Can you imagine?"

I could imagine something. I could. But I shook my head.

I had to walk away with these imaginings in my mind, so I started toward the stairs. He followed me down. We passed others on the stairs heading up, and I thought it would be good to see the memorial and the original cottonwoods before we had to leave. I felt a little embarrassed and awkward because I *wanted* him. I was physically drawn to him in a way I hadn't allowed myself to imagine before. I wanted to lean back into his chest again, to feel the warmth of his hands on my shoulders. I wanted to look at the vast sky above me with his warmth behind me.

"Nell," he said, quietly so no one else could hear. "Will you have dinner with me tonight?"

I looked back at him, thinking yes, but my mouth formed the word no because I am a fool, I am an awkward, lonely fool, and doesn't he have a thing with *Lorrrena*?

He said, "Yes. Say yes. We haven't finished talking. I want to talk some more with you. I want to hear your thoughts. I want to explore this idea. This thing. Say yes."

"The others?"

"Tonight is free. 'Dinner anywhere.' If anyone asks, you have plans."

"Yes, then," I made myself say. "Yes. Thank you," I remembered to add without Ma prompting me.

"Yes!" He made as if to wipe his brow. "That was tough. Got a yes out of you. That Wagon Wheel place we passed? We can walk, I think. I'll meet you at the front desk later, at six o'clock?"

I made a thumbs-up sign because I am an awkward idiot. "I'm going to the grove now. You can come if you want to." *If you want to.* Why would he want to?

"I will in a few minutes, but I need to check in with Brandon and make sure we are on schedule."

We parted, and I walked toward the memorial with a heart lighter and more awake than I'd felt in a long time. The chill wind buoyed me along.

June's grandmother, Marian, stood at the grove, and we walked about it slowly and touched the trees, taking a fallen leaf for a souvenir. I will press it later, keep it in one of my early-edition LIW books, maybe *Silver Lake*, which tells when Pa plants the young cottonwood trees for his five women.

The rock with the plaque on it held a place of honor. I read the text, although I'd seen it before on the website. I didn't feel anything emotional at all, just the facts, ma'am, but something caught my eye. The road. Why was the road here, in this exact place?

I walked out into the road and looked toward town. Charles Ingalls made this road. Pa used to drive this way and eventually wore down two wagon-wheel tracks, which became the road. That was something original that still existed here. I wanted to walk the road back to town, but it was so chilly, and the sun was already low in the sky. Could I get to town on time? I didn't think so. I wish I'd thought of this earlier. Maybe tomorrow. Maybe there will be time. Maybe later.

I picked up a pebble, just a plain gray-brown rock from the roadside. Tossed it in my hand. Looked at the gray stripe of it. No, never mind.

The land was here long before the road, and long before Laura[117]. It's just a rock. Let it stay here.

---

[117] And with this point, I must insist that readers of the *Little House* series take time to read the equally charming and historically accurate *Birchbark House* series by Native author Louise Erdrich, also renowned for her adult novels *Love Medicine* and *The Night Watchman*. The *Birchbark books* are about a 12-year-old Ojibwe girl named Omakayas (whose name means "little frog") and her Ojibwe family's experiences in the 1840s and 1850s near what is now Lake Superior. There are five novels in the series, and they adequately depict life in a Native family in a similar fashion to the *Little House* books. I think they are a suitable antidote to Ma's ethno-hatred and frank racism.

CHAPTER 11

We walked back to the vans, and I got in next to Marian. She had plucked up a few more cottonwood leaves, a twig that showed off the interesting bark, and a handful of fluffy seeds. She put the seeds into a folded sandwich bag pulled from her purse.

"I'm going to try and sprout these at home," she said. "Would you like one?"

Lordy, I'd love a cottonwood tree from one of Pa's. "Yes, please!"

"I'll get them started, and then overnight it to you." God love a grandma with a green thumb!

I had a window seat and turned my head to watch until the homestead was out of sight. And we were almost in De Smet already by that time; that mile and a half went fast. I wondered about wandering in the starlight gay and free, and how long it would take Barnum to round the corner of Pearson's Livery and arrive at Pa's homestead claim.

It was after five by then and the *LauraLanders* were starting to make dinner plans. Some were going to the diner, and others wanted to try the bar and grill on Calumet where the locals drink.

I tried to stay out of the conversation, feigning occupation with my phone, but Amanda asked me point-blank, "Are you coming or not?"

"Not."

A chorus of arguments arose, wheedling me to join either party. I felt *wanted.* I couldn't help blushing. I felt so nakedly visible when I was used to being a nonentity.

"I can't. I made other plans."

"What other plans? Staying in your room?" Lorena turned around in her seat to look at me. Was that scorn on her face?

June looked aghast that I would miss dinner.

"I—have a date." My face glowed fiercely. The ladies in the van whooped and giggled. Mary, Carrie, and Grace could not hide their delight and Kellie said, "You go, girl!"

"Who's taking you on a date?" June wanted to know.

"Now, never mind," Sandy shushed her, but the Jersey girls were ahead of her and provoked me, "Al. It's *Al.* Is it Al? *Almanzoor!*"

I looked at my hands and my face glowed red as a fire truck and they laughed and high fived each other, teasing me. It was totally all right. I was one of this gang if no other, and I rather liked it. I had a stupid grin on my face and couldn't stop smiling.

Lorena, my nemesis, said, "Whoa, Nelly, I had no idea. Have a good time tonight."

Did she mean it? Did that mean we were friends? I had never had a real friend nor enemy like Lorena, and I simply did not know how to read her. Humans are complex. I don't trust myself. I took her at her word, having no other direction to go.

"And don't fall in the *Slaw*," someone added, and the laughter started anew.

"Better wear your *JIN-jam* dress."

"Yeah, these folks are *wilder* than you know!"

"If this Little House is rockin', then don't bother knockin'," Amanda said, forgetting about June. Kellie shushed her immediately, but they kept laughing. The other van arrived just behind us and disgorged its riders. Al seemed unaware of the joshing that had taken place in my van, but he had a self-conscious grin on his own face.

"Have fun tonight, Nelly," I heard sing-songing through the crowd.

Liz at the desk wondered if anyone wanted a cup of tea before the evening began. A few of the party agreed and joined her in the parlor. I climbed to my room and threw myself on the bed, face down, and pulled a pillow over my head.

A date. Good Lord.

I hid under there for a few minutes, then started the shower and picked out some clothes. My wardrobe choices were limited to what I brought, obviously, so it looked like jeans and boots and a sweater. I had brought a nice necklace—a floral enamel locket on a chain that was my maternal grandmother's, old-fashioned and quaint, valueless in my mother's eyes. I laid it out to wear.

My hands were plain. I don't wear rings and I don't polish my nails. I don't bite them, either. It's surprising how many people do. But at least my staple wound was healed. *No more bloody finger.*

I showered and brushed out my hair, leaving it long and loose, and I applied a little bit of makeup. I needed a little something on my eyelashes and lips if I wasn't to fade into the wallpaper. I resisted the urge to ask for help from the other women; they would surely offer me clothes, scarves, perfume, a hairdo, a make-over. *This is me.* I'm a homespun girl—*woman.* I like books. I wear glasses. I am afraid of things. But I'm smart. And I have a lot to offer. Right?

One last look in the mirror while I convinced myself, or tried to, that I was a catch. "You're a catch." I couldn't fake myself out, though. "You're insane." I polished my glasses.

I'm something, anyway.

We met at the front desk. Liz looked at both of us and then raised her eyebrows and smirked a little. I turned away as my cheeks flared pink again. If there was a cure for the common blush, I'd use it. Out the door, and I was on foot, on a date with *Almanzoor*.

Like Laura on her first excursion with Almanzo, I had nothing to say at first. Al smelled not of cigars nor pipes nor cigarettes, but still faintly of his shaving soap or aftershave. Not overpowering. Just a presence next to me. We didn't touch.

The lights were on in the streets, and they were modern fixtures, but somewhere there was an old antique gas lamp. It said so on the hotel's brochure. I mentioned this.

"Yeah, we passed it this morning walking from the first place down Calumet. It's by the old depot."

With that, my stock of conversational gambits was exhausted. We kept walking. The wind was still blowing, no surprise there. What was a little shocking was how much colder it was than it had been earlier. The sunset brought a drop in temperature of twenty to thirty degrees. My hair crackled with electricity when I shook it out of my collar.

We walked along, two Californians in the Midwest, in air so cold it felt breakable.

I don't do dates. I didn't date in high school. I stayed in the library and read, and did extra homework. I became a teacher's aide because I didn't want to go out, where there was competition for friends, the cutest outfit, or who had a boyfriend, or whatever. I stayed in, helped keep track of funds for the French Club's trip to Disneyland, sorted books for the librarian, and made sure the encyclopedias were in alphabetical order. Order, because out of order made chaos. How could you learn if you couldn't find the right book? How could you know what was right or wrong, good or bad?

What's good and right is that you should be safe in your own neighborhood. From your neighbors. What's wrong is not being able to trust because the world was broken when you were too young to know. And now you just don't know who to trust. What had he wanted with a 5-year-old? What the hell is wrong with people? He never knew or cared what he had stolen from me. But I knew it. I was cheated and robbed.

And now I'm handicapped. I have a broken lever or switch that goes off at the wrong time, makes me want to run away screaming when there is no danger, and one that doesn't go off at all when I'm standing next to a psychopath. Or so it feels. Little things—the sickening smell of Vicks VapoRub, for example, or the sound of a sliding door—can set me off. Big things go over my head because I stay low. I don't want to be hurt.

I had said yes to a date like a fool, and it was freezing outside, colder than I thought it would be—but I started sweating. I was starting to panic. It would be better if I just said it out loud, just broke the tension. Then I could go back to my room, pack up, and drive away.

"Look—what do you want?"[118]

"What?" Al looked at me, startled. "What do you mean, what do I want?"

I kept walking. "Just—what do you want with me? I don't have the energy—the bandwidth—to get screwed over. I just don't."

"Whoa," he said. "Stop—will you?" He took my arm, turned me gently.

I could have jerked away but I was tired. So tired of not knowing. Maybe I'd get an answer if I listened to him. All my broken sensors on, blaring, *danger!*

"What do I *want*?" He tilted his head like a quizzical cocker spaniel, the cutest puppy meme ever. "That's easy. I

---

[118] <record scratch again> Like Laura telling Almanzo she was only using him for the ride home, not because she wanted him to be her beau, what came out of my mouth was shockingly rude. Sometimes, Nelly—just don't talk!

want to have a good time. I want to have fun with you. Just fun, that's all. Nothing heavy. No drama, no big scene, no broken windows or screaming. Just a little fun. Is that too much to want?"

Fun for you. What about for *me?*

"I'm not sure what that really means," I said, choosing words carefully. "I don't really—look, I'm being honest. I just don't know how to have fun[119]. Whatever that means. Everything is always serious with me. No joking around. So when you say *fun*, what does that mean? You have fun and I end up obliterated?"

He blew on his hands. "Hey, let's keep walking, okay? Too cold just standing here. At least we can get there and have a glass of wine or something, warm up?"

We walked. He coughed and spoke again. "I'm not asking you to marry me, Nell. I only asked you to dinner. Let's talk some more about Laura and farms and what it means to be a pioneer, and wow, isn't the prairie amazing? Can we do that first? And if I'm laughing and having a good time, and you are at least not crying or running away, we can call that a success?"

While that made me sound like a total freak, which I am, it was strangely just what I needed to hear.

"Go on," I said, in a lighter tone.

"We'll have a glass of wine, or beer, if you like—I doubt they have hard liquor at this place. This ain't *México, chica,*" he said in his thickest accent. "You order dinner, I order dinner. We might even order the same thing!" He gasped dramatically. "We might enjoy our food."

"Oh, my god," I said, in mock horror.

"Then we will—*order dessert!*"

I gasped loudly and covered my mouth. "No!"

---

[119] The original F word, to me. *Danger, Will Robinson!*

"And after that—I will pay the bill!" He threw his arm up across his face in imitation of Dracula's cape. "And then I suck your blood and turn into a bat."

"Perfect." Laughing at my own stupidity. So fraught, everything I do and say.

"Well, maybe not the blood-sucking. But everything else. Would that be fun?"

"Gah, there's that word again."

"Okay, okay, we can't say *fun*. That freaks you out, obviously. How about *pleasant*? Would that be pleasant?"

"Yes, that would be pleasant." My level of trust was elevating. It was such a relief to poke fun at my deepest concerns and show them as just empty balloons. Fear is *false evidence appearing real*, as my therapist used to say.

"Well, let's go for *pleasant* tonight, then, and not worry about fun." Al winked at me with a big grin, and I felt, I swear, safe and secure. I would probably have a pleasant time. I would be okay. I might even have fun.

By this time, we had walked the four long country blocks and gone up the walkway into the Wagon Wheel. Al held up his hand to stop me.

"Allow me," he said. "This will make it more *pleasant*." He opened the door and said, "After you."

A youngish white girl with braces on her teeth and still learning to walk in heels showed us to our table. The waitstaff dressed in black slacks and white shirts in the evening. It felt fancier than it was in comparison to a San Francisco restaurant, but it was just right. Special, but homey, too.

Al ordered a draft beer, and I had a ginger ale. Dinner was steaks of local beef, grass-fed and well cooked. Baked potatoes, the biggest I'd ever seen, from Iowa, and loaded with sour cream and bacon. Cornbread squares, sweet with honey and thick with butter. A lackluster salad, but that's what you get in the Midwest, it seems. Too far to ship anything but iceberg lettuce, so it's shred-ded, with a slice of carrot and a rippled beet slice on top, and some thick pink dressing. Not California cuisine, but it was *pleasant*, and I was hungry after all the walking we'd done.

Al made me laugh. Over and over. He was my kind of prince, and he was charming.

I think I had something like fun.[120]

I could have paid for my own dinner, but Al insisted on taking the check. But suddenly, looking toward the outside windows, we saw snowflakes falling outside, flurries, even.

"It's beautiful!" I had never seen snow actually falling. California gets snow, up in the mountains, but I didn't live near there, and my days and nights were a coastal temperate 68-74 degrees, year-round.

"It is, but this early in the season?" Our server, a thirty-some-thing woman with no wedding rings on her fingers, made a wry face. It was just October, after all. "My uncles are probably rounding up the cattle as we speak," she said. Just last year the local beef ranchers had lost a hundred head of cattle in a two-day blizzard after just such a cold spell, she elaborated.

A blizzard was heading our way, a storm warning had turned to a storm watch, and we had not been following the news, or we would have been told. It was early in the year for such a thing, but not unheard of[121], she told us.

"Get right home, it's getting bad out there."

Al paid the bill. We bundled up in our California "winter" coats and headed back to the inn up the road.

---

[120] But let us not say the *F word* just yet. More adventure remains ahead of us.

[121] Remember the cattle with their faces frozen to the ground by their own breath? Remember the jackrabbits hiding in the hay? Remember how the sun shone after that and they got the harvest in? An October blizzard was uncommon but not impossible. Laura knew. But those innocent Eastern visitors who didn't understand the prairies could get caught in their shirt sleeves, if they weren't careful.

CHAPTER 12

I'd called it windy before, but this was more than wind. It whistled and cut, blowing snowflakes around. I'm a California girl, and we don't get snow where I live, ever. You have to drive four hours before you hit a mountain where snow falls, and the coldest it gets at my little house is down to 35 in a very cold year. It's usually in the 50s all winter long. I felt this cold like a slap in the face—sharp, chapping, stinging blows. The wind howled[122].

In no time at all, my hands were cold, my feet were cold, my nose was cold and running, then icy. I wore my winter coat, but a winter coat for California is not the same as a winter coat for the Midwest. I wore my leather boots and a pair of socks, with a pair of tights under my jeans. My pashmina scarf was more decorative than a useful muffler, and I had brought a knitted cap but had left it at the inn, along with my black gloves.

I thought the falling snow was beautiful, but I didn't have time to admire it. We stood under the eaves of the Wagon Wheel and rethought our plan.

"Better zip up your coat and turn up the collar. We should hurry. It's too cold to be walking around." Al flipped up his nylon

---

[122] Laura could hear voices in the blizzard—panthers roaring in the trees, Native war songs from the Kansas creek bottoms, the sounds of a woman screaming. So much screaming.

hood. "Put your scarf over your head," he said to me over the wind. "You'll stay warmer."

We started off in the dark down the sidewalk, just four blocks from our hotel. My legs were cold under my jeans and tights. Al walked faster than I could, with longer legs than mine. He got a few feet ahead of me, then stopped and took my hand.

"We have to hurry."

It seemed a little overblown to panic in a bit of wind, but perhaps I was underreacting? I overreacted in panic to everything else, but maybe we were in real trouble here. What did I know? I couldn't seem to tell the difference between what was good and what was bad, no matter the circumstances.

In the space of just this time between leaving the warm, bright restaurant, the wind kicked up, and suddenly the blowing snow was everywhere. Streetlights glowed like orange lollipops, with a halo of white fuzz around them. A couple of cars rolled past us and disappeared from view faster than I expected. And they were going slowly, too. All I could see was a line of streetlights away in the dark, and that line was getting shorter. Visibility dropped in just minutes.

The snow wasn't beautiful anymore. It was a thick fog clinging like mud to everything around us. It blew across our legs, smacking in our faces, and my untethered hair snapped in my eyes, stinging. The gutter was clogged already, and snow was drifting. It was happening so fast, or it was happening in slow motion. It was hard to tell anymore; it was so surreal.

Al pulled me along, trotting, half jogging. The wind kept rising, seeming louder, and it was hard to tell if Al was speaking to me or if it was the wind. We made it to the end of the street, halfway to the inn, when all the lights went out, everywhere. Our streetlights were gone. It was dark, with the swirling snow no longer reflecting light. Flakes blew all around us, and I wasn't sure which way to go to get back to the restaurant or to the hotel. We were supposed to turn at this corner, but now I couldn't remember. Turn left? We needed to turn left, but we also had to cross the street, and that made me nervous.[123] I really couldn't see anything, just this swirling, and the darker shadow that was Al next to me.

He turned and yelled something at me but I couldn't understand him. He bent over and cupped his hand, said right next to my ear, "We have to cross the street. Hang on to me."

"Which way? I can't see a thing," I shouted back.

"Just hang onto me. Don't let go," he said. He fumbled with something in his pocket and took his glove off with his teeth. He fumbled some more, and his cell phone turned on a flashlight. He shined it up at the street sign next to us and said, "We have to cross here, both ways. You ready?"

"Yeah!"

He put his glove back on, dropping the cell phone. He grabbed it back out of the snow and brushed it off. Held it so it shone a few feet ahead. I was still clinging to his coat, my whole body shaking with fear and cold.

He tucked my hand into his and said, "Hang on."

Snow eddied around us. As we stepped out of the lee of the building the wind hit us full on.

This was the prairie. We may have been in a town, but there was no tree line, no tall buildings, no mountains. This wind came from Canada, Saskatchewan, maybe, born even farther north than that, from miles away, and gathered power as it came. It screamed down the center of the land mass and hammered the prairie, flattening trees and grasses, and sometimes the people

---

[123] As a child, I practiced for avoiding hot lava, I could beware the Bermuda Triangle, I was prepared for the monster under the bed, but I hadn't thought about getting lost in a blizzard, the way Laura had. We didn't have snow when I was a child. California tract homes hadn't prepared me for De Smet, South Dakota, in a blizzard.

who tried to live here. It was cold and unforgiving. It didn't care if I was dressed for the occasion. If I didn't make it, I wasn't the first nor the last one it had felled.

But Al kept moving and hung onto my hand.

We didn't reach the corner of that extremely wide country street. We missed it. There should have been a curb or a building ahead of us, but we must have veered into the crossroads. Al shined the flash of his cellphone around and pulled me to the left a little. It was so blasted dark out there, and nothing to guide us. Then I tripped on something and fell sprawling on my knees, all fours, but he hung on and I didn't, thank goodness, land on my face. My arm got an awful wrench, though. I struggled up from my scraped knees onto my numb feet.

"The curb," I shouted.

He kicked it and stepped up and pulled me into the lee of the brick wall, of whatever building it was. "See if someone's here," he shouted at me. I hung on to his coat, and we followed the wall around to the windy side again. There was a set of steps and a door at the top. He knocked heavily at the door.

I was glad to be out of the worst of the wind in the entryway of this building, and please let there be someone home. Al swore in Spanish and pounded harder this time, but there was no answer. It was a Friday night, and the building must have been a business. Everyone had gone home, beaten the storm. No one was left at work to let us in. Just us tourists.

We were a scant two blocks from the inn, no further. I was shivering so hard. I stuck my hands under my armpits and crouched down in the corner of the stoop by the door. Ridiculous to be in this position, this place. Lost in a snowstorm like Laura. Could we dig into a snowbank and survive four days on Christmas candy and oyster crackers? I remembered the squares of cornbread we had left in the basket at the restaurant. That might have been the difference between survival and being frozen to death—but we weren't lost in the snow. We were just walking home. Where was my brain, anyway?

Al crouched in front of me to block the wind even more and took off his gloves. "Put these on," he said. "I didn't know it would get so bad." I was too cold to argue, so I put them on, felt the stiffness of the man-gloves and knew they were warm from his hands, but my hands were so cold, I couldn't really feel it.

"Listen, we have two blocks to go. We can't sit out here—we'll literally freeze. My phone is about to die—it's too cold and I was almost out of battery. We can try to go back or go on. What do you want to do?"

"Go on. I want to go home."

"Here," he said. "Fix your scarf." He unwound it from my neck and shook it, the cold shockingly so, snow sifting down my neck, my back; then he wound it back again, over my head and around in front of my face so that my eyes showed as from a burqa, then tucked in the end so it wouldn't flap. He pulled up my collar and tried to zip my coat a little more. I felt like a child, this time safe and cared for.

Al pulled my sleeves over the gloves on my small hands and said, "Try to keep those gloves on. Do you have your phone?"

"In my pocket," I said through the muffling of scarf and collar. I gestured to my right coat pocket and he got out my phone. It turned on and had plenty of battery, but I wondered if it was too cold to function.

"What's your passcode?"

"N-E-L-L."

He shot a glance at me and said, "That's not a very good passcode. Too easy." He punched in the code and then found the GPS function and touched a few more keys. In a minute, he said,

"Okay, I know where we are now. Just hang onto me. It's so dark, I might not be able to find you if you let go. You okay?"

I was far from okay, so cold, so numb, and everything hurt. But I said, "Yeah!" It wasn't fun anymore, but it was interesting.

"All right, *vámonos!* As fast as we can get there, okay?"

"Okay."

Al blew out a puff of frosty breath and took my gloved hand. He stood up and we made our way down the stairs, into the brunt of the wind again, into the blurry, howling whiteness. He held my hand and the phone, and walked confidently across the street, and in a minute, we were on the other side.

I held on as he led me along the side of a building or a fence, something solid on our left side. It disappeared, but he kept walking confidently forward; soon another building was at hand, and we kept going. Then that building was gone, and we crossed another street. Al walked, just kept trudging onward, and I took one more step, one more step, in boots that were damp and heavy and had snow jammed into the tops, and I'm sure they were ruined but I didn't care because good boots on a dead body were less use than wrecked boots on a live one.

At this block, there was no building, but there was a picket fence that I vaguely remembered. I kept one hand dragging along it like a child at play. When it stopped, Al just kept going, and then another fence, wire or chain link, maybe, still waist-high, and I remembered the wall next to the inn was like that, and I knew we were close. I squeezed his hand and we trudged on steadily. That fence ended, and we took about ten steps across a wide, dark space, and then both of us ran clumsily into the snowy boxwood hedge around the inn.

Al dropped my phone, and it fell into the hedge and disappeared. The light went off. But this was the inn's hedge, and we were able to use it to get to the front yard, and once we were inside the yard, it was only a minute until we reached the steps and the porch.

Al pounded on the door. Liz opened it with a flashlight in her hand and said, "Oh, thank god you're here."

Inside lanterns and some candles lent a cozy glow to the room, and the wood stove was blazing.

"She's very cold," Al said, but Liz was already unwrapping my scarf and Marian came over to help. They got my outer clothes off and decided to get me upstairs and into some warm, dry clothes. The women clucked around me with borrowed socks and thermals and down-filled slippers, and Liz brought up a cup of her cinnamon-ginger tea.

I was still shaking, deeply cold, but my fingers and toes stung and tingled. Liz assured me I wasn't frozen; it was too quick for frostbite.

"I lost my phone out there."

Liz said, "Ha! We'll find it in spring, lady. It'll be wet and useless by the time this storm stops."

There was a flashlight on the bedside table and a candle, too. I felt as if I had been blasted with sand; my skin felt so raw. Even my eyes felt as if I had cried a thousand tears. But slowly, under my blankets, I warmed up again and drank my tea.

"Your boyfriend is all tucked into bed, too," Liz said, as she came in again with more tea. "I can't believe you two walked out into a blizzard."

"Lovestruck, that's what it is," said Kellie.

"Sun-struck, maybe. She's a Californian, *fer sure*," Amanda said, trying to sound like a Valley Girl and failing.

"I'm not from here," I said, which I meant sincerely, but everyone treated it like a joke and laughed.

"Get warm and go to sleep," Liz said. "I'll get the generator going so we can have some hot coffee and I'll feed you here tomorrow. We can't have any of you fools walking outside till this dies down."

My phone was lost, or out of my hands, and that meant no weather report, no email, no scrolling social media. It meant no Mom texts, either, which was both a huge relief and a source of angst. If I couldn't see her texts, I couldn't answer, but I was so used to being her pet on a chain that I felt riddled with anxiety about not answering. *She's going to be so mad at me.*

I lay in bed and listened to the wind. I blew out the candle and snuggled way down under the comforter, warmed all through with hot tea inside and dry, warm feet, with a sore shoulder, barked shins, scrapes on my knees and hands, and a cut under my eye, I think from that last run-in with the hedge. Nothing bled; I think it had been too cold to bleed. I would maybe take a bath tomorrow, if they had a gas heater or some way to make hot water in this frigid country. Maybe just a sponge bath.

With the lights out and the sounds of the blizzard on the other side of the windows and the wall, I understood at last what Laura had been through in December 1880 when they tried to get home from school in a blizzard, what Pa had survived on the bank of Plum Creek that Christmas. Something of what the family endured all winter, with no electric lights, no railroads. What a difference a hand in the blizzard could make. How Laura held onto Carrie and was afraid to lose her hand in the melee.

Into sleep. A lost child in the dark. A hand to hold. *Hang on to me. Don't let go.*

CHAPTER 13

Overnight, the storm dropped a couple of inches of snow per hour, and the wind drifted the snow against the inn on one side, while the other side was left with a smear that built up as you walked from the house. The power was back on by 7 a.m. Liz had her gardener clear the front path, and by the time we were eating oatmeal and drinking coffee, the first snowplow had gone by. The winds dropped, and by noon they were no longer stormy, but simply scudding along as usual, pushing snow instead of grass. I couldn't believe that 24 hours ago we had been walking under sunshine in dry prairie grass, but that's how the weather turns here.

We had been scheduled to go out to Almanzo's tree claim on Highway 25 this morning and hear a natural history lecture at Lakes Henry and Thompson afterward. Al had called the naturalist who was supposed to speak to us, but she cried off due to the storm, and so we were left without an agenda. Tonight was the farewell dinner, and then home the next day, provided the airports and roads were open—Liz had said they would be. South Dakotans don't get fussed over a one-night snow shower.

I anticipated a four-hour drive back to Omaha, and a train that left at 11 p.m., so as long as I was in Omaha by dinnertime or thereafter, I'd be fine. But I still felt shaken by last night—not sure I could face that drive by myself if it started to snow. Driving in the rain is bad enough. Snow-driving is just not on my radar. I also needed to find a place to buy a new phone. I doubted Loftus carried burner phones in the general store, but I could be wrong. I wasn't looking for phones when I first wandered through.

Marian and Sandy got out their knitting projects to make use of our unexpected free time. June had a child's knitting spool and was working quickly with a crochet hook to produce a coil of multicolored yarn rope that she said would be easy to sew into a blanket for her doll. June showed me the snow hat she had made for her doll previously, and added, "I'm *glad* it's snowing so I can put this on Addy *for real*."

Carrie was playing with June's doll and asked if she could try the knitting spool. Soon Sandy pulled out a second spool of a slightly different size and another skein of bright ombre yarn, and Carrie and June were set for the hour, if not the day.

The parlor had a television, usually kept behind the doors of an armoire, but today Liz opened the cabinet and turned on the Weather Channel so guests could see what was coming. The anchors kept talking about the unexpected storm and the slight damage wrought. No deaths, although several cattle were caught out in it, and ranchers were rounding up as best they could despite the wind and the drifts.

The next day's weather was forecast to be clear with no storms coming, but travelers were still urged caution and to travel with emergency supplies, etc.

I borrowed some snow boots and a shovel from Liz and put on my coat and woolly hat. I went out to the front yard, trying to find the hedge where my phone was lost. After a while, Al came out and worked on the inside of the yard, digging into the hedge.

It was wet, cold work, but after about twenty minutes he said, "Wait a minute—I think—yes! Got it!"

I stuck it in my pocket and hoped it wasn't destroyed. I'd take it in and dry it, see if it still worked. "Thanks. You saved me again," I smiled up at him.

"It's the least I could do, after dragging you out into a winter storm. I should have checked the weather," he said. His brow was furrowed and the smile didn't reach his eyes.

"It's fine. We got here. It's all good,." I was trying to comfort him; he seemed angry with himself.

"I should have known, that's all."

I take refuge in a Ma saying. "Well, least said, soonest mended."

He stared at me, then cracked a smile. "That doesn't even make sense. Why not 'Hunger is the best sauce' or something like that?"

"I don't know. Maybe I'll save that for later. Anyway, all's well that ends well[124]," I said.

"There's only one problem with that saying." "What's that?"

"It hasn't ended yet."

"True."

"What time are you leaving tomorrow?"

"I don't know yet. If the weather is okay, I might still like to drive past the tree claim first, and we never did go to the cemetery. But I need plenty of time to get to Omaha. I don't know how to drive in snow."

"Come with me, then. I'm going back to Des Moines. It's just a four-hour drive."

I wanted to. And I was scared of that wanting. I had my car, anyway. So I couldn't say yes to his offer. But if I said no, he'd vanish like a good dream, instead of sticking around haunting me like a nightmare. "I don't know."

"What don't you know?"

I glanced at him, then away. I'm pathetic. I can't help it. Driving off alone into the prairie with a guy I didn't even know,

---

[124] A Pa saying.

just met two days ago? I couldn't do it. "I'm sorry—I'm just not ready."

"To drive with me to the train station. Okay." He shrugged. Smiled. It was a *whatever*, a *seriously?* shrug, larded with emotion and bravado, and I knew I was a fool, but I was scared. And I couldn't express it to him. My walls were too thick. I didn't know him well enough to share this secret. And who knew what he might be thinking about me?

"Okay," he said again. "Would you at least like to take a walk with me, Nelly? Take a walk with me around De Smet? Let me buy you some flowers at the De Smet Florist for almost getting you killed?"

"Yes," I said. "I would like that." I said, "I like small steps. I'm just a Cowardly Lion when it comes to big steps."

"*I'd tuhn back if I wuh you,*" he said, Cowardly Lion accent pitch perfect.

So it was all right. He was funny, and he knew the funny things that I knew, and he wasn't mad, *at me* anyway, and he wanted to buy me flowers.

No one buys me flowers.

Al went off to help the gardener blow the snow off the cars in the inn's parking lot, which was nice since I wouldn't even have thought of it. I traipsed back through the side door of the inn, kicked off the borrowed boots, and wiped them off with the old towel lying there.

I was headed upstairs when Marian waylaid me.

"We were thinking about changing our plans a bit—we got off in Des Moines on the way here," she said. "We visited a cousin who drove us up here. But you got off at Omaha. We want to go back sooner, not get stuck in any more snow. Do you think we could ride with you? If you can take all three of us in your car, I mean? Sandy, Junie, and me?"

Three companions for the road, all female—I liked that a lot. And in fact, a huge weight came off my shoulders, because I would be helping someone, and helping myself. I wouldn't have to make up an excuse, and I would be safe. Safer. Not alone. Dare I say, with friends?

We planned to depart the next day at a time that gave us plenty of cushion for rest stops or contingencies, and to have dinner in Omaha before the 11 p.m. train departure. Marian went off to tell her family and change her train reservation, and I went back to my room with a feeling of relief.

My phone had been cold but not wet, and when I plugged it in, not only did it come back to life, but there were a dozen messages from my mother, voicemail as well as texts. I suppose she had also sent me email but I chose not to look. Later. I could deal with my mom later. I was ill-equipped to hang up on her or confront her, but I sure as hell could avoid her[125]. I kept the phone on silent, no vibrations, while I cleaned up for some food and my afternoon walk-date.

I crossed to the diner with Kellie and Amanda for some lunch, trudging through last night's snow like I was born to it. But I couldn't imagine doing it in high-button shoes, wearing flannel underdrawers, and without Gore-Tex. Maybe Ma was right about being prepared, regardless of the weather, if the *season* was right for wearing long drawers or a sunbonnet[126].

---

[125] "Least said, soonest mended." No, wait. How about this one? "If Wisdom's ways you wisely seek, five things observe with care. To whom you speak, of whom you speak, and how and when and where."

[126] Ma (and Nellie Oleson) were right about the sun's damaging UV rays, but their racist preference for whighter skin over brown is reprehensible. And although it was acceptable in the timeframe when Laura/Rose were writing about life on the prairie to use such condescending colorism, the phrase "as brown as..." should be stricken from the English language.

I managed to steer the Jersey girls away from the topic of my date and blizzard adventures as much as I could, asking them endless queries about teaching high school and their plans for the winter holidays. But I checked my phone once too many times and they both pounced.

"What's your hurry, Half Pint? Is Almanzo waiting at the singing school?" Kellie teased.

"They're going driving with Barnum," Amanda suggested. "Maybe out to Lakes Henry and Thompson to pick wild grapes."

I wasn't used to such attention, such friendly banter, and it made me feel warm inside, like I was part of the girl gang. I loosened my armor enough to reveal the truth: "We're going walking this afternoon."

"With Elmer[127]?" Kellie feigned shock.

"No, with Manly. She's going on a prairie walk with Manzo."

"A stroll through town is all," I clarified, laughing along and trying to enjoy the flavor of fun—*fun!*—that is a part of *girlfriends* and *sisterhood*. I may have—possibly—succeeded. It was a lunch to remember.

I met Al afterward for our promised walk to the florist. This took us across drifts that had been hand-shoveled left and right, and a damp street that was already getting mushy with mud in the sunlight breaking through. The wind still blew, but I wore my gloves, hat, scarf, a sweater, extra socks, my high boots that had not been ruined by the damp, and my freshly dried coat. I had my recharged phone with me. I was surely equipped for a three-block walk. If a blizzard were to start, I'd duck into the nearest building.

"Well, here we are again," I said as we walked down Third, in the center of the street since the sidewalks were still blocked.

---

[127] Ida Wright Brown's Sunday stroll with Elmer made me laugh as a child. Elmer like the glue!

We crossed Joliet. Al took my hand and tucked it in his arm as we crossed. I didn't protest. I didn't say anything but I liked feeling his arm, knowing it was there if I slipped, if I struggled.

Al was quiet for most of the walk, companiable but not talkative, then finally said to me, "I have to ask—was last night *pleasant?*" Sheepishly.

I was charmed by his sweetness.

"Ha!" I said aloud. "Well, yes. Dinner was pleasant, and then—well, it was an adventure. And we made it. So, sure. No one died. That makes it fun in my book."

"Whoa," Al laughed. "You have a pretty low bar for fun. 'No one died.'"

"True. The bar is very low."

We reached the florist then and he opened the door for me. "Choose what you'd like. What you would have liked if I had brought you flowers."

Again, the warming feeling rushed through me. If I wasn't careful, I would be in great danger of having real feelings. I might get hurt. Badly[128].

Now, in general, I love spring bulbs—the iris, tulips, daffodils, a straight stalk, no-nonsense leaves, one blaze of bright color, and the gentle opening in a vase. But it isn't spring.

"I tell you what I'd like. I want to choose something to put on their graves. Kind of a thank-you for helping to shape Laura. Thank Ma and Pa for making her who she was."

"We can do that," Al says. "But choose something for you, too."

So I chose single-stemmed roses for Laura's sisters: pink, yellow, lavender, and I chose a red rose for Pa and a white rose for Ma. Then I chose a bunch of mixed freesias, probably the last of the fall bulbs, for myself. They were fragile and

---

[128] But what if it was real? What if I wasn't hurt at all? How pleasant would that be?

sweet-smelling, and so rich in color. Waxy, cheerful, uncrushed. Sweetness and light. The owner, whose name badge read *Stella*, wrapped the freesias in plastic and tissue, but she left the roses in damp paper and then newspaper, knowing they'd end up at the cemetery.

"At least roses dry beautifully," she said. "Some of the flowers people leave just wilt and rot and look terrible."

"That's something I never thought of," I said.

"I volunteer at the cemetery doing clean up during the summer months, when there are lots of tourists. You wouldn't believe what some people will leave. Somebody left a pair of ladies' underwear on Charles Ingalls' grave. I was offended by that. He was a married man!"

"I hope you wore gloves," I said. I could believe it. The slash-fiction and other nonsense going on the *LauraLand* website had inured me to excessive fandom as far as the Little House folks went.

Al told me more behind-the-scenes drama on *LauraLand* and how he ended up moderating the bulletin board and the mailing list; he had helped to upgrade the site and institute the agreement for first-time users that warned them to expect the unexpected.

"Any resemblance to the real historical Laura Ingalls Wilder is coincidental and users shall be held harmless," he said. "It's fiction. *It's all fiction.* Which helps keep us safe from lawsuits or copyright infringement. More or less."

When we got back to the inn, it was getting dark and the wind was getting colder, so we went inside to warm up. I put the flowers in water, all of them, to keep until tomorrow's cemetery visit. We Laura fans had one more evening together before the confab broke up.

The Grange Hall was the site of our farewell dinner; Al had booked a private room there and had it catered with a

New England-style supper like the Ingallses had enjoyed in the 1880s.

Lorrrena[129] decked herself out in full *Godey's Lady Book* style and so had the three Japanese exchange girls. Sandy and Marian did their best with contemporary long skirts and aprons and their sunbonnets, favoring a Halloween look over historical accuracy. June might have walked off the pages of the *American Girls* catalog[130] in her perfect, pretty dress and her hair braided into loops. Al had put on a string tie. I wore a ruffled, tiered skirt and a button-up ruffled blouse with a simple gold brooch at the throat, all gathered from thrift stores. I wore my hair up in braids across my head, not so different from Junie's, which was as close as I could muster to dressing in costume.

Liz laughed and laughed when we came trooping down. She offered some extra aprons to cover our dresses, and actually threw a few at us. "It's always a treat to see modern Americans try to wish themselves back in time," she said. "Sometimes the illusion almost works," Liz added, pointing at Lorena and June. And sometimes not so much. She didn't point, but we knew who was perfectly attired and who was not. And for once, I didn't mind being imperfect. I knew it, and I was okay with it.[131]

We squeezed into shared cars and drove slowly across town to the park with the Grange Hall. I deliberately drove my own rental car on the freshly plowed and cleared roads because I felt too shy to try to sidle up to Al; I endured a great deal of ribbing anyway. Lorena wasted no time in sitting in his car, though. It was worth it, sort of, to be teased by the women in my car. It felt like friendship and acceptance, a tall mug of frosty beer to a

---

[129] Hiss. I reflexively hiss when I say her name. Because I am a shallow, small person.

[130] Kristin, of course.

[131] I didn't mind the teasing. I'm still a petty green-eyed monster, though.

thirsty traveler. And I had a moment of Zen in the car, because it was I who had received flowers from Al, not *Lorrrena*. He had chosen. Perhaps it was not something I could affect with sulks and jealousy and vicious thoughts.[132]

Al had ordered the works for this supper. We arrived to find a massive pork roast with whole baked apples, mashed potatoes and gravy, baked beans, and chicken pot pie, with several fruit pies and frosted cakes for dessert. While none of us stood stock-still, we showed our delight, unlike Pa and Ma, and clapped our hands in glee.

"Just like Laura and Carrie," the Japanese trio kept saying. "And baby Grace!" Perhaps I would have to wash and wipe dishes for my supper as well.

Hunger is the best sauce.

The food was delicious, and let me see if I can do it justice in a most Laura-like manner: The crackled roasted surface of the pork where the fat had crisped gave off its good brown smell; the gravy was thin enough to pour but thick enough to cling to the mashed potatoes, whipped into white peaks. Farmhouse butter and crimson jelly in cut-glass dishes sat at either end of the table. Soft rolls, home-pickled beets, and a vinegar-and-herb dressed green bean tray completed the spread. Sprightly fiddle music piped into the room from someone's playlist, and we ate and ate of the good meat, beans, and fluffy chicken pies until we were full to bursting[133].

As we were taking cups of coffee and tea from the catering staff, Al stood to address the group.

"I was going to make a final toast to Laura, which I will, in a moment. But maybe each of you could say something that you

---

[132] Ya think?

[133] Say what you will about Rose usurping Laura's authorial voice, and their innate bigotry elsewhere; Laura's food paragraphs can make you drool.

learned about Laura, or about yourself, while you've been here. I know it was just three days, but it seems like a week or a month! I would love to hear from each of you."

We murmured and squirmed because speaking aloud before a group, and all—it's a lot to ask of a book nerd. Or a shelf of book nerds. A herd of nerds.

He turned to Amanda next to him, his eyebrows raised in question, to get the comments going.

In her bright, cheerful Jersey-girl accent, Amanda announced, "I never knew that water skiing was invented at Lake Pepin." We erupted into laughter, and it took a minute to quiet down.

"I know that's not really a Laura thing, but that just blew my mind," Amanda said. "But I also learned that I could never, ever live on the prairie. It's too quiet here!"

Mary, Carrie and Grace whispered among themselves. Mary spoke next. "My real name is Kumiko, but my sister is blind, so I read all the books with her, and Mary is our favorite girl. So I call myself Mary when I come to the United States. I learn how to use a Braille slate at the schoolhouse."

Carrie, or the woman we have been calling Carrie, was next. She said, "I did not know that Carrie is *Caroline*, just like the Ma in the story. I admire Ma very much. I am the little sister, so I take Carrie as my name. It is an honor to call myself Carrie, and it is for Ma and the sister Carrie. I learn a lot on this trip."

The third student, Grace, giggled as she always did. It was her expected response. But then she straightened and spoke in her little voice, surprisingly clearly, if imperfectly.

"I am baptize two years ago. They choose a name for me at my church—they call me Grace. It is a name I find when I am reading the *Little House* books and when my friends take other names, I keep my name. I am Grace by baptism." Then she said, "God bless you. And God bless the Little House."

The two catering ladies serving us were obviously very touched by this genuine Christian sentiment, indeed, dabbing at their eyes. I was reminded how little I knew about my sister travelers.

Carrie piped in, "I forgot to say thank you, Grandma, for teaching me knit. *TO* knit."

Marian responded, "You are very welcome!" and laughed along with her protégé. Marian went on. "I learned that there are friends around the world and right at home, and this is something I knew a long time ago, but I remembered it again this weekend."

Blown kisses from the Japanese contingent.

"I also learned that Laura and Rose were both very good bakers. In the books, Laura says she hates the feel of the flour and the dough, but despite that, apparently she made a very good loaf of bread, and so did Rose." Marian sat back in her chair again, dusting her fingers of imaginary flour.

Her daughter stood, fidgeting with her hands. "I learned about the tallgrass prairie and the wildflowers, and if there were a way to bring that home with me, I would do it," Sandy said in her soft voice.

"What did you learn about *yourself*?" Al urged her.

"About myself? That there are new horizons. Different horizons. I needed to get away, and it was a blessing to get out here on the prairie and let my troubles blow away." Sandy made a little smile, as if apologizing for taking up so much time.

"In the wind that never dies!" Kellie burst in. She made as if to hold her hat from the prairie wind, a wild gesture that made everyone laugh.

Roxi from Sarasota said that she had packed too many clothes but had still not been warm enough, and that she was happy to be the only redhead she had seen. "And I love Laura even more now."

Dan, the schoolteacher from Philly, was at the foot of the table. He said, "I really like the people here. I don't know many people like these kind, generous South Dakotans. And I thought they were just fiction. But they are very real. So I thank you, ladies," he said to the caterers waiting with carafes of hot coffee and decaf. They smiled and nodded from their station.

"What did I learn about Laura?" Dan continued. "If these people are not fiction, then maybe the fiction wasn't fiction either. Maybe it is more real than we knew." I agreed with that. "And about myself, I just am happy to feel so welcome in a place so far from home. I feel *welcome*."

It was a lovely word.

Kellie jumped in. "Okay, okay, it's my turn. And I would like to say that the cowboys of Dakota Territory are *very handsome!* The ones at the Bar and Grill are gorgeous!" Laughter bounced from every corner. "I think that Laura and Carrie must have had very good legs, because they had a lot of walking to do. I enjoyed my run here and wish the weather had been better so I could have run a little farther out into the countryside."

"No *boolshit*," Amanda loudly whispered, and we erupted into laughter again.

Lorena was next, and she looked a perfect picture in her costume. "I was so taken by Laura's sewing box. I do a lot of handwork myself, and seeing the tools she used made me feel as if I knew her a little better." She ran her hands down her dress, whether consciously or unconsciously, I don't know.

"What did you learn about yourself, Loreen?" Marian asked across the table.

Lorena winced at the sound of her name mispronounced, but she didn't comment upon it. "Oh, that's a tough one. I would say that I've learned to see with my own eyes and not just assume. I thought I would be bored by the personal possessions, but I was just thrilled to see these real things. That tells me that I am a skeptic by nature, which is true, but also a believer, which I didn't know."

Her pink cheeks gave her a pretty, healthy glow, and I thought if I were Al, I would ask her to marry me immediately.

June was seated between Lorena and me, venturing from her mother's side like a big girl. She had her Addy doll on her lap and blushed when prodded to speak.

"I liked the schoolhouse and the horses best. I didn't know how to drive a wagon but now I do. And Addy was real happy to see other dolls here."

That was so sweet it made my heart melt a little. I was growing very fond of this girl and looking forward to sharing a car ride with her, and maybe some time together on the train home. I have always rather feared children. Or ignored them[134]. But June—she kindled something in me like affection, like affinity, or something. I didn't know what to call it. An alien feeling for sure!

My turn. I was not a loud speaker, so I was glad there was just our small group. "I learned to pay attention to the weather," I said, which made everyone laugh again. "Never go out without gloves and a hat!"

"—and a lantern!"

"And snow boots—"

"And your winter flannels!"

"And a boyfriend!"

"And a St. Bernard!"

"A Saint *Alberto*!"

"And a charged-up mobile phone!"

Al clapped his hand onto his head and groaned. "*Ay*, don't mention it!"

The ladies came to pour hot coffee for us, and I thought I was off the hook.

"Nell, what did you learn about Laura?" Al asked.

---

[134] Laura's experience with the screaming Johnny Brewster comes to mind.

"I am still thinking about it," I said, "But it has to do with size and spaces. She was a very small person physically, but huge in that she created this whole world for us. And here we are in the counterpart of that world, the real world of the *Little House*, the *Little Town*, and it's huge, too. I'm trying to parse the balance between her physical size and the vastness of the prairie landscape. How large or small we are depends on our place in the world, and in our own worlds."

"Well, Professor Nelly, that was lovely," said Amanda, and I knew it was too nerdy when I got started, but he had asked me, so I answered.

Lorena leaned across June and clinked her coffee mug to mine and said, "Righteous, Professor." *Damn!*

Marian said, "I don't know how you think of these things, you university types."

Unemployed librarian. But—she's right. I *am* smart, and it's okay to be smart. *Stop picking on yourself.*

Lorena picked up the baton and asked Al what he'd learned.

"I learned more about the reality of farming in a harsh environment," Al said, rubbing his chin. "I thought Mexico was a tough place to farm, but *hijo le!* It's nothing compared to the wind and the snow and the extremes of weather up here. I can hardly imagine it."

He accepted the pie being placed in front of him and thanked the lady. "Oh, this looks delicious. Okay, right, and about *myself?* I found out what a pleasure it is to be with like-minded people, people who love and cherish the same things that I do—this author, this way of life. I appreciate all of you for coming all this way, and I hope you fulfilled a dream as I did in visiting here."

Alberto/*Almanzoor* raised his coffee cup and said, "If it's not too late, I will offer the last toast to Laura Ingalls Wilder: To our heroine, our inspiration, our brave girl on the prairie. We thank you."

PART THREE

ON THE WAY HOME

CHAPTER 14

In the morning, we placed our suitcases into my little car and I said goodbye to Liz, and then to Mary, Carrie, and Grace as they drove away to Sioux City to catch their airplane home to Washington state. They were unable to go to the cemetery, but Carrie asked me to place her flowers on Carrie's grave. She had purchased some bright yellow marguerite daisies at the supermarket on Calumet. I hugged each of them goodbye, and then we drove to the cemetery, which was parallel to the Ingalls homestead.

It was almost as if they were laid to rest right there in their own yard, just a quarter section away.

It was Sunday morning, and the cemetery was quiet, although Liz had told us that local folks liked to visit their interred families in the afternoon, after church. We were subdued in the presence of the graves, the tall headstone that is Charles Ingalls' and the small marble markers that are Caroline's, Mary's, Carrie's, and Baby Boy[135] Wilder's, with Grace Ingalls Dow and her husband[136] buried together a little way away.

---

[135] But why didn't they name him? Wouldn't they have named him for his father, another Almanzo? Charles, for his Ingalls grandfather? Frederick, for Laura's late little brother? James, the Wilder grandfather? Why did they not name him? They had two weeks, according to *The First Four Years*. It makes no sense to me.

[136] I can't get over Grace growing up and getting married and having sex and then dying. It just bugs me. She is forever the little china doll with a lisp in the swan's down hood.

I laid my roses on each grave, and Carrie's daisies on Carrie Ingalls Swanzey's grave, but I had forgotten the baby boy, so I went back to the car and took the stems of white freesia and laid them on his grave. The adult plots didn't bother me as much as the tiny baby in the cold ground. How sad was it for Ma, for Laura, and Rose, too, each to lose her only son?

Sandy, wiping tears from her eyes, held June by the shoulders and hugged her tightly, as June carried her doll in a motherly grip and whispered, "Hush, hush, it's all right."

★ ★ ★

It was time to go. I walked to my car, catching Al's eye, and he followed me over.

"You be careful," he said. "Just stick to the main roads. It's early in the season, and the ground is not frozen, so there won't be any ice. It should be fine."

"I hope so. It'll be okay, with the four of us together. It's just a few hours. Sandy or Marian can drive if I get tired or freak out or something." I thought he was just talking about the roads.

"Will you text me or send me an email or something, so I know you got there all right? So I know you're on the train?"

"If there's a signal. If I can, I will. By tonight, I'll be heading home." I wanted to see him again. I wanted to talk more. I won't ask, though. No one likes a clinging woman[137].

"Take care," he said. "Thank you for coming all this way."

"It was fun." So glib, just to say that word.

He smiled. "Was it? Oh, good! I'm glad."

I smiled back, but I felt like crying. He pulled me into a hug, and I hugged him back. We were friends now, nothing more.

---

[137] The only clingy thing people like is cling peaches. Not like Nellie in THGY, clutching Almanzo's arm: "Oh, Manny, those horses frighten me, why are they so wild?" Yeesh.

And then there were others to hug, so we all said our farewells and got into the car. It took me a few turns to get back onto Highway 14 and on our way.

"Did you like that little town on the prairie, June?" I asked her to fill the sudden silence in our car.

"I did! I had so much fun. The horses were beautiful. And the schoolhouse. Addy loved it! I can't wait to read all of the books again, by myself." She continued chattering in the back seat with her grandmother, while Sandy sat beside me, scrolling her phone and looking distractedly out the windows every few minutes. I was, surprisingly, not nervous, but Sandy was. So then I felt anxious. But I didn't want to call attention to her. So I just drove.

At Brookings, we turned south onto 29, and then all we had to do was go straight until we reached Omaha. Everything was flat and looked like farms, about as farmy as you can imagine. Red barns or white ones, some with green roofs; silver grain silos, stacks of rectangular hay bales, or round bales left in the field. The occasional solar or wind farm, and flat flatness, damp with mud.

In a little while, I turned on the radio and pushed buttons in the car past the religious music and talk radio, Spanish rancheria music, and right-wingnut news. We found a station playing some pop hits, with an occasional Taylor Swift or Beyoncé song, which June liked and sang along to from the back seat. Pretty catchy tunes at that, I realized, and soon was also singing along, and the other women joined in. I one-upped the radio station and found a Taylor playlist on my phone. We played only Swifty songs the rest of the way.

Just for giggles, I sang even louder, and so did June, and by the time we got to Sioux Falls, we were shouting, "You Belong With Me."

The Sioux Falls traffic silenced my singing, but not June's. We found an exit and stopped for a restroom break at a gas station. Sandy went into the store and bought bags of chips for everyone and some bottled water. Then they switched seats, and Marian sat up front with me. We stayed that way the rest of the drive.

Marian talked about her farm years growing up in Oregon. When we arrived at the point where the highway jogs left at Elk Point, she said we were near the Missouri River, and by gosh, you could actually see the river way off to the right. At least I tried to look, but I was driving, so I just snuck a quick over-the-shoulder peek.

We ran right along the great river again, down at Sioux City, on the border of Nebraska and Iowa, and for just a few minutes, we were driving from one state into another, and maybe even in two states at once. June was thrilled.

She had her arms stretched wide in the back seat, saying, "I'm in two states at once. Right now I'm in two states! This arm is in Iowa and this arm is in Nebraska! This arm loves corn and this arm loves—what do they love in Iowa? Corn? Both arms love corn!" She laughed at her own genius.

I wasn't quite sure if June was geographically correct for more than an instant, but I had to watch the road, so I gave her the benefit of the doubt. To be in two states at once was a sensation I had felt many times in the past few days.

We went back into farmland for another hour, until we saw the signs for Omaha and the interchanges ahead. I needed Marian's guidance to get off 29 and into downtown, where we eventually found the rental car place. I turned in my keys and slapped some plastic on the counter. What the hell. I would pay off the credit card somehow. Someday. Maybe I'd write a book[138].

The clerk drove us to the Omaha train station, which had a single clerk on duty and several people waiting to board the next train that night. Sandy updated her tickets and got a family cabin

---

[138] *Me, write a book?* I hooted.

for the three of them instead of sitting in Coach all the way back to Sacramento. I still had my single sleeper reserved. We checked in our luggage and then asked at the desk and learned that the Omaha Children's Museum was close by.

The four of us hailed a taxi and went to the Children's Museum for the last hour, and enjoyed the exhibits and the little gift shop. It was less than a mile back to the station, so we thought we would walk back and find a place for supper, and then we could settle in at the station till our 11 p.m. train.

June would be tired out after all the walking and wasn't a naturally fussy child. She had bought a book at the museum and looked forward to sharing it with Addy at the train station.

We walked across Jackson, and found a place to eat that was low-key, not too pricey, and very homey. It was a relief to rest our feet after an hour at the museum and walking, despite the long car trip. A cheerful waiter even brought a small plate for Addy. June was charmed by his kindness.

"We have to order barbecue," Marian said, looking at the menu.

"Do I have to? Can I have a grilled cheese? I want to share it with Addie." June had her way, but I had a pulled pork sandwich with a tangy, spicy sauce that I had never had in the Golden State. My opinion of the Midwest improved by the day. I thought I would be back again another time, maybe to visit the other Laura sites.

Finally, we finished our meal and took the long walk in the cold back down South 10th Street to the train station, claimed a bench, and settled to wait. The train was late by more than an hour, due to some trouble on the tracks near Chicago. We got on board about midnight, and all of us were just one step from utter exhaustion. Junie was in tears by then, and I walked with her to their room, holding her hand.

"I'm in the next car, just two minutes away. I'll see you for breakfast, okay? We'll have pancakes or maybe they have Froot Loops!" I kissed the top of her head and asked, "May I give Addy a kiss goodnight?"

Junie nodded, wiping her eyes.

I kissed the plastic doll's fake hair. "Goodnight, Addy. Sleep tight!"

I went to my sleeper upstairs in the next car, and thankfully, my bed was pulled down and ready for me, courtesy of Duane, my car's porter. I flopped back on the thin mattress, too tired to take my clothes off just then. I was exhausted, but also keyed up. Such a long day, and so much to do and focus on. I needed to unwind and stop thinking. Or think and stop clenching.

So tired. So very tired.

After about a half an hour of just lying there, hearing the train moving along and blowing its horn at the crossings, just watching the lights go by, and the darkness, I remembered that I was going to text or call Al, but by then there was not much signal. We were between cities, and I knew we'd pass through Lincoln soon, and then a handful of other Nebraska cities before we hit Colorado's mountains. I couldn't get my text to go through.[139] I gave up and figured I'd deal with it in the morning.

Then, of course, I was too tired to sleep—same old story.

I finally decided to find some herbal tea and made my way down to the end of the car where hot water and coffee were available all the time, except at one in the morning. I kept moving to the next car, and same problem there. I had missed out. The snack bar closed at midnight, but I thought I'd try one more car down the line, and there I saw Sandy getting some hot water at the urn in the corner.

---

[139] But at least no texts from Mom, either.

She was stirring some instant hot chocolate into a paper cup.

I whispered, "Couldn't sleep."

"Me neither." She looked apologetically at her stir-stick. "I only brought this one cocoa."

"That's okay, I came for tea."

She finished stirring and fitted on a plastic lid. She didn't move away while I made my tea. The train was as loud as ever, but you forgot about it after being onboard for a while. The shaking and rocking were constant, too, but harder to get used to. I stood like a sailor, balancing in the aisle.

"Thanks again for the ride. I just want to get home," Sandy said softly, just above the engine noise. Her eyes got teary, and she sniffled and put her hand to her face.

I hardly knew what to do. I said, "Oh, Sandy," helpless against the wave of compassion and terror that flooded my chest simultaneously. She pulled out a tissue and dabbed her eyes, but the tears kept coming.

"Are you okay?" Clearly she wasn't.

"You've been so nice. I'm sorry. There's just been a lot—Junie—" and then she covered her face and cried hard into her hand. I took her cup of cocoa and set it near the water urn, and then took her other hand. We stood like that in the dimly lit train rocketing through the Nebraska dark for some time.

"I'll just tell you, and then you won't think I'm insane," Sandy said.

"I don't think you're insane."

"We came on this trip to get away from my husband. I'm leaving him, I left him already, I guess. He's been—he did something to Junie. I found tissues in her underwear, and she was all freaked out, and I called him at work, and he said there was nothing wrong and whatever it was, I was imagining it, Junie was making it up. And then I went looking in his stuff where I don't usually look, and there were pictures of her. *Pictures. My god.*" She sobbed quietly into her hand, and I put my arm around her, unable *not* to cry, hearing my story in the mouth of another.

A porter came around the corner toward us, and when he saw me, he looked startled and concerned. I shook my head and kept my arm around Sandy. She sobbed so hard, yet still so quietly, into my shoulder. And it didn't get better. She sobbed harder, screaming silently into her hands on the train, in the dim corner. Tears streamed from my eyes.

I put one elbow against the wall to brace myself and wiped my eyes on my sleeve. I leaned around her and grabbed a few paper napkins from the tea urn corner and handed some to Sandy. She was settling down, breathing better, easing up. She finally looked at me.

"I'm sorry."

"No, don't—Please. It's okay." She blew her nose and started to protest, but I shook her arm a little and said, "Really, I get it. It happened to me. I'm Junie, too."

She clapped her hand over her mouth and said, "Oh, god, you poor thing."

"It was a long time ago," I said. Exactly what my mom had told me. But I hadn't gotten over it. Could Junie? What could I say—that it destroyed my life? That I was a terrified, anxious 45-year-old virgin, or damaged goods, or a fucked-up mess, whatever you'd call me?

"But here you are," said Sandy. "And you're amazing."

Jesus. That's the last thing I was.

"No, but I'm all grown up and went to college and got a good job," I said—well, that part was a lie, but Sandy needed to hear that Junie will survive. Junie *must* survive it. "I survived it. We can help her survive it, too."

"You're so smart and sweet and kind," she said. "That gives me a lot of hope—that this doesn't ruin her."

"Yes, but Sandy, you have to listen to her. When she wants to talk about it, let her. Don't silence her. My mother never wanted to hear about it, never thought it was that bad. She ran away from it. And I have no faith or trust in my own mother, or even other women, because of it. Don't be that way with Junie, please. Love her through it. Help her heal. And then she'll be okay. She'll be better than if you ignore it or minimize it."

"That's so hard. I'm so angry right now, and how I failed her. I should have known. I—."

"Sandy—*it's not about you*. It's about Junie. Get into therapy, both of you, okay? And if you have to freak out, do it apart from her. She needs you. Little girls need their mommies." Where there's a will, there's a way. Ma knew.

We went back to our rooms, I to my own roomette, completely wrung out now. So many thoughts went through my head, out of control, like a stampede of buffalo, a runaway oxcart, a collapsing dugout. I sipped my lukewarm tea and then, with the cooled liquid, swallowed a sleeping pill and was able to fall asleep.

But not to rest. Over and over, my eyes snapped open as I heard doors open and slide closed, slam and bang. Whistles and bells, horns and rattles. A cacophony of train noises went in and out of my restless dreams, with a hand snatching me out of the snow. A man's hand pulling at my clothes. Little Junie and I crouching in the corner. The man came up the stairs in the dark, and I leapt up into him, shoving him away, my hands with claws that could rip. I had never been able to stop him before, but with a little girl to defend, I was stronger. I would kill him if he touched her. I pushed him down the stairs into the dark and swirling snow.

I turned around to comfort the crying Junie, and it wasn't she. It was me.

* * *

The train chugged westward as inexorably as destiny, manifest. I opened my eyes again to white light, a snowy arrival in Denver, and the scent of coffee in the corridor.

CHAPTER 16

I washed my face and ran the washcloth over my sticky body in warm water in the tiny train bathroom, cleaned my teeth, and brushed my hair back into a low ponytail. I was not rested, no, I felt like I'd spent the night on a narrow sofa with Mrs. Brewster screaming in the night, a knife flashing in the darkness. I needed Pa's stout door[140] closed between me and chaos. Just one night, I'd like to sleep soundly, with no haunts, no terrors.

I dressed in comfy stretchy pants, my last clean sweater, and my slip-on boots. I followed the scent of coffee to the end of the corridor and took a paper cupful with me toward the dining car. As I passed through the parlor car, I stopped. Al twisted in the armchair toward me and got up steadily despite the shaking of the train around a broad curve in the track.

"You made it! I was worried!"

"I didn't know you were on this train." I was slack-jawed in surprise.

"I wasn't supposed to be, but we got in earlier than planned, and the train was running late, so I got onboard when it came through Des Moines."

"I tried to text you."

"So did I. But no signal."

---

[140] He made doors from slabs of wood in the Big Woods, on the prairie in Kansas, and in the houses he built in Walnut Grove and De Smet, in town and on the claim. Pa and a good door. I'd had neither.

"No signal."

"Breakfast?" He thumbed toward the dining room.

"Well, coffee and toast. I promised Junie I'd have pancakes with her later." I was glad to have a companion. I hadn't the energy to chitchat with strangers. I don't know that I had the energy to talk to Al, either, but the path of least resistance triumphed. We went in, and they seated us together on one side of a four-person table. This put us leg to leg, and no possibility of looking at each other in conversation. It was awkward until another couple was seated across from us and then it was okay because they didn't speak English and just smiled at us. They spoke to each other in a Central European language of which my French-learned-in-high-school recognized few words.

"You look tired," Al said.

"I didn't really sleep."

"Your trip down was all right? No trouble?"

"No, the drive was fine. It's beautiful country, and we saw the Missouri River." I told him about the Omaha Children's Museum and how much Junie had enjoyed it, but then I stopped.

"What?"

"Oh, it's a long, sad story." "Tell me."

"Not here. Later."

Our breakfast came—his omelet and my toast—and more coffee. We could see the Rockies in stunning snow-dusted majesty outside the windows as we ate. Our Euro tablemates saw it, too, and we smiled at each other in mutual admiration of the view.

"Beautiful," ventured the man with a thick inflection. The woman nodded.

"Snow," Al said, then said "*Nieve*," in Spanish, and wriggled his fingers to indicate snowfall. The woman recognized the gesture and said "*sněžení*" in her language, indicating that she was cold by hugging herself and shivering.

The server came by with coffee, and we all said yes, and then the woman said, "*káva*," and her husband copied her.

"*Café*, mmmm," Al added.

The server placed our tickets on the table in passing, and the man asked Al to help with the proper dollar bills. Then, we each said "Goodbye," to their word, which sounded something like "*Sbohem!*"

"I love travel," Al said from behind me as we left the dining car. "You meet so many interesting people. That makes me want to learn some more languages. Two are not enough."

I couldn't get the car door to open in my caffeinated-yet-sleep-deprived state, so Al reached around me to push the pneumatic button again. His arm brushed against me. I warmed to this touch, had felt warmth next to him for an hour now. Back in the parlor car, most of the seats were taken, so we passed through and went into the first sleeper car. My car was two cars farther back, but Al stopped at a numbered door and said, "Sit with me a while in my compartment?"

He slid the door open and pushed back the curtains. The bed had been folded back into two facing seats again, as mine was probably being made just then, too.

"Forward or backward?"

"I'd rather face forward, please."

He waited until I sat in the western-facing seat, then pulled out the folding table that was hidden in the recess in the side, and seated himself with the pop-up table between us. His jasper eyes were kind and I wasn't afraid.

"Okay. Tell me what happened with June?"

I took a deep breath. "Some family drama. Her parents have just split up and—." It all came dangerously close to the surface. My throat closed up. "I don't know if I can tell you."

"Why not?"

"It's very private."

"Is she in danger?"

"She was. I think she'll be safe now. Sandy left her husband and they are going to live with Marian. June'll be safe there. If they get her some therapy."

I had already said the rest of it without words. He rolled his lip with his teeth and looked away out the window. When he spoke, I realized Al was very angry. "Was he fucking around with his own daughter?" His voice was very soft and measured.

I nodded.

"*Hijo de la gran puta!*[141]" He said it again under his breath and clasped his hands together on the tabletop, as if to stop from punching something, someone. "Jesus, Mary, and Joseph, how can guys do that?"

"I don't know how, but they do it." I watched, kept watching, judging him, his reaction, ready to bolt if I had to.

"Poor kid." He rubbed both hands over his face, which he had found time to shave that morning. "Some son of a bitch did that to one of my sisters. My uncle beat the shit out of him when we found out. It makes me so mad." He bit his thumb and looked out the window, his leg vibrating with unspent rage.

I sat and watched him. Should I tell him? Should I go now? Where were we going, anyway? But who wants to hear these stories? About the hands on my knees, my thighs, inside my underwear? The threats. My fear of kidnapping and doors opening in the dark. Who wants to know these details? Who wants to relive that?

"Well," he said after a while, bringing his eyes back to me. "Thanks for telling me. It breaks my heart, and if I ever caught the son of a—*hey!* Hey there—what?"

---

[141] Don't ask me why, but this was about the sexiest thing I had ever heard. Swearing in a foreign language is just — *mmph! Shudder!*

Stupid tears. When he looked back at me, those beautiful mahogany brown eyes, I was flooded with sadness, that I wouldn't get to be happy, that I couldn't get to be close to him or any other man, that I am untouchable, that I am invisible, off limits, violated, tainted, and it was partly my fault because I had never said no. I had just wanted attention from my dad, from a father figure, from anyone.

He was nice to me, until he got me on the table, and the touching began. And even then, at least someone was talking to me, I wasn't alone, I had a hand on my leg and he touched my hair, and then the dress went up and the panties were taken off, and he had something in his hand. No fucking clue. Kids made jokes about wieners and hot dogs, but I didn't know anything about that, so how could I understand? And later he said shut up, shut up, and don't tell, and you'd better keep your goddamned little mouth shut or I'm coming to get you.

All that is good is gone from me because I was small and lonely, and someone paid attention. *At least it was attention.*

Al pushed the flip table up and into the wall pocket and reached for my hands. And the physical act of him taking my hands, holding my hands so gently, just, humiliatingly, opened another level of tears, of flood, of what I could never have. I pulled my hands away and covered my face, knowing how ugly I looked when I cried, and anxiety started to rise that I was trapped in this moving box, and I couldn't run away, crying like an idiot. My face felt like it was on fire.

He pulled me forward, got on his knees before me, cradled me in his shoulder, put his arms around me, and just said, "It's okay, it's okay. Go on, it's okay now."

I didn't think I would ever stop.

CHAPTER 17

When the flood slowed down, and I was all but limp, Al let me go and said, "I'll be right back."

He slid the door open, pulled the curtain, and then slid the door shut, and I was too tired to freak out. I wasn't trapped. I was simply exhausted. He came back in a few minutes with a warm washcloth and towel and offered it to me.

The damp heat felt so good against my face. I thought about staying in that position forever with my face covered by a washcloth but it really wasn't possible. It never is. There's no such thing as forever. I sat up, and he took the cloth from my hand. Stashed it on a hook. Looked at me quizzically.

"I'm okay now. Sorry about all that." My face still burned with shame.

He didn't contradict me, but he didn't agree, either. "You've got a lot going on inside." He sat down again. Took my hands.

"You have no idea."

"Oh, I do. I think I have some kind of idea."

I started to say I was sorry again, but he said, "Just cut it—don't. You gave me a gift just then. Don't take it away from me now! You let me be strong for you, and that was amazing. Thank you."

I opened my mouth again to protest this upside-down way of thinking, but he said, "You don't have to tell me now, you don't have to tell me ever, but if you want to, if you trust me enough someday, I'd like to hear what happened. You don't have to carry this alone." He shook my hands a little when he said that.

My eyes watered again. Spilled over. He leaned forward and kissed the tear track on my right cheek. Kissed the tear track on my left cheek. Kissed my right cheek again, a little lower. Licked his lips and smiled at me. Kissed the tears lower on my left cheek. Gently bumped noses. Pressed his forehead to mine. His eyes were so close I had to close mine. Opened them. His eyes were closed. I could smell his skin, feel the tickle of his hair, the warmth where our heads were so close. His eyes still closed, he cupped his hand behind my head and kissed my cheek again.

I wanted to kiss him. I turned my face just a little and he turned toward me and kissed me very lightly on the lips. Again, on the lips. Again. Put his forehead to mine again. His eyes were still closed. There were tears on his cheeks. Mine? His? My entire body was tingling and awake, electrified by these tender kisses. He drew his hand around to gently touch my face with his eyes still closed. I moved my hands up to touch his face, too.

His face, where a razor had passed not long ago, was smooth with a hint of roughness underneath. His skin was warm, and I rubbed my fingers against his shadow, just a little, to feel it. To see how it felt. He nuzzled my hand like a puppy, kissing my palm, my fingers, the back of my hand, the inside of my wrist. I rested my hand against his face and then drew it away.

He opened his eyes. Sat back into his seat, facing me, but leaned forward on his elbows.

I couldn't hold his gaze. I loved those kisses. Part of me wanted to take my clothes off and run down the corridor. Most of me wanted to submerge like a swamp thing and watch. What was going to happen next? I wanted to turn the page and see.

"Nell. You are—something." He said, "Half of me wants to bite the buttons off your blouse and the other half wants to tiptoe away and not scare you into your rabbit hole."

"Me, too."

He was grinning at me. "Did I scare you?"

"No, it was nice."

"Do you want some more kisses?" He laughed a little.

"Yes, but no. I liked that. I'd like some more kisses. But I'm just really raw right now, I guess. To be honest, I think I would like to take a nap. I was supposed to have breakfast with Junie, and I doubt I have the bandwidth for that. I'm worn out with travel and no sleep and sobbing my guts out and—just not right now."

"Okay."

"If I go back to my sleeper right now—will I see you later?"

"Yes, you will see me later." He opened the curtain and unhooked the door. Slid it open. I took his hand for a moment and then went through the door and down the corridors of the moving train to my own compartment in my own car. I pulled the door closed and the curtains, and pushed the seats together again. Plumped the pillow and curled up. I pulled my coat over me and tucked my head underneath.

I was so tired, I could hardly stay awake. My eyes stung, but the rocking of the train and my own warm exhaustion took me, and I dreamed.

Such a long way to go, such a high, tall mountain. The train car leaned first one way, then another, and the air pressure changed. I could feel my ears popping. I could feel that my head was higher than my feet as the train climbed while I slept. I could feel his light kisses, his tender crooning in my ear, *it's okay, it's okay, go on now.* It's okay.

I was a swamp frog under the blanket of bright green slime. My eyes peeked out. Blink. What the hell does he want with me? You can't squeeze a frog or it will die. He wanted to fuck with me, take what I have, he wanted to break open my shell, my ability to breathe underwater, to walk on land, to capture me in a net and put me in a glass case. He wanted my legs, my tender virgin legs, to tear them open, to spread me wide and look at my lady parts, to see what else he could shove in there.

He wanted to eat me. He wanted to hurt me. He wanted to kill me.

He's at my door. He's at my door.

CHAPTER 18

We pulled into Glenwood Springs and it was past two in the afternoon when I woke up and went to the restroom and then up to the parlor car. I didn't see Al, but Marian was there, knitting. She was working on a beautiful striped scarf in shades of green and brown; it reminded me of the autumn prairie. An open book rested at her knee.

"I'm sorry I missed breakfast," I told her. "I didn't sleep last night, and I just woke up now."

"That's all right, honey, you needed it. It was a long day yesterday! And you did all that driving!"

It was such a relief to have this motherly woman soothe me and make things right. I felt a burst of love and gratitude for Marian right then. I would have hugged her if she weren't covered with yarn, knitting, and a book at the same time[142].

She told me Junie was playing in their room and Sandy was resting.

I headed for the snack bar in hopes of finding something for lunch that wasn't too processed, a possibly fruitless attempt. The attendant, a white lady, was flattening a box and straightening

---

[142] It used to be a thing, reading and knitting. Look it up. Lots of girls had permission to read if they were knitting, although I can't see how they kept their eyes on both at once. Today, I could totally see listening to an audiobook while knitting. But Marian was a little old-fashioned, and she had her book, the hardcover of *Caroline,* under one knee as she knitted.

the napkins. She could have been 40, and she could have been 70. It's hard to tell with some people. The uniform didn't help. Her name badge read *Carole* with an E.

I was awake, but my dreams kept playing with my head. Were those kisses real, or was he using me? Is he trying to take what he can get? He's just a nice guy. *There are no nice guys. People screw you. They take. They take.* I keep staring at the juice and the fruit and the mini-cereal boxes. *People fuck you over.* They ruin you.

What would Laura do? I hadn't even thought of what Laura would do. What, I wondered.[143]

"Are you almost ready?" Carole gave me a tight smile. "I have to close the shop for a little while for my break. Do you know what you want?"

"Who knows what they want?" I said, asking the wind. "How can you ever know?" I selected a cranberry juice, an apple, and a cup of yogurt and turned back to her.

"That's a good question," she said. Rang up my purchases. "Eight dollars."

I pulled a twenty out of my purse and she was looking at the poster on the wall about *Get Your Rail Pass Today* with a colorful photo of the Grand Canyon and two happy people with binoculars.

"You never really know," Carole said. "You just have to trust your gut."

"What if your gut is wrong?" I handed her the cash.

"Your gut is never wrong."

"But—." I started to argue because what does she know?

---

[143] Laura would have reached out and slapped his face, as she had with the Native dude who allegedly wanted to take her horses and become his wife, according to *The First Four Years.* She would have asked nicely, as she did with the boys in LTOTP when they were hounding Miss Wilder, and the boys respected her so much, they stopped just like that. So which is it? Ask nicely or slap his face?

She said, "No, it's true. If you second-guess, it's your brain or your guilt or your conscience or your wishes, but it's not your gut. Your gut is like an animal inside you. It's what crawled out of the muck. It's like this inner beast, and it knows everything. They call it 'the second brain' but it's really your *first* brain. Before we had a brain, we had a gut. And we have forgotten to pay attention to it. Don't forget this—we are nothing more than sea cucumbers with arms and legs and a head that confuses us. Trust me, I know. Listen to your gut. And take good care of it." Carole handed me the change.

"Yogurt is very good for your gut," she added.

"Really?"

"Really. You get nervous, your stomach tells you. You're scared? Your gut tells you that. You're excited? You get butterflies. Stressed out? What happens?"

"You get an ulcer. You throw up. You eat too much."

"All of it. Take care of your gut," she said. "Now, if you don't mind, miss, I have to close up for my break."

★ ★ ★

I ate my yogurt, which had live cultures in it and had been known to correct an unhappy gut, then took my apple and juice back up to the parlor car. Marian was still knitting, but there was no empty seat near her. I sat at one of the small tables and pulled out my phone. There was no signal there in the mountains, but I was going to look up that second-brain thing when I got a signal. Maybe Carole was right.

I ate my apple and wrote some thoughts I had about the trip to De Smet in my notes, which I would post on the *LauraLand* site, along with some photos, whenever we got a signal. There was supposed to be WiFi on the train, but the Rockies are not the place to cry about no WiFi. In any case, the view was spectacular, and I was glad there was a parlor car to enjoy it.

The parlor car had full windows up around the ceiling, allowing for a wide view of the scenery. We were following the course of the Colorado River and somewhere in there, before we got to Grand Junction, is the spot where rivers run the other way, toward the West instead of the East. Where I no longer have to fight gravity and history and genetics, but my path becomes a little easier, little smoother. Where the river runs down. Where the water flows clearly and smoothly.

We followed the river for some time. In a while my phone buzzed and I had a text message. "Hi"

From Al. It looked like he had sent it an hour or so ago.

I sent back a "Hi," but it didn't go anywhere. Too many mountains.

I settled in with some music on my earphones and tried to heed my gut.

My gut said, *Thanks for the food* and *I don't like to look down the mountains. Only look up.* My gut said, *I hate the trestles. Look away.* My gut said, *Stop worrying. He'll turn up eventually. Don't chase him.* We were traveling together, still stuck together on this vessel, so we'd cross paths again. I could trust my gut on that.

Then it said, *Pay attention to the countryside. You may not ever pass this way again.*

My gut didn't say that—my brain did. We were still in steep mountains, with sheets of snow on every ridge. We'd be in Grand Junction at five p.m. and passing into Utah. We were heading into beautiful red rock country again, but it would be dark by then, and I wouldn't see a bit of it. We'd catch the sun again in Winnemucca.

My gut said, *Everything's cool.* My brain said otherwise. *Don't be a fool!*

What if he thinks I'm stupid? What if he's seen enough drama already? What if he's married, or a wife-beater, or a terrorist, or a drug-smuggling human trafficker? *What if, what if, what if,* spinning like the wheels of a noisy motorbike, too fast for these mountain passes.

If I think like that, I'll be sick. My gut told me that, too.

★ ★ ★

New passengers in the Rockies tended to be flannel-clad mountain guys, tanned-face skiers in Gore-Tex, and toothy Mormons always dressed as if for church. I don't know how I could tell they were Mormons. But they all seem to have those gleaming Osmond teeth. I hadn't seen an Amish passenger heading this direction. Maybe they only went east.

I played some rounds of Solitaire on my phone and spent time with Sudoku puzzles, with a soundtrack of acoustic country instrumentals[144]. It seemed fitting for the terrain. I took deep breaths when I started to feel nervous, and my gut was fine. *The gut is your second brain.*

The sun peeked out for a little bit in the afternoon, dazzling the eye with its glare off glittering peaks as we pulled into Grand Junction. Al appeared, too, from his sleeper compartment, where he'd been having a nap. He came through the parlor car with a magazine in his hand. I had my face toward the entrance and saw him come in. My gut sat up and noticed, doing the butterfly dance. Al came right up to me and asked if he could sit for a minute.

OK, gut, I'm listening. "Sure."

"I just came through to get a soda or something. Gotta wake up—or I won't be able to sleep tonight."

"Carole in the Snack Bar can help you with that."

---

[144] John Denver had set me up for such expectations.

"Is that her name?"

"It is."

"Did you sleep?"

"I did. You did, too."

"How can you tell?"

"Sheet print on your face."

He rubbed his face. In a flash I could see how he had looked as a child. My gut squirmed.

"We have about ten minutes before the train goes. Want to get some fresh air? I know I do." He stood and held his hand out to me. I got up and quickly slipped my phone into my back pocket.

"Let me stash this in the sleeper."

"No, we don't have time. Let's walk. Stretch and breathe."

We took the nearest set of stairs down and out onto the platform.

The air was sharp and cold at 4500 feet. Grand Junction station was regal despite its old brick and faded paint. The gold leaf was gone from the sign and the wooden windows needed new enamel. Al took my hand again, and we walked toward the front of the train until the platform ended. The engines were still beyond us, but we couldn't walk that far. It was snowy-slushy out near the tracks.

We saw the distant canyon range catch the last salmon-colored sunlight, then, in an instant, purpling into darkness. We walked down toward the back end of the train, blowing puffs of white breath and skirting hurried travelers. The conductor blew his whistle and we ran to the nearest door. Al scooted me up the stairs ahead of him. We were back in the coach section and had to pass a number of cars to reach the parlor again as the train picked up speed again.

In the glass doors between cars, I could see my cheeks were pink and my face looked alive, so awake and aware. My gut said *This is what fun feels like.*

"On to Utah," said the conductor, passing through behind us. We stopped him to book a table for 7:30 in the dining car.

"Hey, I want to go check on Junie and her family," I said over my shoulder. We weren't exactly traveling together, but I wanted to see my little friend and ask how she was enjoying the sleeper cabin.

I went through to their car, grabbed a handful of tissues from the coffee stand, and stuffed them in my pocket. I knocked on the compartment door. Al went on to his own space without me. Sandy opened their door and invited me in.

The room was larger than my little sleeper, but it still wasn't large. There was a sofa sleeper currently in the sitting position, with an open bunk overhead. Their family-size compartment had its own sink and mirror. Junie was on the floor; she had made a tent from a bath towel for Addy and was reading *Little House on the Prairie* with her head and book inside the tent, too.

"How's it going?" I said softly. I thought there might be more tears, but Sandy shrugged. She looked worried but not fragile, so I was a little relieved. "Do you mind if I talk to her?" I received a nod. I nodded back. *Roger that, Sandy.*

"That looks like fun," I said aloud so Junie would hear me. "Can I come into the tent?"

"Yes, you can try it!" Junie's voice came from within.

"Can I borrow another towel?" Sandy pulled one from their little cabinet by the sink, and I draped it over my head and got onto the floor with Junie. I wriggled until I got my face under Junie's towel and then mine covered both of us, sort of.

It was silly. We both giggled at how silly it was to be under towels, pretending we were in a tent. On a train.

"Hey, I'm sorry I missed out on Froot Loops. I slept late. I'm a lazy slug."

"Slug bug!" June didn't punch me, but she grinned, familiar with the game.

I cleared my throat. I leaned my head closer to Janey. I whispered. "Your mom told me about some of the stuff that happened."

"What stuff?" She whispered back. We were conspiring. We were sharing a secret.

"You know. The thing with your dad."

Scowl.

"I'm pretty mad about it," I said. "Mad at your dad, I mean."

"He didn't mean anything by it. He said—."

"Junie, listen to me, okay? This is really important. What he said doesn't matter. The only thing that matters is *you*. You got scared, right? He made you do some things you didn't like. He was wrong. He's still wrong even if he's mad at you."

Junie looked down at her doll. She wasn't laughing and having fun anymore.

"No, look at me. Do you trust me? Good. This is how I know that he's wrong." I took a breath, and then I said it. "Because my neighbor did that to me, too. When I was younger than you. That's right. It happened to me, too.

"And I was so scared and hurt, and I felt like I was dumb because I didn't know, and I couldn't stop it from happening. But it's not your fault when that happens. You're just a little kid. Right? Like I was just a little kid. When grown-ups do that to kids, it's bad. They're wrong. And they know it."

"I didn't know that grown-ups could be wrong. You're supposed to do what they say." She met my eyes.

"Right? But some grown-ups do bad things, and it's wrong. My neighbor said I was a liar, and my mom said I made it up, or I made a big deal out of nothing. But it was something. I was really scared."

"You don't look scared now." Out of the mouths of babes. Perhaps I wasn't.

"Well, I've been working on it. It was a long time ago. And I had a friend who helped me out."

"Who?"

"Her name was Laura. I didn't have Addy and I didn't have my mom or dad to help me, but I had Laura. She was in all those books, and I knew if I had a friend like Laura, I'd be okay. And I am."

"I love Laura!" Junie smiled widely.

"So do I!"

"So do I," Sandy chimed in from the other side of the compartment.

"I wanted to tell you about my experience so you would know you aren't alone," I continued, still speaking softly. "Things can be scary and hurt your feelings, but it doesn't have to take away all your fun and your good feelings and your good times. You're safe with Mom and Grandma now, right?"

"Yes."

"You know what else I did a lot of? Talking! I went to a talking doctor, a therapist—it could be a man or woman therapist, but mine was a lady—who let me explain what happened and helped me to learn how to feel safe again."

"Mommy said we should go to a sy, sy—I can't say that word."

"That's a talking doctor. Sometimes they're called psychologists, sometimes therapists. They're usually really nice, and sometimes they have toys for kids to play with. Sometimes there's a couch to sit on or lie on if you feel like lying down. They're really smart and they can help make you feel better inside."

"Where inside? In my—down there?" She pointed at her crotch.

"Oh, girl. I'll tell you where: In your," I patted my heart. "And your," I patted my belly. "And in your head, and in your dreams, and everywhere. So do me a favor, and go see a therapist with your mom, okay? And then if you want to, I'll come to Sacramento and see you, and you can tell me about it, if you want to. Or send me an email. Or a nice notecard in the mail. Or call me! On the phone!"

"On your own cell phone?"

"Yep."

I drew my head out of the towel-tent and fanned myself. It was hot under there.

Sandy looked as if she would cry again, but she kept it together and said, "What are your dinner plans? Would you like to have dinner with us?"

"I would love to but I'm having dinner with someone already."

"With *Al!*" Junie laughed out from under her tent. "Nelly's *boyfriend!*"

"Hush, you!" I said, rubbing her head like a dog through the towels, and she giggled some more.

"But breakfast tomorrow, or lunch?" Sandy persisted.

"Maybe lunch? I haven't been sleeping that well, so by breakfast, I look like I was hit by a truck. Lunch."

"Lunch."

"I'll see you later, Junie-gator, if not before then."

"After a while, crocodile!" Junie pulled the towels off her head and sat up with her book and her doll. I wrote my cell number on a piece of Amtrak notepaper, and June tucked it into her book as a page marker.

"See you mippo, silly hippo!"

"That doesn't even make any sense!" She laughed like any little girl did, freely and without restraint.

CHAPTER 19

I went back to my little bunk and looked at my face in the tiny mirror on the wall of the compartment. Smoothed my hair. It was early yet. I wasn't hungry. But I saw my car attendant, Duane, in the corridor and stopped him. I asked him to make up the bed right away because I hadn't slept and I was probably going to bed soon, right after dinner. Or immediately. I was fine, just tired. So very tired.

I went back through three cars to the parlor car where Al was still flipping through a back issue car magazine with a beer bottle in hand. I sat next to him in the empty swivel armchair and looked out at the dusk, seeking distant lights, but in the Utah desert, there are few.

But there are stars, if the clouds will part. We will wander gay and free.

He smiled and put his magazine aside. "You want to have a drink before dinner?" An attendant in the parlor car had taken up his station behind the bar. Al picked up his bottle and showed me it was empty. "I've had one. I could have another."

"If you want."

"What about you? What do *you* want?"

"I'd like wine—just whatever, white wine."

A few minutes later he was back with a split of Champagne and a glass for me and his own beer. He set out the paper napkins. "Their wine selection was crap, but I thought you might like this."

"Perfect." I stood up and picked up the split and the glass. "Bring your beer." I turned and went down the parlor car toward the sleepers. I didn't look back.

"Where are we going?"

I looked back as we went through the first set of doors and jostled into the first sleeper car. I walked a little faster, my sense of speeding accentuated by the dark countryside speeding along outside. At the second set of doors, the technology balked, and I punched the button several times. The door would not slide. Al caught up and nudged the second button, at foot level, for when your hands are full. It didn't budge. He put his arms around me and hugged me for a minute, but I pushed the button again and the door popped open. I scootched out from under his arms and walked down the car.

Duane was in the end of the car talking with another attendant. "I put your bed down," he called.

"Thanks, Duane." I kept walking, and Al had the sense to slow his pace and stroll casually. I went on through to my own sleeper car, and a minute later, Al was at my compartment door. I went in and he stopped at the door, looking in. He eyed the bed. I pulled him inside and slid the door shut, pulled the curtain, and made sure the catch was locked.

And then.

I reached up and pulled his head down. We met with fire, kissing, absorbing the flavor of each other, tasting, tasting with the depths of hunger I had not known. His hands were in my hair, loosening my hair from its band and twining his fingers into its depths. He kissed my neck as I pushed off his jacket and fumbled with his shirt buttons. Under the blue cotton, there was skin, smooth brown skin, and I tasted it, kissed it, and smelled his male scent. His hands in my hair turned my face up to his again, his mouth warm and searching, but gentle, and I felt his shadow burn against my cheek as I tasted his mouth, his face, felt his breath, his lashes against my cheek, our mouths sliding off each other, and I felt his hand sliding up my shoulders. For the first time, he let his hand drop to my sweatered chest—my left breast—and I gasped a little, surprised at how sensual that felt, how erotically tingly and right, and I leaned up into his hand and he pressed in, kissing me deeply.

The train shook and wavered, and he planted his hand against the wall to steady himself and pulled me into his arm, against his chest. I pulled back a little to breathe and adored his face, couldn't stop touching him, running my fingers on his arm back to his chest, cupping his cheek, and feeling his rough, stubbled skin. It so delighted my touch that I pulled my fingers down and lightly scratched with my fingertips. He closed his eyes and turned his head into my fingers, kissing them, and the train bumped and swayed.

There were buttons to undo and a furred belly to stroke and a buckle at the center to open, and behind that, jeans that were tight against his skin. I dropped to sit on the edge of the narrow bunk, and he turned toward me, his arms planted above on the low ceiling. He looked down at me. I could unzip him, see the full length of him beneath the layers of clothes but I backed away a little, and he bent, banging into the door behind him, and turned instead to sit next to me.

I kicked off my boots and, with an impish look, turned slightly away—I had to—and pulled my sweater over my head. Shirtless in front of a man—impossible!

Goosebumps ridged my skin, and he stroked my bare back, my arms and shoulders. I turned back to face him. He leaned forward to thumb across my bra, hooking a finger under my strap and pulling it gently down so that my creamy breast showed. The edge of pale brown areola peeked out, and he thumbed over this again so that my nipple appeared, then he bent to suckle and lick in a burst of agonizing pleasure that I never dreamed existed. I leaned into it and, in fact, grabbed his head and straddled him, climbed onto his lap. He sucked, then gnawed gently at my nipple, then pushed over to the other, brushed down my strap and seized my nipple in his mouth. He sucked hard and desperately, like a thirsty, thirsty man.

My nipples were both out now, and I, who never fucked a man, never had enough moxie to touch a man like this, was straddling this man, this delicious, thrusting, rock-hard man, and showing him my naked nipples.[145] He unhooked my bra and dropped it to the floor somewhere, stroked my body, squeezed my breasts, and buried his face between them. I felt so much desire, so much burning want. I rode his hardness between my legs, through my stretch pants and panties, and I knew then what it meant to want to be fucked, to want that hardness in this tender, pulsing place.

I knew he needed to come up inside of me, and I knew the opening was not blocked; it was torn open long ago, and I was not afraid of him going in. But I wasn't sure it would fit, because I could feel how big it was underneath me, and I was a little afraid to see it and touch it with my hand.

He turned and lay me down on the bed, unstraddling him, and moved to pull off my pants.

But I said, "Let me," because I needed to be the one to show him my body and give myself to him. *You may kiss me goodnight.*[146]

But first I unzipped his jeans. He turned and kicked off his shoes and in a swift movement he was bare, all jeans, socks, boxer shorts off. This long, lean, brown man was completely bare and wrapped around me, nuzzling my breasts again.

---

[145] Who am I again?

[146] It's all about enthusiastic consent. It always has been.

I raised my hips and slid my pants off, showing all to him: my curly hair, my red velvet flesh, the secret dark soul of me, the barrier that had been broken, and I felt like he should go inside there, just ram his way in. I wanted that. I didn't know how to ask for it and what to call all these parts and motions, but it felt so right and good, it was powerful in a way I had never understood or comprehended.

We were lying together entwined on this narrow bed, perhaps not unlike the sofa in the Brewsters' bedroom. Al played his hand up and down along my breast, down lower to my belly and he rubbed there and trailed his fingers up my rib cage, up to my throat, my jaw, where he took my face in his hand and kissed me, kissed me deeply, opened up his soul to me, sucked my very breath out. His hands conjured some gentle dance that made me begin to rock in a rhythm with him, pushing against his pushing and pulling back and pushing in again.

I was broken but made whole again, because I wanted someone and that someone wanted me. He rolled one knee between my legs, and for me, this was the test; this was the moment I could scream and cry. But I dared to go on. I opened my legs a little as he kissed me and teased my nipple with his thumb. I felt his hardness at my hip and dampness there; I didn't know it would be damp like that, but his hardness drew a moist trail on my hip as he moved against me.

He pushed his knee a little farther, and my legs spread a little wider; he licked his fingers lightly and trailed them down my breast to my nipple and over, down my body like a mountain range, down to my hip, my naked hip.

And then he licked those fingers again, and I knew where he was going, and it scared me, but I must—and I wanted him to touch me there and see my whole self, my entire raw nakedness. But I didn't expect the jolt that came when his fingers passed over my clit and stroked the red folds between my legs. He didn't go in, and I was torn between fear and pleasure; I wanted him to touch that spot again.

What does a person say? How do you tell a person to fuck you at the same time you want them to love you?

He felt my dampness there, and, on his elbow, leaned over, and he was on top of me. Al's legs were between mine, and suddenly his hardness was pressing at my gate, pressing, forcing inward, and it was so big, so very big, and it hurt.

I panicked and suddenly kicked and pushed at him, shaking my head. "No, no, I can't, it's too—."

He stopped, pulled back, and rolled on his elbow. He looked into my eyes and kissed me softly on my cheek. "What is it, *amor*, what? Tell me?"

I rolled my face into his arm where I can't see him, he couldn't see me, and said, "I'm scared. I haven't done this. It doesn't seem like it will go in. I think there's something wrong with me down there. I'm afraid it will really hurt."

Al pulled me into a hug and said, "Nelly. Really? This is your very first time?"

I nodded against his arm, not wanting to break the contact, wanting to go on but not sure all the parts worked as they should. I was so old for something that should be second nature.

"Oh, my god."

"I'm sorry."

"No, that's amazing. That's wonderful. I'm so—honored. Do you want to go on? Keep going?"

"I do, but I'm scared it won't go in. I'm not sure—I just don't know how, you know. I know *how*, but I mean, how?" *Nervous Nelly! Bah, so awkward!*

"It's okay, it's just different. It's a different kind of loving someone, is all. It's touching. You like this?" He stroked my face gently, tracing downward.

"Yes."

"You like this?" He gently caressed my breast.

"Yes."

"This?" Rubbed my nipple.

"Yes, very much."

He bent and kissed me gently. "That?"

"Yes."

He kissed and kissed, and I felt each one a little deeper and more searching, longer than the last one. "That?"

"Mmmm, yes."

He took one of my hands and placed it against his chest. "Do you like that?"

"I do."

"I love it," he said. "Touch me, don't be afraid. It's just part of me. My body, your body. It all feels good when someone touches you with love. When someone is gentle."

I traced his chest and down his side as far as his hip, and he guided my hand forward to his belly, where I nudged against him, his flesh, still hard, still waiting for me.

"It's just me, it's just another part of me, my beautiful girl. Touch me if you want to. It's all right either way. You're safe with me—and be brave. Don't be afraid to try, okay? Stop if you want to. It's up to you how far we go."

He shifted on his elbow a little, and added, "But I'll be honest with you. I'd really like to keep going."

"I would, too. But if I pull away or get scared—don't be mad."

"I won't be mad. How about you just say a code word, like—I don't know, how about, um—*orangutan? Artichoke? Banarama?* Say the code word, and that means, 'I need to slow down,' if it gets scary for you, and we'll slow down or stop?"

"Okay."

He sat up then, mindful not to bonk his head on the overhead bunk folded against the wall, and opened the split of Champagne.

He poured it in the glass and handed it to me. Then he reached over me for his beer and clinked it to my glass.

"Congratulations. I'll see you on the other side."

I laughed, and took a sip, then another. I just looked at his beautiful face, his lean, long body, and the dark hair that whorled across his chest and belly. I sipped some more Champagne and then offered it to him. He sipped from my glass, and then bent to nuzzle my nipple with his cold, moist mouth. Again, the tingle and shock were surprising, delicious, and I wanted more, so much more.

I sipped again, and the glass was empty. I felt bubbles buzzing in my head. I set the glass aside.

He leaned over me then and we kissed, gently, then growing in heat and want, so much damp, heat, want, need, and he deliberately kissed down my neck, finding a spot on my tendon, my collarbone, that tingled and sang when he kissed and nibbled. I arched my back and found my hands reaching for him, for his hips, his muscular thighs.

And then he lifted himself over me again, and I thought, *this is it*, but he knelt between my legs this time, and reached over to arrange the pillows and whispered, "Scoot back a little, sit up a little."

A little awkwardly, I pushed back and reclined against the pillows, and he was looking at me, every inch of me, and his flesh was poised, waiting to enter me. I wanted to touch him like he wanted, and I shut my eyes to shake away what I'd seen before and now just saw him, and when I touched him there, his eyes widened and then closed, and I knew he liked it. I stroked him lightly, and it was just skin, just warm skin that leapt a little, squirmed when I touched him, and he said, "You had better stop that or it will be too soon."

He came forward and kissed me again, and that kiss went deeper, longer than before, parted me in a way I have never quite been parted, and my velvet was damp with wanting more of him, wanting to feel that thrusting. He touched my thighs, pressed me back into the pillows again, and then he was licking and kissing my breasts again, then my belly, and before I realized what he meant, he had planted his mouth on my opening and was kissing me in a deeper and more soulful kiss than I knew possible.

I closed my eyes and was lost on a wave of moist heat and wonder, deep pleasure in the center of my being. This wetness seemed to engulf him, and then he rose to my mound and rhythmically sucked and licked at the fold and the rise, and I held his head and bucked against him when this wave of intense white-hot spasm came up from the center and rose inside me like some giant fucking scream of joy. I held his head and writhed against his face, his shadow burning my thighs, my core pulsing and pulsing in waves I had maybe dreamed of but didn't remember. It eased back a little, and he rose up and rubbed his face in his arm very quickly, and then came up and lay on me, his arm under me, holding me close. I was still pulsing and rubbing against his body, and he pulled a little and nudged my legs open again, and I felt him there, his heat against the gate.

"Okay?" he asked me softly, in my ear, kissing my cheek. "Okay, *amor*? Okay?"

I could have said, *orangutan, banana, monkeyshines*, but I wanted him. I nodded, wanting him, wanting to hear him purr *amor* in my ear, and he said, "Okay?" again, and his heat was right there, slipping in the moist flesh, pressing, and there was one place where it wasn't quite so tight, and he gently pressed as if to test the pressure. Then he slid right across my clit and I put my hand over my mouth so as not to scream with all the sensation in my body. He pressed in, pressing into the tightness of a hundred thousand empty nights and broken glass, pressed against the broken glass again and withdrew.

I drew a deep sobbing breath, thinking it was over.

He pulled my hand from my mouth and kissed me, deep, tongue playing with my tongue. Then he pressed inward, and back, and farther in, and he was kissing and kissing me and his flesh dragged across my clit on every stroke, and I bucked with him; I felt it opening inside and then he pulled back and on his hands he looked down, breathing heavily, and saw himself pressing inward, and he looked at me again and said, "You're okay?"

"Yes."

And he said, "Okay, because I—," and he thrust, "I'm gonna—," and thrust and thrust again. His face crumpled, and he went and fell with his face in my neck, "Oh," he said. "*Ay,*" and "*Amor,*" and I found myself stroking his back and his hair and crooning to him as if he were my own child.

Nothing had ever been so scary. Or so easy. Or so right.

★ ★ ★

After that first time, he held me for what seemed hours, and I felt like I was floating in the ocean. The train rocked and shook with every passing mile, climbing and curving, and we lay coiled together like twins, as if we'd been born that way. And then his body awoke again, and I wasn't afraid to try another time, another way. This time, I straddled him, and that was another discovery, how controlled it was when I slid down and rose at my speed instead of his, and watched his face at such close, intimate range. And still later, when I got up to check the time, he rose behind me, and I raised my leg to the bed and he cupped me from behind and climbed inside, gripping my hips while I held the narrow rocking walls of our little space. And it was after midnight when we curled together and slept. We had forgotten about dinner entirely.

Before dawn, he slept, but I was awake and saw the sun rising through the curtain, the Nevada desert brightening at once, unlike the slow dawning of the prairie or the always-bright city where we lived.

He slept, and I watched him sleep with the wonder of a new bride. When Laura and Almanzo explored their new house, their new barn, their new cow, their small kingdom, the text says nothing of *consummation*, but somehow I knew that this was how she felt—that they had explored Eden together and found it good.

I lay in the warmth of the sheets, the heat we had made. I was whole. Made new. I was woman. Whoever it was, whatever it was that had taken control of me last night, drove me to tear off my clothes and beg for hot, sweet love, I wouldn't have thought it was the same frog who watched the world go by from the slime, with her nose in a book and her ears turned off.

I couldn't have guessed it would be me.

CHAPTER 20

We crossed into California about 8 a.m. and ate breakfast as the train chugged through Truckee. It was downhill toward Sacramento now and then home, back to no job and my darling *gatos* and an empty slate, but things looked different to me now. I had things to think, say, and do.

The train would stop at the end of the line, back in Emeryville, and Al would catch BART across to San Francisco, back to his neighborhood, his restaurant, his urban garden, and his dreams.

We sat on the same side of the table at breakfast, his nearness, my place in the corner no longer suffocating. I could speak a new language now of touch without talk, of delight in silence, of shared memory. After breakfast, we went back to my little compartment, where Duane had made up the bed into seats again. We sat, holding hands, talking endlessly about everything in our minds, about all the things we had seen and learned on this journey.

We kissed again and again, spinning out the last hour down the foothills, but when we were getting close to Sacramento, I went back to see Sandy, Marian, and Junie again, to say goodbye and that I'd see them soon.

Junie had her new museum book in her backpack and *Little House on the Prairie* under her arm. Addy was wearing a new little sunbonnet and apron and held a miniature Charlotte doll strapped to her plastic doll hands with an elastic band.

I hugged June and whispered, "Don't forget. We're twins now, okay?" I kissed her cheek, and then asked if I could kiss Addy's cheek.

"Kiss Charlotte, too."

Kisses diminishing in scale. I could kiss the whole world right now.

I hugged Sandy and Marian, too. They invited me for Thanksgiving in Sacramento, and I thought that would be a fantastic alternative to the guilt-harangue-passive aggression of my mother's family holiday.

I accepted with alacrity. "We could have jackrabbit, like in *Silver Lake*, or goose?"

"Yeah!" Junie jumped at that. "And all the pies that Almanzo loved. And mashed turnips, and apples 'n' onions fried together?"

"We can all cook it! Team Laura!" I was quite pleased with the plan. Nothing LIW ever did displeased me.

I said goodbye to them and promised to wave from the window. Went back up to my compartment and Al was gone, but he returned with a couple of snacks from the snack bar. He handed me a yogurt. "Carole the Snack Lady says this is good for your gut."

"It is."

The last two hours sped by with the creeping exhaustion of hurry-up-and-wait, the anticipation of finally getting off the train, and reluctance to part with this newfound whatever you'd call it. The less you want something to end, the faster it comes.

But in no time, we were crossing the train bridge over the Carquinez Strait and rounding the edge of San Francisco Bay, with palest blue sky, the brown hills forming a bowl, fog just muscling in through the Golden Gate.

I handed Duane a $20 when I got off, and he winked at me. "Good man," he said, shooting his eyes at Al.

Al hauled my rolling bag as well as his own and wouldn't let me carry anything except my laptop[147] and purse. He waited with me at the taxi stand for my ride, since he could simply take the next BART leaving for San Francisco.

We stood to the side for a few minutes, holding hands and still joking over yogurt and our guts. Mostly, I just wanted to keep touching him. But I'm not going to cling like a peach.[148] I wanted to climb up into his lap and never leave him. I knew, somehow, that it wasn't a good strategy for future success. Call me a savant, but—hey. Perhaps this was something I could touch and *not* screw up.

He took my chin in his hand and leaned down to kiss me lightly. "I will call you."

"Please do."

"Soon. Text me when you get home."

"I will." My ride showed up just then.

Al kissed me again and stepped back. I could have waited with him at the station, watched him sit, wave, and take off, but I couldn't do that. It felt too much like being left behind.

So I went home.

---

[147] How many miles had I lugged that thing, and nary a moment's work? Nice paperweight.

[148] Although I wanted the taste of him to flood over my tongue and fill my mouth with sweetness. Like Laura's canned peaches!

CHAPTER 21

I dropped my bag at home and then went out again to get my boys at the vet. They were very angry with me and said so loudly all the way home. But once I let them out of their cages, they relaxed. Fergus eventually sidled up to me and deigned to be petted, and then Tommy ran up and sharpened his claws on my jeans. *Welcome home* is what that meant.

My neighbor Iris showed up when she saw my blinds raised.

"Your mom thinks you've been kidnapped. She filed a missing persons report. The cops were over here the other day questioning me about your disappearance. I told her you went away, but she thinks I'm in on it, somehow. She printed up fliers and posted something on the Internet. You'd better call her."

"I lost my phone." It was a lie. I still had it, but I had ignored my mother. I suppose the prairie chickens had come home to roost now.

"She's—" Iris hesitated. "Intense."

"I know."

My mother had been busy.

I texted Al, "Made it home," plugged in my laptop, and checked email. I hadn't even looked at it for days, and there were unanswered messages from my aunt, two cousins, and Dave, my former boss. Shawn and Makenzie from work also pinged me, and there was a message from an officer at the Santilena PD asking me to call when I get the message in re Missing Persons Case #LS-3457.

I didn't know whether to be flattered or horrified.

There was a one-word email from *Almanzoor*: "Hi."

A second one immediately after. "I miss you already."

That made me so ridiculously happy that I teared up. "He likes me, boys. He really likes me!" Fergus drooled and Tommy licked himself to show their excitement.

I had to call my mother, if nothing else, to at least call off the dogs. I didn't want to. I'd almost rather be missing, if missing meant I'd feel whole, untrammeled, human for the first time — ever. And I was done with needing her permission, her approval. Her denial might have been her escape method, her only ability to manage the guilt, the inability to keep me safe, but it didn't work for me anymore.

I had to find a way to tell her that. And apparently I'd have to wade right into the shitstream to say it.

Not high on my priority list.

However, I sent a quick email back to the police officer telling him I was home and safe from my travels, and that I had lost my phone. I would call him the next day to clear up any other questions, as soon as I got a new phone. Of course, I already had a phone. But *I* was going to decide how I shared my time, going forward—on *my terms*.

I spent the evening cleaning up after myself. I started some laundry and put together dinner from the reserves in my cupboard. Tomorrow, I'd need to go to the store for kitty litter and cat food, to say nothing of the people-food I needed. I'd also get some flowers for Iris for putting up with the Wrath of Mom.

I had the strangest sensation of vertigo. It felt as if I were still on the train, going around a long bend. My inner ears were out of whack with the solid world, and I hoped it wouldn't take long to get my land legs back[149].

I ate a bowl of soup and some canned fruit cocktail[150] at about 7, by myself at my table, and realized anew how dull it was to be eating alone at my kitchen table when I could be in the dining car with a glass of wine, a flatiron Signature Steak, a handsome man, and the view of the high desert or the rolling prairie outside our window. That inspired me to write a post for my blog and to consider writing a review of the book I'd found at the Discover Laura Center, for the book review blog I was about to start. I considered filming a short video of myself discussing books. All of it sounded pleasant—nay, *fun*.

The words were already starting to coalesce in my mind and jolting out my fingers.

But, of course—the doorbell rang. And I knew. I just knew it was my mother. I would have given my left arm, my first-born child, and my ability to balance a pencil on my chin if only she had not come over. But she was there.

My stomach did the thing it always did when I was nervous, which was turn to liquid fire.

I opened the door.

"Where have you been?" She burst into the house, brushing past me, her keys jangling. All five foot-nothing of her, in a matching blouse and slacks, heels tapping,[151] the perfume that makes me want to sneeze. It smelled like a floral black pepper.

"Hi, Mom. I—"

---

[149] Or would I always go on feeling like I lived in two worlds: the here and now, the long ago?

[150] Alas, I was out of cling peach halves.

[151] At this time of night? Of course. She was brittle as dried gum and as perfect as a mannequin, always.

"Do you know how upsetting it is to have to tell the police I don't even know where my own daughter is? What on earth has gotten into you? You don't just pick up and leave. Where did you go?"

"I went to South Dakota."

"South Dakota! What on God's green earth were you doing there?"

"I went on a trip. To a museum. Laura Ingalls Wilder—."

"And you couldn't call me? You couldn't pick up the phone? You just walk away from your house, your car, and your job, and let people think you've been kidnapped? Of all the irresponsible things to do. You'll be lucky to have a job when you go in. You'll be lucky they haven't fired you."

"They already did. Listen—."

"I knew it! I can't believe you—you sit there and answer me as if it's no big deal. What is wrong with you?"

"Mom—."

"And just how did you pay for all of this, I'd like to know? Credit cards, I suppose. Digging yourself into debt and—."

"Mom, stop. Listen, I just needed some time to think—."

"You never think about what you do. You never *think*. Your whole life, you've been nothing but selfish."

If she had ever said anything different, I might have been hurt. I might have been something other than hurt. I might have cared. I might have listened. I might have learned not to hate myself and what had happened in my life. But she didn't pause even for an instant.

"—nose in a book, head in the clouds, never listening to anything anyone says to you. Here we are, worried sick over where you are, and you've been on *vacation*? Chasing after some stupid character in a book?"

"She's the author."

"Author, schmauthor, who gives a goddamn who she is? Wake up, Nelly! When are you gonna wake up and get on with your life?"

"Wow, Mom. That's amazing."

"And all of this fuss because I told you about Felzman's funeral? Move on! Move on, Nelly. It's over. Move on." She stopped to pull out her cigarettes.

"Not in the house."

"I'll jolly well smoke in the house, my girl, after what you did to me this week."

"Okay, enough. Stop." I reached forward and took the cigarette from her hand. "No smoking in my house."

"What in the world has gotten into you?"

"I've had enough."

"*You've* had enough? I—."

"Stop! Just stop. You need to go."

"I came over here to see if you're all right, and you're telling me to leave? That's just what I would expect. Here you go, sulking again, because you didn't get enough sympathy as a child."

And that was it.

I walked to the door. With my hand on the doorknob, I said to her, "Please leave."

"I'm not leaving until you've snapped out of it and stopped all this nonsense."

"You get your wish. I've snapped out of it. I'm calling the police if you don't leave. Now."

"Nelly, now, just stop this stupid nonsense. You're getting all upset again. Everything's fine, it's fine now. You're just tired. You haven't eaten, am I right? You're hungry?"

"You need to go." I opened the door.

"All this fuss over a cigarette. All right, I won't smoke in the house, if that's such a problem. My god, this is a fine way to treat your own mother."

"Goodbye, Mom."

"Fine." She jangled her keys. "I'm going home. I'm tired anyway. But this isn't over. We'll hash this out in the morning."

"Will you go?"

"I'm going, all right? I'm going. For the love of god, I can't believe you'd treat your own mother this way."

I closed the door. Not much of a fiery last stand. So many years, so long, that I didn't have the stamina to bust it down in one battle. But the tide was turning. For me, it had already turned. I was not that Nelly anymore. And I'm afraid, no, *I know* she knew it.

★ ★ ★

When Laura was 12 years old, they moved to Silver Lake and watched the railroads being built. Her Pa was the paymaster, and sometimes the railroad men got angry and drunk, and wanted to be paid early and extra. Pa held the angry crowd at bay with the help of Big Jerry, the biracial alleged horse thief. When the mob gathered and threatened to take what they wanted, Laura and her mother waited in the dark, in the little shanty, waiting in terror in the darkness, for the angry mob to go away. Laura was afraid, and Ma sat with Laura and stroked her hair in the dark, rocking and stroking Laura's sun-dried hair, until the danger was past.[152]

Laura Ingalls Wilder never had to deal with a mother who blamed her for whatever bad things had happened. At least, in the novels, she didn't.

---

[152] That may have been the first time the two women were on equal footing. Where Laura shifted from girl to woman, and Ma slipped into wise woman. The position shifted back for a few years, but that scene was the first inkling of equality between them.

Now, Rose was another story. Rose Wilder was both very close and very distant from her mother. There was something wrong with Rose, maybe from the start, or maybe just from puberty.[153] Rose grew up willful and angry and resentful, and somewhere in there, she and Laura butted heads. Rose described her mother as cruel, belittling, and controlling. And that I couldn't believe. Not my Laura.

All this time, I had identified with Laura, beautiful, intelligent, capable, all of the things I wanted to be. But what if my real literary twin was Rose? Bitter, aggressive, angry Rose? The mother of the Libertarian Party. The thief of her mother's stories, while Laura was trying to write them. Pissed off at her mother. Vicissitudes and vitriol.

Was that me? Could I be Rose instead of Laura?

I couldn't.[154]

I know the Laura in the stories wasn't real, either. I know she's an amalgam, a hybrid of what is true and what is formed to tell the story. We tell stories, and sometimes they're true, and sometimes just what we wish was true.

The story is this: That forty-five years ago, there was a girl named Penelope who called her parents Dad and Mom. Dad went away, and Mom tried her best to raise Nelly on her own. But Mom worked long hours, and Nelly was left on her own a little too much; no one was watching, and the neighbor was so

---

[153] Rose self-aggrandized, telling the story of the Wilder newlyweds' home burning down, and "it was my fault." Laura was clear that it was not Rose's fault. In the *Rose Years* books, the Rocky Ridge era, Rose stays out all night with their family friend Paul Cooley in a field, learns how to telegraph from a drunk, and then takes off for San Francisco, a Bachelor Girl painting her face, and horrifying Paul. He basically backed away and said, "Whoa, Rose, WTF are you doing?" I look back at this scene and say, yep, her mental illness was starting to show.

[154] Could it be my mom? Uh, yup.

nice, and why couldn't he help by keeping an eye on Nelly? And things happened.

Things happened that shouldn't have, and Mom couldn't face that there was culpability, that her judgment had failed, so she didn't believe, she blamed, and the lies went round and round, and everyone caught in this web was stung. Even Dr. Felzman, who died by suicide, had perhaps more stains than I upon his conscience.

Shit happens in this world. The grasshoppers come. A bipolar woman, screaming, holds a knife in the dark. Someone takes your precious doll away and throws it in the mud. Your beloved sister goes blind. You shoot and miss the herd of antelope, and the town starves. You miss the turn and fall down a snowbank in a blizzard.

Sometimes you trust the wrong man.

And you keep going. You don't get over it, like you get over a skinned knee. It becomes a part of you and makes your story. I'd be lying if I said it had made a patina on my soul. If I said I was beach glass, battered and made smooth by time.

It's not a joke. It fucked me over. But it didn't kill me. It's not going to.

When I first saw Marian and Sandy and Junie and Addy all sitting in a row in the lounge car, I could see the scope of generations of fucked up, from behind me, and ahead of me, leading down the years and on into eternity. Someone fucked my mom over. Someone fucked me over. Someone fucked with Sandy, maybe with her mom, and definitely screwed over Junie. Who was next? Could we stop it and save poor Addy?

Yes. It stops with me—no more. And I'll see to it that Junie stops the chain of trauma. Our stories will change. Our endings will, too.

You must learn to trust your gut. And that will help you trust the right partner.

★ ★ ★

The next day, I texted Al to say hi.[155]

He texted back. *Saturday. Alemany Farmers' Market. 6 am-3 pm. Then dinner?*

You're working?

Yes, join me?

I think I will. It might be fun.

---

[155] (I miss you and want to see you, to sleep with you, so much.) But this I did not text.

Author photo credit: Courtesy of Julia Park Tracey/Sibylline Press

ABOUT THE AUTHOR

Author Julia Park Tracey's ancestors and their stories have given her a trail to follow, from New York and New England to the Deep South and the Pacific Coast. *The Bereaved: A Novel*, the story of her great-grandmother's loss of her children to the Orphan Train, was named by *Kirkus Reviews* in the top 100 indie books published in 2023. Likewise, *Silence*, about Julia's seventh great-grandmother, a grieving Puritan mother, was also named to the Kirkus Top 100 in 2024.

Julia, a lifelong fan of the Little House books, put her train-traveling time to use as she toured with her previous historical fiction, and penned this novel as she herself crossed the American prairie. She is a member of the South Dakota Historical Association, as well as a life member of the Jane Austen Society of North America. She has written for academia about Jane Austen, Virginia Woolf, Vita Sackville-West, and the Harry Potter phenomenon.

ACKNOWLEDGMENTS

This story wouldn't have been possible without the inspiration of Laura Ingalls Wilder, my lifelong imaginary friend in books. Thanks to my grandparents, Ruth Crum Bailey and Raeford L. Bailey, for the gift of the yellow boxed set of Little House books, illustrated by Garth Williams, of which I still have eight out of nine (no idea where *Big Woods* went).

Thanks to my dear husband, Patrick Tracey, who helped me invent names and details. And to my daughters, who told me I needed more hot sex in the story. Thanks to author Christina Mercer, who reminded me about the heroine's journey. And thanks to Sang Kim, Suzy Vitello, Suzi Steffen, and Catie Giusta for being early readers, and Vicki DeArmon, for encouraging me to pull this funny old thing out of the drawer. Thanks to Alicia Feltman for creating a gorgeous cover and to Anna Termine for her wisdom.

Thank you, gals. I love you!

★ ★ ★

Most of this was written on Amtrak trains, including the Coast Starlight, the California Zephyr, and the Southwest Chief, during a book tour in 2014 for my *Doris Diaries* book series. Thanks, Amtrak!

The quoted text from a fictional coffee table book about Jane Austen's doors in Chapter One was copied from my own travel article about Jane Austen, posted on my website in its entirety, if you want to read it: https://www.juliaparktracey.com/what-would-jane-do-a-literary-pilgrimage/

QUESTIONS FOR READERS

1. Do you recognize The Heroine's Journey in Nelly's long railroad trek to De Smet, South Dakota, and back? Can you identify any of the archetypes in the story: The Witch, the Child, the Wise Woman?

2. Are there parallels between the covered wagon journeys across the plains of Laura Ingalls Wilder's pioneer days and Nelly's cross-country journey to visit the site of Laura's novels?

3. How does this novel flip the narrative between Laura and Nelly in the Little House books, and the Nelly and Lorena of this novel? Do you feel empathy with Nellie of the Little House books, considering she might have also had childhood trauma?

4. Is Nelly a feminist?

5. Is Nelly a victim or a survivor?

6. How do the footnotes work as a device for reading Nelly's inner thoughts? Does Nelly's inner voice match her outer voice?

Sibylline Press is proud to publish the brilliant work of women authors over 50. We are a woman-owned publishing company and, like our authors, represent women of a certain age.